I0741983

The Dreamer III ~
THE PEOPLE OF THE WOLVES
is due to be released in 2018!

Look for updates on *The Dreamer Book Series* at
www.dreamerliteraryproductions.com

The Dreamer II

THE GATHERING

By E. A. Meigs

Dreamer Literary Productions, LLC

2018

First Edition Paperback

I dedicate this book with much love to
my mother and father.

 Fonts used in this novel 

Papyrus was created by Chris Costello in 1982.

Garamond was designed by Claude Garamond in the early 1530's.

The Dreamer II

THE GATHERING

Introduction

The Dreamer II ~ The Gathering is the second in The Dreamer series. This book continues the saga which follows the life of a young Neanderthal man, as told from his perspective. The tale takes place during a time in history when Europe was experiencing brutal climatic changes and man's position on Nature's food chain was indeed perilous. *The Dreamer II ~ The Gathering* is written as a "stand alone" novel, meaning it is not necessary to have read the first volume in order to understand the storyline. The Introduction from Book I: *The Dreamer ~ The Beginning* (below) is included for those who are unfamiliar with the era in which The Dreamer Book Series takes place.

* * *

When the last Ice Age was well underway approximately 40,000BCE (Before Common Era), nearly one-third of the earth's surface was hidden beneath a thick layer of ice. Since a substantial percentage of the planet's moisture was frozen solid, the world's oceans receded and coastlines were greatly expanded. At that time the Eurasian landscape consisted of vast wind-scoured tundra and small pockets of woodland which were populated by at least two groups of people: the Neanderthal and the Cro-Magnon. These populations probably coexisted in parts of Europe and Asia for only a relatively short period of time, geologically speaking. They lived a seasonally nomadic lifestyle and each hunted the same game. We can only guess at what their lives would have been like: their languages, their social behaviors, their spirituality. Due to the passage of time and the impermanent nature of most materials they would have used in their day-to-day lives, there is little to tell us about their existence besides the tantalizing clues left by their remains, their tools, their art, their burials and…their refuse.

Analyses of fossilized Neanderthal skeletons show that the males averaged five feet, five inches to five feet, six inches. The tallest Neanderthal man found to date was five feet, nine inches. The females were five feet to five feet, one inch. Their bones were about one-third stouter than ours. They were heavily muscled and had tremendous upper-body strength. The Neanderthal had the largest brain size of any known humans. Initial DNA tests showed that they likely had fair coloring: red to auburn hair, green or hazel eyes, and pale, probably freckled skin. Later genetic research on Neanderthal individuals found in different parts of Eurasia revealed that some had brown hair, brown eyes, and dusky skin.

The Neanderthal roamed the earth for roughly 200,000 years before their trail went cold around 37,000 to 42,000 BCE. That said, the Neanderthal may have persisted to eke out a living for some time after that, but we have no evidence of it at this writing. However, since most modern humans outside of sub-Saharan Africa share between one to four percent Neanderthal DNA it is almost certain that the Neanderthal are still with us even now, albeit in diluted form.

The Cro-Magnon first appeared in the European fossil record around 42,000 to 47,000 BCE. Over a period of tens of thousands of years they migrated out of Africa, gradually making their way into Eurasia. They were anatomically constructed more or less the same as most modern men and women. Cro-Magnon men averaged about five feet, nine inches in height, but it is thought that some taller individuals may have been upwards of six feet, five inches. Like the Neanderthal, their brains were also bigger than those of today's people. They are believed to have had dark coloring: dark brown to black hair, brown eyes, and tan or olive-toned skin. (Blond hair and blue eyes are a relatively new development in modern humans, having first appeared about 6,000 to 12,000 years ago, long after the pinnacle of the Ice Age, but possibly coinciding with the end of that last great glacial period.)

* * *

It is my humble opinion that after so many years of existence in a world which often presented extreme challenges, these intelligent beings would have been at the top of their game in leveraging the available resources in order to ensure their own comfort and the continuation of their species. Some indications suggest that early man was potentially much more advanced than is generally credited (more on this topic in the author's note at the end of the book) and it is my guess that we will continue to be surprised by what is revealed when ongoing and future anthropological studies peel back layers of time, as we search for ourselves in the lives of our ancestors.

* * *

An animal index is presented at the end of this novel for the convenience of those who are unfamiliar with the Ice Age animals of Europe. It gives basic information about most of the animals mentioned in this book. It might be useful to know, for example, that a wisent is a European bison, and that the animal to which North Americans refer as a moose is called an elk in Europe.

* * *

This is a work of fiction and it is not intended to hold up to scientific scrutiny. I merely seek to tell a story that is set amid this ancient backdrop. I have peopled it with those whose lives—when broken down to their most basic elements—would not have been so different from ours: sharing care and concern for loved ones, enduring all life's hardships, and reveling in serendipitous moments of love, beauty, and joy when they grace us with their presence.

Awna
Tor
Tris
Morning Star
Black Wolf
Ru & Saree
(& Hork)

 **Chapter One** 

I stand amid the smoky murk inside a dimly lighted cavernous dwelling. A huge creature lounges on a raised platform at the rear of the chamber. It has glossy brown skin that shines like that of a seal which has just emerged from the sea. It appears to be dozing. I study its peculiar skin markings, consisting of numerous blue-black lines and crisscrossing patterns. Then, as I closely observe this unusual being, its eyes open. They are large and piercing, dark in color, and the whites are full of fine red veins.

The shocking sight of those penetrating eyes startled me to wakefulness. It was much like unexpectedly finding myself eyeball to eyeball with an irate bull wisent. But as a rosy dawn ushered in the blushing promise of a bright summery morning, I was eased back into my present place and time. The fam-

-ilar cries of sea gulls and the persistent rhythm of waves washing the beach helped to sooth my sense of apprehension. I shrugged it off as a preposterous dream brought on by too much seal hunting.

My mate Morning Star slept peacefully as she lay encircled within my embrace. I smiled as I gazed at her adoringly. I still had not gotten over the novelty of seeing her smooth bronze skin pressed up against my summer-tanned but comparatively pale freckled flesh, her glossy black hair mixing with my long red curls at the head of our bed. And I am overflowing with joy at the recent knowledge that a new life has already been sown in my beloved. We have been paired for only three idyllic moons and that time period had been deliciously blissful, especially after I had spent so many lovelorn years thinking that we would never be allowed to be together. We were of two peoples, Morning Star and me; my family belonged to a clan of the Old Ones while Morning Star's kin were of The People from the East. Although bondings such as ours were not unheard of, they were also not common. My pairing with Morning Star was the only one of which I had personal knowledge and had only come to pass due to the strong friendship between our families and the unusual circumstances that convinced her parents to allow us to be joined.

We Old Ones have lived on these lands since times untold, but for the last few generations The

People from the East have gradually moved into our long-held territories. There had been relatively little friction between the two groups, probably in part because most of The People lived in a small village about a day's hike from our woodland family compound and that has meant that there was not much likelihood of frequent interaction. In fact, the only local members of The People who lived outside of the village were Morning Star's family. Her father, Black Wolf, has been the life-long close friend of my Puh, Tor. They were boys together, hunted together, and raised their families together. Morning Star's mother, Little Fawn, and my Muh, Awna, have nursed and parented one another's children, prepared food side by side, and offered moral support to each other at times when their men were away from home on long hunts.

Despite the close relationship of our respective families, Old Ones are sometimes held in low regard by The People, who are taller and very fit but lighter in build than are we, with tan colored skin, brown eyes, and straight black hair. The Old Ones, in stark contrast, are often somewhat shorter than The People, with stocky, well-muscled physiques, fair-freckled skin, green eyes, and curling red hair. Other distinctions between the Old Ones and The People include some beliefs we Old Ones share. For example, we believe that some members of our people are Dreamers: those gifted with night visions that have some relevancy in past, present, or future happenings. I had inherited this ability from my aged Great Gran and it had allowed me to see when my Puh was in trouble earlier this year. Morning Star's father, Black Wolf, and I had set out to find and rescue Puh, and that, in turn, had presented me with the opportunity to deliver Black Wolf from a perilous situation. This stroke of luck, and Black Wolf's gratitude, eventually led to my current happiness with Morning Star.

I nuzzled Morning Star's neck affectionately, breathing in the scent of her. She opened her eyes and smiled at me sleepily.

"The sun has not yet cleared the horizon; what has roused you into wakefulness, Tris?" Morning Star asked.

"It was nothing," I told her. "It was just a silly dream."

Morning Star snuggled closer and kissed me lovingly.

"Let us chase that silly dream away," she murmured into my ear. I eagerly returned her kisses. In a moment the dream was all but forgotten.

* * *

The sun had risen and its golden warmth temporarily painted the white sands, turning them a soft yellow. A gentle wind propelled processions of deep blue combers laced with white foam toward the shore. At this time, Morning Star and I had a great hunger and thirst. I poured a little water from our water bag into a dried gourd cup and handed it to Morning Star. She smiled broadly at me as she took the proffered cup.

"Thank you, dear Tris."

I nodded in return, refilled the little vessel and downed my share. Both of us were still naked of clothing in the cool morning air, but we are in no hurry to dress. Morning Star moved to sit behind me and she began to work my mass of unruly hair. She used her fingers, but she also had a small smooth forked stick that helped to work through the tangles. Morning Star had remarkable patience with my thick, waist-length mane. Soon after we arose every day, she faithfully tackled the chore of arranging my hair in the traditional way of the Old Ones. She removed the knots, divided the hair into multiple sections on either side of my head and then, twisting each section in the direction of the natural curl, produced a number of rope-like coils. This process served to conveniently wrap-up all those pesky loose ends. After all the hair was coiled, she gathered it into a substantial bunch at the nape of my neck and bound it tightly, using a leather thong to bind my hair in a criss-cross pattern until the entire length was thus contained.

I had never thought much about the chore of keeping my hair tidy until Morning Star and I had begun our lives together, but I did notice that she spent far less time plaiting her lovely shining long black hair into braids and I soon came to the conclusion that straight hair is much easier to deal with than bushy hair like mine. But I did not mind too much, especially at times like this when Morning Star struggled to hold onto the bulky snake-like coils.

"Tris, dear, your hair is nearly impossible," Morning Star said with a good-humored laugh, "but I love it just the same!"

Any excuse to feel Morning Star's hands on me made the most mundane of tasks worthwhile. When she finished, I turned to her and pulled her to me for yet another of the countless kisses we would exchange today.

"My hair never used to get so completely disordered before you and I became paired," I teased her gently.

"I am afraid that it might be my fault." Morning Star grinned. "I love to run my fingers through your hair when we lay together at night. And before I know it, it is all undone."

"I guess what is fair is fair…" I began, "since I also manage to make a mess of your neat braids every night, as well."

We were sitting on the woven bull reed and hide-covered matting that made up our bed underneath the canopy of our lean-to. My dog Raena looked at us keenly, hoping that we might soon arise for the day and begin to do something that would be of more interest than our many romantic interludes. She was not to be disappointed. By now, both Morning Star and I needed to make our morning trek over the nearest dune to the little hollow where we usually relieved ourselves. I gave my sweet mate one more kiss and stood up and stretched. Morning Star got to her feet, too, but rather than making an effort to leave our shelter, she wrapped her arms around my waist and leaned against me, her head resting between my shoulder blades in the middle of my back. She had not yet plaited her hair and it felt silky where it touched my skin. I reached for my spear; I never ventured even so far as the dell between the dunes without a weapon and Raena. I had never seen any large predators this close to the coast, but that did not mean that it might not happen. I did not actually expect to meet with troublesome creatures, but Raena would provide warning if any threat was near, and Puh was within shouting distance if we needed assistance.

"Ready?" I asked Morning Star. She nodded.

Wordlessly, we walked hand-in-hand over the dune with Raena trotting along beside us and, as was our habit, we quickly scooped small holes in the sand with a shell trowel. I stood facing the sandy hillside and urinated into one of the holes. Morning Star squatted behind me, just behind my legs. Oddly, this was one of our many rituals that I treasured, especially when she held on to the backs of my knees to help balance herself. I would have had never guessed that being paired with a mate would be quite like this. Inasmuch as I had long cherished so many hopes and wishes for a future with Morning Star, I had not foreseen that our lives would become as lovingly intertwined as this. Even the most commonplace and simplest of undertakings would come to be so significant, simply because I was now doing them with Morning Star.

Feeling much better, we returned to our lean-to and Morning Star began to braid her hair. I looked out over the landscape at the orange sun as it arose over the distant treetops. We would need to don clothing soon. Here on the open beach where there was nothing except our manmade structures to protect us from the sun's rays, sunburns were a constant problem. It was too warm to wear much clothing, so we only wore enough to cover the most sensitive skin on our bodies. Some spots, like the tops of my shoulders, my back and forehead, and the bridge of my nose, were perpetually burned, peeling, and scabbed at this time of year.

Morning Star must have been thinking along the same lines. She brought my loincloth to me and helped me to tie it on. As I secured my sheathed knife to my right hip, Morning Star put her head through the neck opening of a long rectangular garment made of lightweight deerskins. She arranged it so it hung evenly front and back, and then belted it around her waist. Every morning when she dressed, the same thought crossed my mind: it was a shame to hide such a lithe figure under such a crude covering. I might get used to the sight of her body someday and maybe I would not resent seeing it hidden under shapeless clothing then —even the rather skimpy outfit she now wore—but at this time, I very much preferred to see her unclothed. Morning Star suddenly glanced my way.

"Tris, my love, you are staring," she said.

I smiled.

"Yes. I am staring," I admitted. "Staring at you. It is one of my favorite pastimes." I wondered if this was how all newly paired men felt. Did my Puh still feel the same way about Muh? Did Morning Star's father Black Wolf feel the same way about his plain-featured, lumpishly plump mate, Little Fawn? Morning Star smiled back and stopped to embrace me. She gazed into my face. "What are you doing?" I asked lightly.

"Staring at you," she said simply. "Do you not think that I like to feast my eyes upon you too?"

* * *

We have been at the coast for nearly two moons. It was almost time to pack up our summer accommodations and the many drying stages used to preserve fish and seal meat, and return to our forest home. It did not seem so long ago when we had first arrived and started the annual ritual of digging up our summer home's building materials from where we had left them the previous fall, buried at the edge of the woodlands near the dunes. The earth kept the structure's poles and sealskin hide coverings more or less intact from winter storms, although we did replace parts of the configuration every year as poles and skins rotted out or became damaged.

The simple round building that housed the rest of my family was perhaps eight paces across and it was easy to erect and partition. It provided all the protection from the elements that was needed. Mid-summer weather tended to be mild; days were sunny and warm with enough of a breeze to keep the temperatures from becoming too hot. Occasional rain showers beat through now and then, but if we were fortunate, they happened just often enough to keep us from traveling inland to find potable drinking water.

Now that Morning Star and I were paired we had our own small shelter, located a short distance away from the rest of my family. Our lean-to did little more than protect us from the sun and damp, but we did not care. We had each other and we spent most of the time when not actively gathering or producing food or indulging in long walks at the edge of the surf, making love in our little home. Rainy days posed no hardship on us, as we joyfully whiled away the time, happy in one another's arms. My dog, Raena, lying nearby with her head on her paws, would look at us once in a while and sigh heavily as if to say *they are still at it.* We did not care about that, either. All we cared about was to have as much time as possible to be alone together.

But there was more to a summer on the coast than enjoying the weather and basking in the rapture of our newly-paired state. There was also a lot of work. Once our homes were built near the crest of the dunes where they would be safe from the surf but open to the cooling winds that would also help to keep the numerous biting insects at bay, we had to set up our fish traps and the many drying frames which would be needed to preserve the various meats harvested from the ocean. Puh and I actively tended the traps every day. Every now and then we killed a seal that had chosen to heave its great bulk up onto the beach near our drying racks, possibly attracted to the scent of our catches as they were suspended under the sun's desiccating rays. Raena's frantic barking would alert us to the invader, and Puh and I would come at the seal from opposite sides with our spears.

I had mixed feelings about killing the seals. Although they had a grace while sea-bound that gave them the appearance of almost flying through water, on land they were cumbersome and at a distinct disadvantage. Somehow it unsettled me; it seemed too easy. However, I was grateful for the meat and oil that each animal provided, and also, for their remarkably water-repellent hides.

* * *

Driven by hunger to join my family, Morning Star and I strode down the shore together, our noses taking in the smell of roasting fish. As we approached, I could see that a gutted but otherwise whole codfish was encased in beach clay and that it had been baked in the fire pit on red-hot coals. The clay covering was now broken open, allowing eddies of steam to escape as the fish cooled.

"We could smell the aroma of fish while were coming up the beach," I said as we neared the group. Raena gazed around tentatively as she edged toward the fire pit where the fish lay, but she stopped in her tracks when my thirteen-winters-old sister Ru blocked her way, standing guard over the fish with a forbidding look. Muh was nursing my youngest sister, thirteen-moons-old Mi, and simultaneously encouraging eight-winters-old Twie to finish dressing. Three winters old sister Saree was squealing merrily and dancing just outside of Muh's reach.

"*Noooooo!* I do not want to wear clothes!" Saree broke into a run to dash away, but Puh intercepted her with an adroit move that nixed her escape and he brought the wriggling youngster back to her mother.

"Saree, you must mind your Muh," Puh spoke quietly, as always. "You will cook the same as that fish if you do not protect yourself from the sun. Look at my shoulders; do you want your nice skin to look like mine?"

Saree took a gander at Puh's sun-scorched upper body, many times blistered and peeling, and so freckled that the individual spots now merged together.

"It would not bother me!" Saree insisted stubbornly. But she allowed Puh to dress her.

"You would be bothered when your little bottom is too sunburned to sit on," Muh said wearily.

Muh was six moons pregnant with her eleventh baby. As her eldest surviving child, I had witnessed all but one of her pregnancies and it almost seemed to be a perpetual state for her during the seventeen winters I had been alive. This attested to the fact that my family had been unusually successful in making a comfortable living and extremely lucky to have so many thriving children at a time when many families were struggling to bring two or three to adulthood. Besides the four sisters who had accompanied us to the coast, I also had a brother, Ty, who had stayed home with Puh's grandmother, my Great Gran, because at 64 winters of age she did not care to make the long trip. Our old dog Rooph was also left behind. He would have been all too willing to hit the familiar trails, but at this stage of his life, he was far too lame to physically accomplish the trek.

Muh smiled in greeting at Morning Star.

"How are you feeling?" Muh asked.

Morning Star smiled, too.

"I feel very well, Awna. How are you? You are not too tired, are you?" Morning Star was also an oldest sibling in a large family, so she was well acquainted with pregnancies.

"No, I am not too tired," Muh assured her. "I am looking forward to the day when you and I will hold our babies side-by-side. You are only about three moons behind me. Our babies will grow up together."

"I am eager for that day as well. I hope the time will pass quickly." Morning Star rubbed her still-flat stomach as she spoke.

Ru prodded the cooked fish with her finger.

"It is cool enough to eat now," Ru announced. "Come and get something to eat!"

Ru was already portioning the fish into shell bowls and gave the first to Twie, and then to Saree, who bounced up and down in anticipation. Puh held out a large shell to Ru.

"Fill this for your Muh, Ru," Puh requested.

"Yes, Puh," Ru obliged.

"Many thanks, Pretty One," Puh said with a nod.

Ru gave him a rare smile at the compliment and for a moment, she actually did look pretty. Even though most Old Ones were not considered to be adults until they reached 15 winters, girls often seemed to mature earlier and Ru was a prime example of that.

She was a second mother to her younger siblings and she was also required to work very hard to help Muh manage the household. As a consequence, Ru often seemed authoritarian and somewhat humorless.

Puh took Baby Mi from Muh to allow her to eat in peace. Morning Star and I also received our slabs of fish. Puh returned to Ru to get his share, holding Mi in one arm and a shell bowl in the other. As Ru filled the shell Puh leaned in to give her a kiss.

"Many thanks. Now sit and fill your own belly, Ru."

"Yes, Puh," Ru nodded, tossing the leavings to Raena, who would devour most of the fish's remaining meat and carcass.

After our meal was finished, Puh and I walked out to the drying racks where the last of our seal meat was waiting to be packed for the trip home. The fish fillets dried faster and were already bagged and sitting on our travois sled. The seal meat contained more fat and took longer to attain the level of dehydration needed to be stored for long periods of time. Raena walked with us. This had been her first summer at the shore and she had learned her duties quickly. She kept watch over the racks to keep the sea gulls from stealing too much of the drying flesh. Sometimes she and the gulls engaged in a tugging contest over a particular piece of meat, but she always won. And, of course, she dined on the prize. But she earned everything she ate, so we did not begrudge her an occasional meal from the racks.

Puh touched the hanging seal meat.

"Hmmm," he said. Puh took down two pieces and struck them together. The sound of their impact made a dull clack. "These should be ready to pack later today." Puh gave one chunk to Raena and hung the other back on the rack. "Let us go back to our camp and gather our shovels. We can expand the storage hole so that it will be ready to receive the poles and seal hide coverings tomorrow morning after we dismantle our shelters."

"Yes, Puh." I said as I nodded and followed him back to the dunes. Whilst I walked behind Puh, I had a good view of his lean but powerful build. I had always been told that I resembled my father. I was unusually tall for an Old One and Puh was not, but we had the same light red hair and the same pale green eyes. Our facial features also closely mirrored one another's, except that Puh's was lined and scarred from 32 years of exposure to weather and various hunting mishaps—including those he had garnered while helping me recover Morning Star after she had been stolen from our pairing ceremony. I had beaten my rival to win Morning Star in The People of the East's Challenge Circle, but the losing party had gathered a group of men to help him kidnap my new mate. Then, Puh, Black Wolf, and I had to pursue them in order to get her back. When I first fell in love with Morning Star while we were still small children, I had no notion that we would have to endure so much before we would be allowed to be together. But it had all been worth it. Worth it many times over.

As I came to walk abreast of Puh, I took note of the healed slashes across his chest. It had taken a solid moon before the skin had finally regenerated enough to cover them. Puh would always carry the marks left by the cave bear that had attacked him and his brother Mror while they were hunting last spring. When the huge bear had come at Puh, brave Uncle Mror had stepped between them and stabbed the marauding animal with his knife. The bear then went after Uncle Mror instead of Puh and started to carry him off, dragging Uncle Mror toward a nearby canyon. Puh followed, continually thrusting his spear into the bear's side and it was then that the bear had turned, and hardly breaking its stride, taken a hasty swipe at Puh with one of its massive paws. This was revealed to me in the first of the vivid Dreams that had inspired the long trek Black Wolf and I had embarked upon to find Puh and Uncle Mror. Incredible good fortune had been with us; Black Wolf and I had located Puh where he, Uncle Mror, and the bear had fallen into a deep pit, a trap. The bear and Uncle Mror had not survived the fall, but Puh had landed on top of the bear and, although very hungry and nearly expiring from thirst, he was still alive. Puh had made a rapid and complete recovery, and although he still had a gaunt and angular physique, he had regained the weight he had lost during the ordeal.

As we neared our camp, we could see that Muh, Morning Star, and Ru were packing the food supplies that had been gathered during our stay at the coast: small plums, rose hips, and assorted berries. Like the meat, most of the fruit had been dried. We would be living off these and various additional dehydrated foods, such as venison, elk, or aurochs, for a good part of the coming winter.

Picking up shovels made from modified giant deer antlers, Puh briefly explained to Muh that we were going to enlarge the storage hole. Muh nodded absently in response.

"Tris and I will be back shortly," Puh assured Muh. She nodded again.

I held both the shovel and my spear in one hand, and paused to give Morning Star a kiss in passing. Puh kissed Muh, too, and turned to leave.

"May I come, too?" Twie asked.

"No, Little One," Puh said gently as he shook his head. "Stay here and help your Muh pack. We will be leaving in the morning and we must make ready to hit the trail as early as possible."

Twie took his words calmly.

"Yes, Puh."

"I do not want to leave," Saree piped up in her chirping voice. "I like being at the beach! It is warm here!"

Puh grinned at Saree's notion that the shore was impervious to the change of seasons.

"It will not long remain warm here," he told her. "Winter comes to the coast, too."

"It does?" Saree looked crestfallen. "Does it snow here, like it does at home?"

"I have never seen it, but I am sure that there is snow and ice here, just as there is everywhere else," Puh replied.

"Poop," Saree remarked. This was her new favorite word when she was disappointed about something. We neither encouraged nor discouraged her use of this term. Left to her own devices, she would outgrow this phrase.

Puh and I carried our shovels and spears a short distance to the place where our building materials would over-winter. The long, narrow ditch had partially collapsed since we had removed the contents of the hole, so we began the process of excavating the loose soil until the cavity was restored to its former dimensions. We left the shovels stuck in the ground near the shallow gorge and returned to our family.

The sun was now high in the sky, so we all took sanctuary inside the little shelter where Muh announced that she would cut everyone's hair. This was an annual occurrence. One of the Old Ones' beliefs was that our hair provided us with a conduit to a second sense that allowed us to more intuitively commune with the natural world around us. For a hunter, this was a great boon. So we Old Ones cultivated our hair to great lengths, only trimming it once a year each summer.

Puh would be first. Muh unwrapped his bundle of coils and Ru stepped forward to help Muh pull the hair out to its full extent since it was long enough to reach down to the backs of Puh's thighs. Muh laid the ends of the hair across a piece of smooth driftwood and a using her sharpest blade, cut off a hand's breadth of Puh's hair. Puh stood, his long hair billowing in the wind, all at once surrounding him in a cloak of faded red, the few shining silver strands catching the light the way the sun sparkles on the surface of the ocean. Saree took up the pile of newly shorn hair before it could blow away.

"Puh-Puh, may I have this?" Saree asked.

Puh shrugged.

"If you want it, you may have it. But why do you want it?"

Saree stroked the little bundle of curly hair.

"I made a doll, but I have always wanted to have a doll with hair…not just grass hair, but a doll with real hair. So I would like to have all the hair that Muh-Muh cuts off today."

Puh and Muh traded amused glances.

"Are you going to try to put it on the clay doll you made yesterday?" Muh inquired.

Saree had worked a lump of clay that still looked like a lump of clay, except that it was a smiling lump with two finger-poke impressions for eyes. Saree nodded.

"All right, Saree." Puh said, "I will melt some glue later this evening and I will help you glue hair on your doll."

Saree wrapped her arms around Puh's legs in a hug.

"Many thanks, Puh-Puh."

As the day wore on, all except Baby Mi, whose hair was not yet long enough to be cut, and Morning Star, who severed a little length off her own hair every few moons, had received our trims. Saree collected all the cuttings, which ranged from Puh's lightest red to Ru's darkest red. But Muh's hair was still in its usual pile of coils, affixed to the back of her head with the slender ivory rods that Puh had given her as a pairing gift years and years ago. Muh began to put her tools away.

"But Muh, we have not yet cut your hair," Ru said.

Muh smiled.

"I do not cut my hair this summer. I do not want to do anything that might diminish my strength. I want to be sure that I bring forth a big strong baby for your Puh. Maybe another big son like Tris." Muh reached out to touch my hand and gave it a squeeze. "When Morning Star and Tris's baby is born, my baby will have a new nephew to play with who might grow to be the size of his father and he will need to keep up!"

"But what if you have a girl instead of a boy?" I asked teasingly.

Muh shook her head.

"After all those girl babies in a row? No, it will be a boy."

"What if I have a girl baby?" Morning Star chimed in, smiling impishly.

Puh let out a silent laugh.

"Given the size of Tris and that of your parents, Morning Star," he said, "she may still be big enough give any man with dubious intentions pause."

Morning Star giggled. She was a woman of The People who was slightly smaller than average, but her parents were both quite large. Black Wolf towered over almost everyone except his mate, Little Fawn. How my comparatively diminutive Morning Star had been born to those two giants was a mystery to anyone who was apt to ponder the question.

* * *

Later that day, Saree appeared in front of Puh with her bald doll and the now quite disheveled stockpile of assorted hair.

"Did you bake the doll in the coals?" Puh asked her.

"Yes, Puh-Puh." Saree said. Even at her young age, she knew that all clay objects had to be cured in the fire pit if they were expected to last.

"Good," Puh patted her head and gingerly took the doll from her. Seeing the misshapen blob of hard clay with its deep-set eyes and sappy grin made Puh smile. He set about melting a quantity of glue that had been leftover from the last time we hafted new spearheads to shafts and when it was malleable, he dipped the top of the doll's head into the glue until it was well coated. "Saree, bring the hair to me."

The glue was too hot for Saree to touch, but Puh's tough hands had no trouble pressing the array of curls to the sticky clay pate. He painted more glue over each application until finally, the doll had a respectable, if not slightly maniacal-looking, head of hair. When the hot glue had cooled, Puh returned the doll to Saree. She hugged her new toy and gazed at it lovingly.

"Many thanks, Puh-Puh! Many thanks!" Saree said, beaming with pleasure at her doll's new head of hair.

Twie gave the doll a fleeting look, wearing a markedly underwhelmed expression.

"It looks like a tuber with a very bad fungal growth," she declared.

"It does not!" Saree's chin trembled and tears came to her eyes.

Puh wrapped his arms around Saree and lifted her off her feet.

"Now, now," he said softly. He cuddled the silently sobbing Saree but managed to give Twie a stern look at the same time.

"I am sorry," Twie apologized to Saree, "I did not get a good look at your doll. Let me see it."

Saree sniffled a bit, but gave the precious item to her sister.

"Saree, this is...um...a *beautiful* baby. You must be very proud." And she returned the doll to Saree, who was still in Puh's arms.

Saree's tears cleared up like a sudden passing rain shower and her sunny disposition returned.

"Again, many thanks, Puh-Puh, for giving my baby hair," Saree said as she kissed Puh. "Now she will be able to tell where the deer walk and hear the whispers of the moon."

Puh returned Saree's kiss and stroked her long, loose curls.

"*The whispers of the moon?*" he repeated. "Does it whisper to you?"

"Oh, yes!" Saree exclaimed. "It says *I am watching over you.*"

Puh snuggled her tighter.

"That is good because you are a busy little bee who needs watching over." And giving her one more kiss, he set her on the ground again. "Come on, Tris. Let us pack the last of the seal meat and take down the remaining drying frames."

I had expected that this would be our next chore. It did not take long to bag the last of the seal meat and disassemble the frames. We gathered twigs and cut bull rushes from the edge of a nearby pond until we had enough to make a protective layer at the bottom of our storage ditch. It would help to keep some of the earth's dampness away from the materials we would store there.

We then carried the wooden poles that made up the frames to the cache area and placed them on top of the small branches and rushes. Tomorrow morning, we would take down our shelters and add those to the pile, covering the wood with the seal-skin hides that enveloped our summer homes and finally, bury the whole thing under a thick layer of dirt.

After our evening meal, Morning Star and I left as the youngest children were readied for bed, and set out for a last walk on the beach. Raena paced alongside us. The moon was nearly full but it was almost obscured by a thick fog. As we strolled through the eerie mists, incoming waves swept over our feet and then withdrew again, the foamy edges gradually disappearing into the sands. We could not see the combers as they rolled in, but I could hear them and feel their impact on the shore through the soles of my feet.

Morning Star stopped and picked up a few white shells which she had been able to discern in the semi-darkness.

The Dreamer II: THE GATHERING

"I have so enjoyed our summer here," she remarked. "I was not sure how I would like being at the coast, but I was curious to see the place where all the shells in my necklace had come from." Morning Star indicated the ornament that hung from around her neck. It had been my pairing gift to her, assembled from shells I had gathered over the many seasons I had come to the shore. I had carefully selected shells of various types but of the same color and size, and produced a necklace that I hoped would please her.

The gift turned out to be more than a simple present. When Morning Star was abducted from our pairing ceremony, she had used most of the shells to leave a trail for us to follow so that we could retrieve her from her captors. Now, the necklace consisted of only ten or twelve shells, where originally there had been hundreds.

I had offered to restore the necklace to its former state but she politely declined. The bare twine with the small number of shells looked somewhat pitiful to my eyes, but she was pleased with it as it was, so I let the matter rest.

"I am glad that you have liked being here," I said to her. "Maybe your family would like to come to the beach with us one of these summers."

"Maybe," Morning Star nodded. After a moment, she added, "Da would not like all this sand, though. He would never be able to rid himself of it."

I opened my mouth to laugh. Black Wolf was an astonishingly hairy man and I could just imagine that his fur would catch and hold quite a bit of sand.

"I can tell you are laughing," Morning Star elbowed me. "You Old Ones may laugh and cry without sound, but I heard the air rush out of your mouth!" She laughed, too, "My mother would be telling Da to shake himself off outside like a dog before she would let him indoors!"

Chapter Two

Heavy rain beats the ground and roaring blasts of thunder make the earth tremble. Puh is sitting on the turf amongst weeds, his loose hair wetly plastered to him like a soaken garment. He is staring vacantly into space. Not moving. Just staring.

I awakened with a terrible sense of foreboding. It was still dark out. A strong wind had blown away the previous night's fog. I looked out the opening of our lean-to and gazed up at the nighttime firmament, now crystal clear. The moon, low in the sky, threw long shadows across the dunes. Morning Star was still asleep, her back to me but curled up so that I am wrapped around her slumbering form. Raena stirred and gazed at me intently. The air was quite cool, so I adjusted the position of our blanket until it covered us more adequately. I tried to go back to sleep, but the stricken mood I sensed in that Dream stayed with me for some time. The sky was beginning to brighten in the east when I at last fell into a light doze.

* * *

There was always a feeling of regret when we left the coast each summer. Not only would we leave behind the easy carefree ways of the season, but knowing that it would be a long, hard trudge home with Puh and me pulling the well-laden travois sled and Morning Star, Ru, and Twie toting packs. Only Muh, who carried Baby Mi, and little Saree were not burdened with transporting our belongings and the quantity of food that we had gathered at the shore.

Even though our sled poles ran through the ruts created by many prior trips, it was still an arduous journey. Although Puh and I took turns taking the lead pulling the sled, our chests and shoulders would bear the marks of the sled harness for many days after we arrived at home. We stopped around midday for a short break during which we ate a bit of dried fish and snacked on fresh berries, washed down with a much needed drink of water.

The sun was well into its decline when we reached the home of relatives who always put us up for the night when we traveled to and from the beach. It was a good opportunity to visit, trade goods, and rest before finishing the trip home. This visit, however, was not as happy as it had been in years past. We had always looked forward to our stays with Uncle Mror and his clan. Most Old Ones were rather soft-spoken and not overly talkative, but Uncle Mror was an anomaly—a jolly lively man, and a Keeper of Stories. He was universally loved and he loved all in return. But after he had so selflessly stepped in to save Puh last spring and he and the bear had fallen into the trap, his spirit had flown. His household still looked much the same, but it somehow seemed empty without him.

We were affectionately greeted by Uncle Mror's mate, Aunt Vee, and their three sons: Bror, Dor, and Lor. My cousins ranged in age from 19-winters-old Bror to 15-winters-old Lor.

Aunt Vee was of small stature, but she always had a large personality. She was an energetic and funny woman, but now she seemed somewhat de-flated. Aunt Vee still smiled and made us welcome but there was an ever-present sadness in her eyes. Not only had she lost her mate, but both her parents had passed in the months following, and now she and her sons were all who were left at the sprawling dwelling that had once housed many more people.

Aunt Vee was busily readying a veritable feast, but she soon settled everyone comfortably around the hearth.

"I knew you would be here on the day before the full moon, so I have been preparing for your stopover," Aunt Vee said. "You must be very hungry. The food will soon be ready. Bror and Lor brought in a deer this morning, so we will have plenty of fresh meat on which to dine.”

Saree had climbed into Bror's lap. Bror was of average height for a man of the Old Ones, but he was extraordinarily heavily built, much like his father had been. Bror owned a huge frame and he was so muscular that he could hardly put his arms down by his sides or stand with his legs close together. Yet, he was a gentle presence and Saree had no qualms about placing an arm around his thick neck or putting her fair cheek up to his coarsely bearded face.

“You and Lor killed a deer?” Saree asked. “Was it a boy deer or a girl deer?”

“It was a buck. A yearling,” Bror answered. “He was well-fed after feeding on lush foliage and grasses all summer.”

“Ah,” said Saree. She then brought forth her new doll. “See what I have, Bror? I made the clay body and face. Puh-Puh helped me to give her hair.”

“Yes, I see,” Bror replied with a soft smile. “It is important to have hair. What have you named her?”

Saree paused in thought.

“I do not have a name for her yet.”

“You must give her a name,” Bror said. He turned the doll toward himself and for a moment, seemed to struggle to maintain his composure after he got a glimpse of the doll's deranged demeanor. “Everything must have a name.”

"That is true," Saree agreed. "I shall have to think of something that fits her. Something pretty like she is."

"Well, that is easy, then," Bror nodded. "Name her for someone you know who is pretty."

"Muh-Muh is beautiful," Saree stated.

"Yes, Muh-Muh is beautiful," Twie echoed.

Muh smiled at this. She was leaning back against Puh, nursing Baby Mi and looking as though she could fall asleep at any moment.

"I do not feel beautiful at this moment." Muh paused and her grin widened as Puh whispered something into her ear and kissed her. "But many thanks, Saree, for saying so."

"How about your big sister?" Bror prompted. "Ru is pretty."

Saree shook her head.

"Ru is bossy."

Ru frowned at Saree. It was not a pretty look.

"Ru has a job to do," Bror said lightly. "A big sister has to do a lot of important work. She only seems bossy sometimes because she is taking care of so many things."

Saree shrugged. Then an idea seemed to come to her.

"Maybe I will call my baby *Hork*."

Puh looked closely at Saree.

"Who do you know by that name?" Puh inquired.

Saree shrugged again and held up Hork to the firelight so she could better admire her.

"I do not know anyone with that name. I just like it. Hork. That is a beautiful name."

Our evening meal was soon ready. Saree ate while seated comfortably in Bror's lap and he seemed to enjoy her simple patter. He patiently answered her many questions and helped to cut the larger chunks of meat into pieces that she could easily consume.

Puh, as always, took Mi from Muh so that she could eat without holding a restless baby. Aunt Vee seated herself next to Muh so they could chat.

"I am sure that you are eager to be home again," Aunt Vee began. "How long will it be before this infant is born?"

"Yes, I am very eager to return home," Muh replied. "The baby should come sometime this fall." Muh caressed her bloated stomach. "I am hoping for a boy this time."

"That would be nice," Aunt Vee concurred. "You and Tor are lucky to have so many lovely daughters, but another son would be wonderful." It was unspoken but understood that Muh and Puh might wish to have a boy after losing my 16 winters-old brother, Dak, when he was killed by wolves last year. That tragedy was never far from Muh's mind. Then changing the subject, Muh looked over at Morning Star and me and smiled broadly at us as she took the opportunity to make an announcement to our extended family.

"I am not the only one who is expecting. Tris's mate Morning Star will also have a baby in the coming months. It will not happen until next winter, but it is surely happy news."

Aunt Vee stood and approached Morning Star and me, wrapping her arms around us.

"That is indeed wonderful news!" She said. "Best wishes to you both for a robust well-born child."

"Yes, many thanks, Aunt Vee. We are very pleased." I returned her hug, as did Morning Star.

"You are so lucky," Aunt Vee went on. "I am so envious. I miss the days when I bore children and when my men were still boys. How I wish I could have another child!"

No one knew quite how to respond to this. Bror broke the awkward silence as he, too, approached us and with Saree still in his arms, took each of our hands in turn.

"Best wishes for a healthy baby," Bror said; his rough hand over mine as he squeezed it heartily. Turning to Morning Star, he grasped her hand as well. "Best wishes, Morning Star."

"Many thanks, Bror," I said. Morning Star chimed in her thanks, too. The other brothers followed. I felt somewhat guilty about my good fortune. I knew that Bror, Dor, and Lor were all at an age when they were considered ready for pairing, but the numbers of Old Ones had been in decline for a long time and nubile women were few and far between. It did not escape my notice that my cousins' eyes followed Ru hungrily and that she kept close to Muh and Puh. Ru was well aware of their interest in her.

However, the mood soon changed when Twie spoke up.

"I miss Uncle Mror's stories. If he was here right now, he would be telling one," she said.

There had been some speculation as to whether or not Bror, as the oldest son, would take over his father's role as Keeper of Stories. He certainly knew all the oft-told traditional tales of the Old Ones by rote. But Bror had not yet given any indications as to his inclinations regarding this subject.

Twie turned to Bror.

"Do you know any good stories?" she asked.

Bror looked a little surprised.

"Why, yes. I know many stories."

"Would you tell us one?" she asked.

Bror seemed to ponder the question for a moment.

"I will tell you the story of *The First Dreamer*," he said.

> *Many, many winters ago, many more than you could count, the Old Ones did not know what it was to have Dreams. They had dreams, of course, but they were*

regular dreams: dreams of hunting and running and of kissing pretty girls.

I did not remember the part about kissing girls. Bror went on:

The first Dreamer was a young woman named Briwa. She was sleeping as always when a startlingly vivid vision came to her. She saw a star falling from the sky. It was chased by a fiery tail as it bore down on the earth and as it neared, it was so brilliant that for a long moment, it lighted the nighttime sky. The Dream was so realistic that it brought her out of the depths of a sound sleep. Briwa had to see if the sky was in fact going to pieces. She went to the doorway of her family's home and was amazed to see that almost right away, a star blazed across the sea of shining lights that sparkled in the blackness above. Soon, it was followed by another star that streaked through the sky from a different direction. And then there was another, and another. But it was not long before she recognized the star from her Dream as it appeared seemingly from nowhere.

By now, Briwa knew that she had to awaken her family. She realized that this much fire falling from the sky was not a good thing. They were barely shaken from their slumbers when they all felt the impact of the star colliding with the earth. The heat from the star set fire to the woodlands and Briwa's family only just managed to escape from the flames by retreating to a nearby lake and taking refuge amidst its waters until the fire had passed by.

From then on, Dreamers would sometimes be born to Briwa's descendents."

Bror paused and looked at me.

"Maybe your new baby will be a Dreamer, too."

I nodded and smiled, but did not otherwise reply. Bror gazed fondly at Saree, who had fallen asleep in his lap.

"It grows late. I shall put this little one and her Hork to bed." Bror rose and carried Saree indoors. Muh nudged Ru.

"Go in and make sure that Saree is properly put to bed," Muh instructed. "Take Twie with you."

"Yes, Muh. Come on, Twie."

Twie obediently accompanied Ru into the earth-bermed home of Aunt Vee and my cousins. It was an unusually large domicile that had housed generations of Aunt Vee's family and it consisted of many rooms. When it was time for us all to be settled down for the night, we were granted a cozy little chamber in which to sleep. Bror's story made me wonder: would I Dream before morning?

* * *

The light is weak and the air is smoky. There is a feeling of unease. Men are angry and they are

The Dreamer II: THE GATHERING

I awoke to Morning Star's kisses. Although there was no sunlight inside the earthen dwelling, I knew that the new day would soon be upon us. We enjoyed a leisurely romantic interval before the household came to life. When Morning Star and I emerged from our room, we found Aunt Vee already outdoors by the hearth, heating leftovers from last night's feast. The rest of our family was soon in motion as well. Morning Star, Muh, and my sisters wished to go to the nearby river to wash, so Bror and I gathered our spears and escorted them to the water's edge. Many animals, predators and prey alike, go to water sources to drink early in the morning, so it would never do to let anyone go to the river without protection. As always, Raena came along, too. She was eager to drink while the rest of us began our ablutions. Muh, Ru, and Morning Star took care to wash their faces and limbs in the cold water but my younger sisters just dabbed the water on their faces without much regard as to whether or not they were actually becoming cleaner.

Bror and I also splashed some water on our faces and hands as well, but we were too busy keeping a lookout to worry about any real scrubbing. We stood on the upper bank of the river where we had a good view of the surrounding area and watched the women and children.

"I am so glad you have found happiness with Morning Star," Bror said. "She is a beautiful mate and so agreeable. And soon you two will have a little one of your own. The first of many, no doubt."

I turned to Bror and took in his wistful expression.

"Many thanks, Bror," I responded. "I feel sure that you will soon have happiness with your own mate. I wish that for you with all my heart."

Bror's expression suddenly became hopeful.

"Have you foreseen that in a Dream?"

"I would like to say that I have, but no, I have not. All the same, I do feel that your day is coming. You will be a good mate. And a good father. Saree adores you."

Bror smiled at the thought.

"Saree is a winsome child and I very much enjoy spending time with her. But I must admit that I would prefer to instead be spending time with your eldest sister."

I was not surprised by this revelation but I was not sure that Bror would have much luck in winning Ru. She was standoffish toward men and had an infinitely prickly nature.

Bror must have sensed my thoughts.

"I know you may think that Ru would not be receptive to my advances, but I do not think that she is as aloof as you would guess." Bror hesitated. "When I look into her eyes, I see something more, something deeper. She has a tender heart if only it could be reached."

Now I was surprised. When I looked into Ru's eyes I generally saw either sparks or ice.

"Well, Cousin, I do wish you all the best. If you care for Ru, she would do well to accept you. She could not find a finer man."

Bror smiled. "Many thanks, Tris. I hope she agrees. And I hope that your Puh still agrees, as well."

"You have spoken to Puh?"

Bror nodded, "Some time ago."

* * *

We returned to the outdoor hearth where Puh was holding Baby Mi and talking to Aunt Vee, Dor, and Lor as the final breakfast preparations were concluding. Aunt Vee encouraged everyone to help themselves to the various foods and then she turned to Puh.

"Let me hold Mi while you eat. That is, if she will come to me. I have seen that you always hold the baby at mealtimes and it seems to me that you might like to eat at least an occasional bowlful of food without trying to juggle an infant at the same time. Besides, I would so dearly love to hold a baby again."

Puh looked a little startled by this request.

"Mi, would you like to visit with your Aunt Vee?" Puh asked Mi.

Aunt Vee held out her hands toward Mi. Mi seemed a bit unsure, but allowed Aunt Vee to take her from Puh's arms.

"Oh, she is heavy!" Aunt Vee said as she smiled broadly. "I had forgotten that even a baby of this age can be quite an armful! Awna, I do not know how you carry her around as much as you do!"

Muh was quite tall for a woman, as tall as Puh, so seeing little Aunt Vee holding the plump and sturdy Baby Mi made the disparity in their sizes even more than was usually obvious.

"Well, it may help that I am a bigger woman, and besides, I am used to it. I have been toting babies of all ages for many years. I am done eating now. Let me take Mi so that you may have your breakfast, Vee."

Aunt Vee shook her head.

"No, let me hold her for a while longer. I can eat later. You will leave soon and I never know when I will be able to cuddle another infant again."

* * *

Later, as I was checking our sled harnesses, Muh approached me.

"What did you and Bror talk about while we washed at the river?" Muh inquired. "You two seemed to be very deep in conversation."

I looked into Muh's face to get a sense of why she was asking. I noted her smile and light mood. I grinned back at her.

"Just the usual sorts of things. Bror said that I was very lucky to have Morning Star."

"Did he speak of his own hopes?" Muh persisted. "Last year he asked for permission to court Ru but your Puh and I have seen no evidence of his courting. I was hoping he had divulged his intentions to you."

"Yes, he did. Well, in a round-about fashion."

"What sort of round-about fashion?"

"Bror said he would like to spend time with Ru."

Muh seemed disappointed.

"Is that all?"

"He said something about making advances…" As the term came out of my mouth and I saw Muh's eyes widen, I realized that I had not phrased my words well. "I do not think he meant anything disrespectful."

"No, Bror would not be disrespectful." Muh's smile returned. "He is a rare man. Better than most." Muh put an arm around my neck to pull me down to her height and she kissed my cheek. "But not better than you, my son. Nor your Puh."

I returned Muh's kiss and then bent to finish tightening the harnesses.

"So are you hoping that Bror still wishes to be paired with Ru? Is she not a little young?"

"*A little young?*" Muh repeated. "Ru is older than I was when I was first with your Puh. But she will be 14 this winter and most girls are paired by the time they are 15. Yes, I am hoping. Why else do you think I sent

her in after Bror last night when he put Saree to bed?"
Muh had a mischievous glint in her eyes.

My mouth dropped open with amazement as I realized that Muh was actively plotting to advance Bror's chances with Ru.

"If that is the case, well, I do not think that you need to worry about Bror fulfilling your hopes. It will be Ru who will need the push toward pairing."

* * *

The day became hotter and hotter as we progressed farther inland. We halted our trek more frequently to drink water and rest in the shade of the trees. I knew we were almost home as familiar scenery came into view and I saw Raena's ears perk up. Soon, I understood why Raena was so attentive: I recognized the well known woofs from our old dog, Rooph, and I heard many chattering voices.

We were still some distance from our home when Morning Star's family came down the path to meet us, followed by a limping Rooph who was panting heavily in the heat.

It was hard to tell who was happier to see us, Morning Star's parents or Rooph. Black Wolf ran the last few steps down the trail and swept Morning Star off her feet, pack and all. Like all of us, Black Wolf wore minimal clothing in this sweltering weather and he looked almost animal-like in his coating of black fur as he neared us and snatched-up Morning Star. If I had not known who he was, I would have been rather alarmed to see such a huge hairy man—sporting a chest-length beard and a head-full of stiff braids sprouting out of his scalp—descend upon my beloved mate.

For all his formidable appearance, Black Wolf seemed overwhelmed at the sight of his long-absent child and, after he hugged Morning Star, he sunk to the ground at the side of the path and sat with Morning Star in his lap, eyes closed, forehead to forehead with her, holding her tight. Morning Star hugged him, too.

"Oh, Da! It is so good to see you again!"

Morning Star finally struggled to free herself from his embrace and in turn, joyfully wrapped her arms around her mother and her younger siblings in greeting.

Little Fawn had tears in her eyes as she heaped kisses on her oldest daughter.

"We have never been away from you for so long. It seemed the summer would never pass. We have been waiting for this full moon, knowing that you would return home on this day. We arrived at Tor and Awna's compound this afternoon to await your arrival and when Rooph started to bark, we knew you were near, so we came down the trail to meet you. You are well?"

"Yes, I am well. In fact, I am more than well." Morning Star paused and placed a hand on her stomach. She gazed at me and took my hand. "Tris and I have a baby coming."

Black Wolf was still sitting on the ground, with his arms resting easily across his knees. He looked at me keenly.

"That did not take very long," Black Wolf said.

I shrugged. Was there a correct response to that remark? I very much doubted it.

Luckily, the sentiment was lost in the many words that were being shared at that moment. Muh and Little Fawn were absorbed in an excited conversation and Black Wolf and Little Fawn's children were busily engaged in gabbing with my littlest sisters; they were their playmates and they had been away for the last few moons, so there was much news to impart. And Saree had to show off Hork. The other children looked unsure as to how they should receive Hork, but they politely made her acquaintance.

Puh and I stepped out of the sled trappings and joined Black Wolf at the edge of the path. It felt good to sit down and rub our shoulders where they were reddened and grooved by the straps of the harness. Rooph planted himself between my feet, whining and licking my face. I tried to soothe him by softly cooing to him and stroking his long fur. This prompted Raena to seek my attention, too, and soon I was petting both dogs at once.

The Dreamer II: THE GATHERING

Black Wolf put a weighty hand on my shoulder and smiled at me. "I am glad to see that you and Morning Star are so contented."

"Many thanks, Black Wolf. I am grateful every day that you allowed us to be paired," I replied. "I am happier than I ever knew was possible."

"Hmmm." Black Wolf gave me a long glance. "You appear a little different. You look thinner."

"Like a buck at the end of rutting season," Puh said quietly. He was seated on the other side of Black Wolf. Black Wolf looked back and forth between us several times. He had known Puh since they were boys and he was well accustomed to Puh's dry humor. All the same, he could not contain himself:

"*Like a buck…*" Black Wolf sputtered. "Wait until it is you who has a daughter who is paired! That is my daughter your son is rutting with!"

"That is life, Black Wolf. How do you think Little Fawn's parents felt about you?"

This was an intriguing concept to me. It was hard to think of Little Fawn, so enormously tall and hulking, and now so matronly, as a prim maiden whose parents who would be concerned for her virtue. Black Wolf shook his head, causing his many braids to bounce.

"Oh, her parents were very satisfied with me. They were quite pleased to find a potential suitor who was actually taller than their daughter. Little Fawn was at least half a head taller than the tallest man they knew.

Her mother and father thought we were meant to be together."

I touched Black Wolf's arm briefly before speaking. "I would like to think that Morning Star and I are meant to be together, too."

Black Wolf smiled and nodded.

"Yes," he said. "You and Morning Star love one another. That is more than most have."

This was true. Most pairings were pre-arranged and their prime motive was to raise a family and ensure the continuation of the clan. In rare cases, such as my Muh and Puh, and Morning Star and me, we had paired for love. We were the lucky ones and we were well aware of it; unlike Black Wolf, who had paired with Little Fawn simply because he was very tall or Uncle Mror, who had paired with Aunt Vee in order to have part of her clan's enormous hunting territories. Both couples had eventually found a sort of happiness together, but I did occasionally get the sense that Black Wolf and Little Fawn barely tolerated one another. Maybe this was normal after a couple had spent many long years together, but I had never seen my Muh and Puh exchange a harsh word or show any sign of displeasure in one another.

* * *

After a short rest, we resumed our trek homeward. Black Wolf helped Puh and me to bring in the sled. As we pulled our burden down the remainder of the trail, I could smell the aroma of roasting meat and I was glad to know we would soon fill our empty stomachs.

Great Gran was aged, but she was spry and still well able to take care of herself. She and my brother Ty were tending the many victuals that were cooking on the outdoor fire pit, but they broke away to welcome us home.

The heat did not seem to affect Gran. Her touch was cool as she embraced me. She looked at me as she always did, peering deeply into my eyes. She was smiling but seemed she somewhat subdued.

"Are you well, Gran?" I asked as I stooped a bit to look into her face more closely.

"Yes," Gran answered. "At least, I am as well as one could hope for at my age. But you are changed. You are thinner."

"Like a buck..." Puh began.

"Do not get started on *that*, again!" Black Wolf cut him off.

Gran moved on to greet the rest of the family and encouraged everyone to commence eating as soon as they were ready. Not that we needed much additional incentive. It was not long before we were all seated on mats around the hearth and feasting on the delicious array of foods.

As usual, Puh tried to take Mi from Muh so that she could eat.

"Not yet, Tor," Muh said, "I want to nurse the baby. "You eat. I will be ready to give Mi to you by the time you have allayed your hunger."

Puh leaned toward Muh, inspecting her carefully for a few moments.

"You are pale," he told her. "Are you sure you would not like to eat a little something first?"

"I am all right," Muh assured him, "I am not hungry. My back hurts. I just want to sit."

Puh seemed concerned. I could not help but notice that Muh was indeed very white, despite the hot humid conditions that had almost everyone else red-faced and sweating. Puh put a hand to the side of Muh's face.

"I think you are over-heated. Rest in the shade. I will get you some cool water. Let me have Mi."

Muh shook her head.

"No, I will nurse Mi. But I would like a drink of water."

Puh left Muh to begin nursing Mi and entered the in-ground home to retrieve a cup of water from the water bag stored there.

"It is much cooler in the house. You should go inside and lie down," Puh said to Muh.

By now, we were all concerned about Muh. Her eyes had closed while she was nursing Mi. She looked pained.

"I do not want to move," Muh responded.

"I will carry you," Puh volunteered.

"No." Muh paused and grimaced. "My back hurts," she said again.

Puh looked around helplessly. He searched for Great Gran. Their eyes met and Gran immediately got to her feet and kneeled at Muh's side. After Gran made a brief assessment Gran said one word. "Ru."

Ru stopped eating and approached. Gran motioned to the baby,

"Take Mi for now."

"Yes, Gran," Ru nodded. Mi allowed herself to be removed from her mother's breast without complaint, but she seemed confused. Mi looked back at her mother as she was carried away.

"What do you mean, your *back hurts*?" Gran questioned Muh quietly.

"I do not want to even think this, but I believe I am in labor." Muh gasped and stifled a low groan. She then opened her eyes and grasped Puh's hand, "I am so sorry, Tor!"

Puh hugged and kissed Muh.

"Never mind. All that matters is that you are well. Hold onto me and I will carry you inside."

"No, I will get blood all over the place!"

"Then there is going to be blood all over the place. You are going inside," Puh insisted.

"Puh, let me help you carry Muh," I said as he lifted Muh off the ground.

Puh shook his head.

"Just make sure that neither her head nor feet hit the doorway frames on the way in."

"Yes, Puh."

Gran walked along side Puh and me. As Puh settled Muh into the bed chamber, Gran whispered to me. "Have Morning Star take the children from here. She does not need to see this in her condition."

"Her condition?"

"She is with child, is she not?"

I nodded dumbly. We had not yet said anything to Gran about Morning Star's pregnancy.

"I have foreseen this," Gran went on. "Prepare yourself. This will not end well. Have Morning Star get the children away from here. I will need Little Fawn's help. We will need Black Wolf to go to your Aunt Vee's to get assistance."

"*Assistance?*" I repeated. I could not imagine how Aunt Vee or my cousins could do anything if Muh was having a miscarriage. But Gran had already reentered the house.

Morning Star was hovering nearby and had heard the end of my conversation with Gran.

"I am to take the children away for a while?" she asked.

"Yes, my sweet." I embraced Morning Star and kissed her. "Just for a while. Take Ru and Ty, too. And Rooph and Raena. Go up to our home on some pretense… you have to air it out or something. I will come up and let you know when it is over."

Morning Star and I had our own little home up the hill from our ancient family compound. It would be a safe and convenient place for them to sit out this ordeal.

"Yes, Tris. Please tell Awna how sorry I am. I know how she was so looking forward to this baby."

"I will." We gave one another a last, lingering kiss before parting.

Black Wolf and Little Fawn were inside Muh and Puh's house when I returned. I informed them that Morning Star and my older siblings had taken the younger children up to my home. They nodded grimly as they stood hunched over under the low ceilings. I stood in the middle of the doorway to my parents' bed chamber. Gran was holding a small bundle and slowly shaking her head. She sensed my presence and looked at me.

"The children are gone?"

"Yes, they are at my house."

"Good."

Muh was strangely quiet. Puh was staring at her, aggrieved.

"What has happened?" I asked.

"Your Muh has lost the baby," Gran whispered, indicating the bundle in her arms. "It was a boy. He was stillborn." She sighed and tears appeared in the corners of her eyes. "It will not be long now. You should go and see your mother."

I quickly squeezed past Gran through the narrow opening. I knelt at Muh's side and took one of her hands. It was cold. Muh opened her eyes slightly.

"Tris!" She gasped my name, "I know…the feel of your hand…so big and strong… remember…that I love you!"

I was flustered for a moment.

"Of course I remember that. And I love you, Muh." I hesitated a moment before continuing. "Morning Star asked me to tell you…"

"Yes, I know…" Muh cut me off, still gasping for breath, "tell her that…I love her, too…"

Gran turned to Puh and whispered.

"Awna does not have much time left."

"No, you are wrong. You are *wrong!*" Puh said fiercely. "She will be fine. Awna has always been strong! She will live to see many more winters."

Muh was lying cradled in Puh's arms and it soon became apparent even to Puh that no being could lose this much blood and survive. Muh was fading fast in an ever-expanding puddle of deep red blood. She barely had the breath to speak. Her voice was scarcely audible.

"For all…I worried…about losing my Tor…it appears…that I…that I…am the one… who will go first."

The Dreamer II: THE GATHERING

"You will never lose me," Puh said fervently as tears streamed down the sides of his face. "I have loved you from the first time I saw you and I will love you until my eyes behold their last." He bent to kiss her lips.

"And…I love you…my gentle Tor…"

Moments later Muh passed peacefully.

Chapter Three

If there was ever a time I had to define when it was that I left my childhood behind, I would have to say it was not when I thought it would be. It was not when I turned 15 winters old and was first considered to be a man. It was not when I took a mate. It was not when I learned that I would be a father. It happened when I lost my mother.

Great Gran had expected that she and Little Fawn would prepare Muh to meet her ancestors, but Puh would allow no one else to touch her. All pleas to assist were met by Puh's quiet but adamant *leave us*.

We finally granted his request.

Gran, Black Wolf, Little Fawn, and I stood outside the hillside dwelling of my family, suffering from both shock and despair. Moments ago, everyone had been enjoying a happy homecoming and now our lives were irreversibly changed. Little Fawn was already weeping. Black Wolf's tears flowed as well as he placed an arm around Little Fawn to console her. Suddenly my legs seemed to go weak. I slowly sank to the ground and held my head in my hands. Sobs choked me. I cried as I had never cried before. Part of me rejected the hideous scene I had just witnessed. It was not possible that my mother, who had always been so vigorous and full of good health, had left us so quickly. But a larger part of me realized there was no denying what had happened before my very eyes. Muh was gone. Her beauty, her grace, the care and love she so lavished on her family, all forever gone.

Someone touched my arm. I looked up and through my blurred vision, I saw that Great Gran was crouched next to me. I drew her nearer and we wept together until I was distracted from my grief by the billowing smoke that poured from the chimney.

I wiped my still-streaming eyes and looked toward the earthen dwelling as the long shadows cast by the setting sun were enveloping the scene. The smoke was caught in the slanting rays, appearing as slices of light in the murky air. The chimney belched acrid fumes. It was then that I realized Puh must have been burning all the blood-soaked hides and furs in their bed-chamber. Muh hated being unclean. Puh would be washing the blood from her and then he would dress her in a fresh garment. His need to take care of her overrode his heartbreak at this moment.

As dusk set in, Gran began to rekindle the fire.

"What is Tor burning?" Little Fawn asked. "It smells like burning hair!"

I stood and approached Little Fawn and Black Wolf. They put their arms around my shoulders. I wiped my face before replying.

"I think that Puh is burning their bedding and anything else that was bloodied."

"What are we going to do?" Little Fawn sniffled. "We cannot leave Tor. There are all the children to care for. He will not let us in the house and Tris, your home is much too small to hold all of us! Where will we stay?"

"Give Puh a little time to absorb what has happened," I urged. "If need be, we can set up a temporary shelter nearby."

"That is not our only issue," Gran said as she joined us. "Mi is still nursing. Ru is a competent older sister, but she cannot nurse an infant. I can help Ru with the children but I am 64 winters old and if something happens to me, Ru would be left alone to mother her younger siblings. She must have help. Black Wolf, can you take Ty and go to Vee?"

"Mror's Vee?" Black Wolf questioned incredulously. "She is older than I am, and I am 34 winters old! She is mother to three grown men; she will not be nursing any babies!"

"Of course not!" Gran said indignantly. "But she can certainly help manage a household! And her sons can help Tris bring in wood and meat for the winter. Tor is not going to be himself for some time. If this family is going to get through the coming winter, we must take action. Right away."

"Yes. That makes sense," Little Fawn concurred. "I can nurse Mi. My baby Dewdrop is only a moon older than Mi and I have plenty of milk."

Black Wolf nodded and he seemed heartened at the idea of having something useful to do.

"If Ty and I leave first thing in the morning, we would return late the next day."

"What about me?" I asked.

"Your father needs you," Gran and Black Wolf said at the same time. They looked at one another, somewhat taken aback that they had thought and said the same words at the same time. Gran went on. "You are closer to your father than anyone else. He will need your support."

"Yes," Black Wolf agreed and then he added. "He will let you in before anyone else. You will need to talk to him and at least get him to agree to let us into the house for the night."

"But first I must go home and tell Morning Star and my siblings what has taken place." That was the last thing I wanted to do at that moment, but it had to be done.

A low moon illuminated the path to my hillside home. Morning Star was seated amongst our younger siblings in the crowded little room, but she sprang to her feet when I came in the doorway. As soon as she saw my face, her shoulders slumped and she put a hand over her mouth. I embraced her tightly and rocked her in my arms. My eyes began to flow once more.

"Tris, what is it?" Ru demanded.

"Is Muh all right? And the baby?" Ty asked anxiously.

All I could do was shake my head for a moment. With effort, I collected myself enough to talk.

"Muh…had a miscarriage…she…she has passed," I finally said.

Ru's mouth dropped open. She instinctively gathered Ty and Twie to her as tears began to pour down her cheeks. Twelve-winters-old Ty was already taller and heavier than Ru but he gratefully accepted her comfort. Twie looked stunned. The youngest children, my littlest sisters Mi and Saree and Morning Star's sisters Sky and Dewdrop, were asleep on our bed. I went over to Twie and lifted her up in my arms.

"Twie, do you understand?" I asked.

Twie shook her head.

"I understand your words but I do not believe them. I cannot believe them. Muh is really all right, is she not?"

I was fighting a losing battle with my composure. I could not answer.

* * *

Sometime later, I left my home to return to the family compound. Black Wolf, Little Fawn, and Gran were seated around the fire pit, absently nibbling on foods left over from our abandoned meal.

"Has Puh come out yet?" I inquired.

"No," Black Wolf answered.

I had expected this.

"I will try to talk to him," I announced.

I stopped in the doorway of my boyhood home. The thick earthen walls usually kept the rooms cool during summer, but the now-faltering fire had made the space rather warm.

"Puh?" I called hesitantly.

There was no reply. I called out again, only louder this time. "Puh?"

Silence.

"Puh, may I come in?" I found myself overwhelmed by grief and soundless sobs wracked me once more. "Puh, *please*! Please answer me!"

All of a sudden, Puh appeared in the darkened entryway to his bed chamber. His reddened eyes were hollow. His expression was one of absolute devastation. Without waiting for an invitation, I went to him. By now, neither of us had any tears to be shed. Extended weeping and dehydration after two days of pulling the sled down the trail had left us dry. But we needed no words or tears to understand one another. We momentarily leaned against each other until at last Puh sighed. "I need to start digging."

"Right now?" I asked. It was nighttime.

"Yes," Puh said. "If tomorrow is another hot day, it will be easier to dig now while it is cool."

"I will help you."

"Many thanks, Tris." Puh said with a nod.

As we exited the house, Little Fawn and Black Wolf wrapped Puh in a hug.

"Tor, we will stay here as long as you need us," Black Wolf assured him.

"Many thanks, my old friend," Puh said flatly. He seemed utterly spent. He walked away without engaging in further conversation.

I explained that I was going to help Puh dig Muh's grave and that they should go up to my home and collect the children so that they could be put to bed in our absence. I then followed Puh the short distance to the burial grounds. It was an easy walk through an ancient pine grove to the open meadow where many piles of stones indicated the place a loved one had been interred.

Puh had brought shovels, but he set them down and began to gather tinder and pieces of deadwood. He started a small fire to light the area where we would dig and to help drive away mosquitoes. Working together, it did not take long to excavate the correct size hole and reach the permafrost layer. We would need to place wood inside the pit and make a substantial blaze. It would likely have to burn most of the night to thaw the frozen earth so that the pit could be further deepened to a suitable depth. Once the fire had caught, Puh sat down to watch the flames. I sat next to him.

"Go home, Tris," Puh said quietly.

"I want to sit with you," I responded.

Puh shook his head.

"Go home. It is a big fire. No animals will bother me. I want to be alone with my thoughts. Please go home." Puh turned and met my eyes. I could see that he meant what he said. I did not want to add to his distress.

"Yes, Puh," I replied. "I will go home but I will be back first thing in the morning to help you finish digging."

Puh nodded. I started to walk away when Puh called after me. "Many thanks, Tris."

"Yes, Puh."

* * *

Back at the main house, I found that everyone, including my Morning Star, was inside. The younger children were in bed, but Ru, Ty, and Morning Star's sister, Petal, were still awake with the adults. Little Fawn and Gran were kneeling at the hearth, heating food for those who were hungry. I realized that not only was I famished, but I was quite thirsty as well. Morning Star had anticipated this and immediately brought me water, refilling my cup until I told her that I had had enough.

"Have any of the little ones expressed any concern about Muh?" I asked.

"Not since Puh first brought her inside," Ru answered. "I told Saree that Muh-Muh was very tired and needed to rest."

"And thankfully, she has been too absorbed in taking care of her beloved Hork to take interest in much else. She is determined to be a good mother to homely Hork. Saree has even tried to feed her leaves and pebbles," Morning Star said. "I am grateful that she has been too busy to need any explanations regarding her Muh, yet." Morning Star managed a weak smile. "I am also grateful that I was apparently not beautiful enough to have my name selected as a possible moniker for Hork when Bror suggested that Saree name her doll for someone pretty."

"What do you mean *not beautiful enough*?" Black Wolf said, looking up sharply.

"You are the most beautiful woman I have ever known," I assured Morning Star, giving her a kiss. And, indeed, she was. "Much prettier than any doll. I think that Saree has picked the perfect name. If there was anything that was ever to look like a *Hork*, it is Hork."

While I waited for the food to finish cooking, I found myself walking toward my parents' bed chamber. Morning Star came with me. A seal oil lamp was lighted, lending a soft golden glow to the small room.

The Dreamer II: THE GATHERING

Muh was lying on her side, semi-curled up. Puh had dressed Muh in her best garment, the one she had worn at my pairing ceremony. Her long dark red locks were loose. Puh had always loved to see her with her hair down. Puh had painted her face with delicate lines of ocher that emphasized her high cheekbones, her large eyes, and full lips. The tiny deceased infant was wrapped in an otter pelt and placed in Muh's arms. Except for the ghastly grayish-white color of Muh's skin, she might have been taken as one who was sleeping.

I felt as though I could start weeping all over again, but my eyes were so swollen and sore that I squelched the urge. Morning Star and I stood over Muh, holding each other tightly. Morning Star seemed to fight back her tears as well.

"Poor Awna," she said at last as few drops escaped from her eyes. "I loved her almost as much as I loved my own mother. Our families have spent so much time together over the years that it is almost as though we are actually one family instead of two."

"Yes," I agreed. I was too emotionally drained to say anything else.

Morning Star kneeled by Muh and touched her hand.

"She is so lovely, even in death."

* * *

The next morning I arose at sunrise and joined Puh

at the burial ground. Puh was already at work and had almost completed the job. I took up a shovel and we continued to dig until we again hit permafrost. By now, the ground level of our hole was nearly as high as I am tall, so we decided that it was deep enough. Puh and I scrambled up the slope at the end of the long narrow cavity and then leaned on our shovels to rest for a moment. This gave me an opportunity to briefly examine Puh. He looked gaunt and haggard. His long hair was becoming unkempt; the once carefully arranged and neatly lashed coils were now coming loose.

As we gazed down at our handiwork, Puh spoke hoarsely.

"I want to bury your Muh before the youngest children awaken. That would be the right time. But Tris, I do not know how I can do it. I cannot put her in the cold hard ground…nineteen years together, eleven pregnancies…she bore nine children with no complaints. She spent so much time waiting and worrying for me."

"I hate the thought of burying Muh, too, Puh," I began, "but we have to do it."

"I know." Puh nodded and sighed. He seemed to need to talk. "I was 13 winters old when I first met your mother. She was a year younger than I, but right away I knew that she was the girl I wanted to be paired with. She said the same thing about me, but even so, I felt that I must make a very special gift to show my great love for her. I traded for pieces of walrus ivory and began to whittle them down into rods for putting up her hair, instead of those wooden sticks she used. I spent so much time carving them down to the right size, my family thought I had gone mad. I did not tell them what I was making. They saw me continuing to whittle for no apparent purpose, the rods becoming slimmer and slimmer. When at last I thought that they were right, I then etched designs into the ivory. They were supposed to look like vines and leaves, but I am not a very good artist and they did not much resemble anything but random scratches."

"Muh cherished those ivory rods. She dressed her hair with them every day." I said.

"Yes." Puh smiled a little. "She did."

* * *

Puh accompanied me back to the family compound. Morning Star tried to ply him with food and water, but Puh would only drink a little. He claimed that he was not hungry. Black Wolf and Ty were preparing to hit the trail and the youngest children were still asleep. We needed to carry Muh and the premature baby from the bedchamber to the burial ground as soon as possible. Puh and I quickly constructed a litter that would allow us to transport them in the most dignified manner we could manage. Using great care, Puh then shifted Muh and the baby to the litter. When she was arranged to his satisfaction, he looked up at me from the floor where he knelt. His eyes were those of a man trapped in a nightmare.

"I will take the end at her head," Puh told me and he went to stand at the front of the litter.

We each grasped the poles and lifted as one. Leaving Great Gran and the dogs to stay with the slumbering children, the rest of our family and friends followed Puh and me to the burial grounds. An orange sun climbed through the branches of the trees and the clouds were stained in a brilliant array of purples and pinks in the slowly brightening sky. Black Wolf and Little Fawn carried the armloads of furs that would be used to line the grave. When we arrived at the site, each of us was again in tears. As Puh stood back, we kissed Muh and held her hand one last time. Black Wolf went down into the hole and arranged some of the furs. Standing there, head and shoulders above ground level, he addressed Puh.

"Let me place Awna on her nest of furs. I am tall enough that I can reach her from here. I will be gentle, I promise."

Puh looked at Black Wolf for a long moment. I could see that Puh had planned on moving Muh, but there was no doubt that Black Wolf's suggestion was much less awkward than Puh trying to carry Muh and the baby into the narrow ditch, himself. Black Wolf could sense Puh's indecision.

"Please, Tor. Let me do this," he said.

Puh nodded. Black Wolf reached out with his long arms and touched Puh's forearm sympathetically. Then, he gingerly picked up Muh, with the infant still in her embrace. He carefully laid Muh on her side, just as she had been positioned on the litter. Before removing himself from the grave, Black Wolf kissed his fingertips and then placed them on Muh's forehead.

Puh took the last of the furs from Little Fawn. These would be used to cover Muh and the baby before the grave was filled.

"I will do the rest," Puh said to us. "Many thanks for being here…for all your help. I will do the rest," he repeated pointedly.

And so, we left Puh alone to finish the interment process. Muh was situated next to my brother Dak and two more siblings who had not survived infancy. I liked to think that she would have been pleased to know that she was near those long-mourned offspring.

* * *

We expected that Puh would rejoin the family after he had refilled the hole. Black Wolf and Ty left us to embark on their journey to Aunt Vee's and the rest of us made some attempt to get on with life. Hungry children needed to be fed, the sled still needed to be emptied, and wood needed to be hewn. While Gran, Ru, Little Fawn, and Morning Star unpacked the contents of the sled, I went into the nearby woods and began to chop a large oak tree that Puh and I had previously selected. The tree crowded other oaks, so culling this valuable hard wood would allow the surrounding trees to thrive.

Usually Puh and I would be doing this work together but for the time being, I would need to do this chore on my own. All the same, I was glad to have something to occupy my mind. Doing something physical helped to allay the powerful grief which still assailed me in unexpected waves. I would be chopping away with no particular thoughts in my head and then, all of the sudden, I would get a mental image of Muh or I would remember something she had said and then tears would escape from my eyes once again.

Coping with Muh's death was hardest when I visited the family compound. Morning Star and I did what we needed to do to help keep both households running, but we were relieved to be able to return to our own home where we could pretend that things had some semblance of normalcy.

Black Wolf and Ty arrived with Aunt Vee the next day. Bror and Lor had set out for the mountains to visit the home of Black Wolf's cousin, Gray Elk, a man known for breeding and raising especially fine dogs. Both Raena and Rooph had been procured from Gray Elk. Last spring, Bror and Lor had made deals with Gray Elk for some of this summer's puppies and they had gone to retrieve the young dogs before the start of the fall hunting season. The middle son, Dor, was left at home so that upon his brothers' return, he could inform them of all that had taken place. Now that Aunt Vee was here, it meant that Little Fawn, Black Wolf, and their younger children could at last go back to their own home, although poor bewildered Baby Mi had to go with them so that Little Fawn could continue to nurse her. Eventually, after Morning Star had given birth to our child, she would take over Mi's nursing, but in the meantime, Black Wolf and his family would return to visit on a frequent basis so that Mi would still have regular contact with us.

* * *

Some days later, I brought in a deer and butchered the carcass outside of the little home I shared with Morning Star. Raena watched with interest as I cut up the carcass and handed slabs of fresh meat to Morning Star. Some of the meat would go down the hill to feed those at the family compound and some would be consumed by Morning Star and me over the next day or so. The rest would be dried or smoked and added to our winter stores.

I was glad to be done before an imminent thunderstorm rolled through. I had listened to the approaching rumbles of thunder and felt occasional raindrops as I made the last few cuts. I was washing my hands when Ru strode up to us. Morning Star smiled in greeting.

"Ru, you are just in time to take home some deer meat," she announced.

Ru looked at the heaps of meat noncommittally.

"Maybe later," she said distractedly and then Ru turned to me. "Tris, I need your help with Puh."

"What is he doing?" I asked.

"Nothing."

"Then I do not know how I can help," I shrugged.

Ru seemed exasperated that I did not understand.

"I do not mean that he is doing nothing, as in nothing unusual, I mean that he is literally doing nothing! Puh has not come home yet! He sits at the grave, day and night. He will not talk. He will not eat. I bring him food and water several times a day and he will drink a little but that is all. Do you not see?"

"Oh." The skies suddenly opened up and we were swept by the torrential rains. "Let us discuss this indoors."

Morning Star escorted Ru inside while I made sure that the hide tarpaulin I had been working under adequately covered our newly harvested meat and the deer skin.

I was thoroughly wetted by the time I joined them. Morning Star gave me a section of soft chamois hide to wipe my rain-soaked face, limbs, and torso. Even if the rain was inconvenient, it was good to know that this storm would likely break the hot spell.

The Dreamer II: THE GATHERING

Morning Star began to dry off my back as I talked to Ru.

"What do you want me to do?" I asked. After all, even though I was very sorry to know that Puh was suffering so, it did not seem there was much I could do to relieve his grieving. As Ru had said, any time I had approached him while he was at the grave site, he had refused to speak or acknowledge anyone.

"Tris," Ru spoke passionately, "you are the only one who can exert any influence on him and failing that, you are the only one big enough to physically remove him from the grave site."

I shook my head at the thought of what she proposed.

"Ru, I know you are upset," I said. "We all are. But we must give Puh time to grieve in his own way. Even if I could, I would not forcibly drag him away."

"But listen to the storm. He cannot sit outside in this weather."

I nodded. This was true. Morning Star was already gathering up foodstuffs and a small water bag.

"I will bring these things…" Morning Star started.

"No," I interrupted her, "There is no use for all of us to get wet. You and Ru stay here. I will bring your offerings to Puh and see if I can get him to come in out of the storm."

As I went back out into the pelting rain, I had to shelter my eyes with a hand at my brow. The now-naked deer carcass still hung from a tree branch and it swung around at the whim of the gusting winds. I made my way through the violently waving brush and swaying trees, cringing at each crash of thunder and blinding bolt of lightning.

The scene that met my gaze as I approached Puh brought back the memory of my last Dream at the coast. Puh sat on the wet ground, his hair completely undone. He was drenched through and through. Puh was still attired only in the loin cloth that he had worn since our trek home from the shore and he was thoroughly sunburned and covered in mosquito bites. He seemed leaner than ever, his scarred face almost skeletal. He stared straight ahead, but he did not seem to be focused on anything in particular. Seeing Puh and the patch of bare dirt with Muh's pile of stones, one for each winter she had been alive, was a heartrending sight.

I was unsure of what I should do, so I simply sat next to him. I knew Puh would not accept the food and water, so I just set down the parcels. I, too, was wearing only a loin cloth and the heavy precipitation stung where it hit my flesh. I suspected that a bit of hail was mixed in with the rain. I noticed that Puh's eyes moved and he gave me a sidelong glance. I looked around, trying to seem nonchalant. Raindrops were dripping off my nose. I cleared my throat.

"Nice weather we are having," I stated.

A flicker of reaction showed in Puh's eyes. Lightning arched overhead with a loud, sharp crack. Puh continued to stare.

I noted that there were fresh animal tracks in the dirt where it was sheltered in Puh's lee. Deer, rodents, and one bear had walked all around Puh and the grave. I looked at Puh, astounded. Apparently, he had sat so still that the animals had become accustomed to his presence and were neither alarmed by him as a potential hunter nor saw him as a possible food source. The wildlife had come close enough to sniff him but it was evident that they did not do more than investigate this curiosity before moving on.

I decided to do the same as Puh. I sat motionless.

Time passed and the storm raged.

At last, the rumbles of thunder became more distant and the rainfall lessened.

"I know why you are here, Tris." Puh spoke in a raspy voice without turning to address me. "I cannot go home. I cannot bear to be there without Awna. I cannot stomach the thought of eating. I cannot sleep. The little sleep I do get, I dread. I am haunted by dreams of your Muh. I see her in everyday life. I relive making love to her. I have nightmares of all the blood and nightmares that she is still alive and I must dig her up from the grave and release her from her earthen prison. All I know is that I want her back. I just want to hold her in my arms once more."

I acutely regretted my lack of eloquence. I wanted to comfort Puh, but the only thing I could think of to do was to draw closer to Puh and put an arm around him.

"I wish I could say or do something that would ease your anguish," I said after a time. "I do not know what else to do except to be here for you."

At that moment, Great Gran appeared at the head of the path that led back to the family compound. When she saw us, she stopped in her tracks as though taken aback by the sight of us, before continuing to approach us.

"You men!" She said harshly. "Sitting out in the rain as the worst storm of the summer roars through! I had to step over two fallen trees as I came up this path! A tree could have come down on your foolish heads!"

Puh seemed startled at this unexpected verbal assault. Gran's expression softened as she neared us. The rain was now falling only in occasional drops. Great Gran knelt at Puh's other side and she pulled his head to her shoulder. It was disconcerting to see Puh, the strongest man I knew on so many levels, laid so low.

"Oh, Tor, your life is not over," Gran murmured to Puh as she stroked his wet hair. "You are not ready to hear this yet, but you still have a long life and a future ahead of you. You have been lucky to have had a mate who was beautiful, kind, and most importantly, who gave you her heart without reserve. Tor, you have given Awna a happiness that she would not have found elsewhere."

"I also gave her much worry and grief," Puh spoke, his voice husky with emotion.

"Love and happiness, and worry and grief, are two sides of the same stone," Gran replied. She then looked at Puh and went on, "one who has loved so greatly once, can love greatly again. In the meantime, your family needs you. They still must eat, growing children need hides for new clothing, and firewood must be brought in for the coming winter. Do not bring about the doom of your loved ones as you let yourself be consumed with pain. You can carry on mourning as you carry on with life."

Before Puh could respond, we heard Saree's piping voice. "Puh-Puh! Puh-Puh!"

"Saree!" Gran said sternly. "What are you doing this far from home by yourself?"

"I need my Puh-Puh," Saree answered, undeterred. "I heard Aunt Vee say that you were going to Puh-Puh, so I followed your foot prints in the mud to find him!" Then, without hesitation, Saree climbed onto Puh's soggy lap and put an arm around his neck. "Oh, Puh-Puh, you have to help me! You must fix Hork! I tried to feed her, I put a pebble in her mouth and now it is stuck in there. I cannot get it out. Help me, Puh-Puh."

Saree held out Hork for his inspection, who was indeed afflicted with a stone wedged into the permanent smile that had been carved into her face. This gave Hork's usually demented appearance a rather saucy element, as though she was sticking out her tongue.

An instant change came over Puh. He wrapped his arms around Saree and kissed her face several times.

"My poor Little One!" Puh said. "Of course I will fix Hork."

"Puh-Puh," Saree's voice sounded muffled as she tried to talk whilst pressed up to Puh's shoulder, "You are squishing me!"

"So I am." Puh ceased to crush her to him. "I am sorry, Little One. Let me see Hork."

Saree gave her precious Hork to Puh, looking at him adoringly and with complete confidence that he would remedy Hork's current difficulties. Puh pulled the rock from Hork's clay lips and Saree beamed with pleasure.

"Many thanks, Puh-Puh!" Saree hugged Puh. "Many thanks! Now I can feed Hork some leaves. And maybe a caterpillar. How could she get those things down her gullet with that pebble stuck in her mouth?"

"That would present a conundrum," Puh agreed. A little shakily, he rose to his feet with Saree still in his arms and began to walk toward home.

Chapter Four

Puh could no longer live in the place that had been his home throughout his life, so he built a lean-to nearby. He did not have the lean-to all to himself, however; Rooph insisted on sleeping there with him.

Besides our usual late summer chores of hunting, harvesting berries and grapes, and cutting firewood, Puh and I also needed to do some construction. We needed to enlarge the tiny dwelling Morning Star and I inhabited to make room for our eagerly anticipated new child, and we had to build Puh something more substantial to house him throughout the coming winter. Morning Star and I only required the addition of a little cubbyhole and that was a very quick project —completed in a just day. Puh's new home took a little longer. As usual, we dug into the hillside to take advantage of the earth's insulation to keep us warm in the winter and cool in the summer. We shored-up the ever-growing cavity with wooden supports as we burrowed, and we created a fireplace with a chimney hole overhead to finish the project.

* * *

Aunt Vee was exceptionally skilled at preparing foods and fortunately, she finally managed to coax Puh into eating. It quickly became apparent to all of us how Uncle Mror and Bror had managed to maintain their incredibly muscular well-fed physiques. What was somewhat puzzling was why Dor and Lor were so slender in comparison to their older brother and late father; unless one simply assumed that they took after their diminutive mother.

In any case, we were all relieved when Puh at last began to take sustenance. It did not take long before he was restored to his former state; still lean, but at least he was no longer distressingly thin. Even though Aunt Vee produced special foods she hoped would entice Puh to eat more, like Muh, she had no success in getting Puh to put on any extra weight.

On the other hand, Morning Star's 15-winter's-old lissome figure showed definite signs of impending motherhood. I must admit that I have been enchanted with her figure for as long as I could remember, but these delightful changes brought about a fresh fascination that sometimes made Morning Star giggle when she reminded me that there would come a time she would be as round as an apple. I promised Morning Star that no apple would ever look so charming.

* * *

The Dreamer II: THE GATHERING

Puh still struggled with deep sadness over Muh's death and, as Gran had predicted, although he was more or less functioning normally, he was not himself. He was absentminded and often would stop in the middle of a task and stare into space. If someone spoke to Puh during one of the spells, it would take several attempts to get his attention.

Puh still spent much of his spare time sitting by Muh's grave. When first I saw him walk in that direction, I was alarmed to see that he was not carrying his spear. Ever since I had seen the bear tracks at the burial ground, I made an effort to be more cautious when I left the family compound. We had been marking our borders with urine for generations and that had kept away most animals, but the borders did not include the burial ground. Those bear tracks were proof that even if large animals were not coming near our homes, they were still moving through the area.

My own spear in hand, I stopped at Puh's little dwelling and grabbed one of his and then quickly followed him down the trail.

Puh was kneeling on the grass by then time I got there, with one hand on Muh's pile of 31 stones. His eyes were streaming. I felt as though I was intruding on his grief, but he could not continue to come here unarmed.

Puh did not hear my approach. He did not realize that I was there until I placed a hand on his shoulder.

"Puh," I said, "I have brought one of your spears. Bears come through here. You must be prepared in case one of them comes along."

Puh shrugged.

"The old bear that rambles through here has never bothered me," he responded.

"You have seen it more than once?"

Puh nodded.

"Sometimes he comes up and licks my face. I think he likes the salt he finds there."

I was horrified at the thought of that old boar bear coming so close to Puh. Although most bears seek to avoid humans whenever possible, when close encounters do occur they are not typically happy events. The slash-mark scars Puh wore on his chest were a testament to the fact that bears were not always so mild tempered.

"But, Puh…" I was speechless. Puh had returned to staring into space, one hand still on Muh's pile of stones. More tears leaked from the corners of his eyes. Was he courting death? Did he hope that the bear or some other creature would put an end to his misery?

* * *

However, Puh did seem to make a concerted effort to come back to life for his children. When Black Wolf and Little Fawn brought Baby Mi back for a visit every so often, Aunt Vee again wanted to hold the tot, but Puh would gently but firmly insist on holding Mi himself. Poor Mi clung to Puh and cried when it was time to leave. Each time Puh watched them depart and saw Mi's despair, he looked so terribly aggrieved. During one of these farewells, Morning Star stood by Puh and wrapped her arm around one of his, the same way she sometimes did with her own father.

"Tor," she said softly, "I know it is hard to see Mi carried away. Take heart, it will only be for five or six more moons and then I will nurse Mi and she can stay here with us."

Puh nodded and smiled somberly at Morning Star.

"Many thanks, Morning Star. I do take heart. I am so very grateful to Little Fawn for taking care of Mi and I am also so very thankful that you are willing to step in after you have given birth to your own child." Puh laid a rough hand along side of Morning Star's face. "Speaking of hearts: you have a beautiful heart …to go along with your beautiful face. I am so glad you are part of our family."

Morning Star seemed touched.

"You are kind to say so," she responded demurely.

"Poor little Mi," Aunt Vee said as she joined us. "I hate to see her so sad when they leave."

Despite her words, Aunt Vee had been looking decidedly chipper lately, more so than she had since Uncle Mror's passing. She seemed to enjoy having youngsters to care for, even if she missed her own sons at the same time.

Saree sauntered up to us, Hork tucked under one arm. She tugged at Puh's hand and when he turned to her, Saree held up her arms in a wordless request to be picked up. Puh lifted Saree off her feet, taking a few moments to brush some dirt from her cheek and stroke her curly hair. Saree snuggled into him, still holding onto Hork.

"Puh-Puh, when will Muh-Muh be rested?" Saree asked. "Ru said that Muh-Muh was very tired and needed to sleep, but I want Muh-Muh."

Actually, Ru had tried to explain to Saree that Muh had passed, but Saree could not understand the concept of death. She seemed to grasp the notion that animals died to provide food and other necessities of life for us, but in her mind, the same did not hold true for people. We had given up on trying to reason with her. Puh rocked Saree back and forth.

"I know. I want your Muh-Muh back, too." Puh hugged Saree as much to draw comfort from her as to give it.

* * *

More than a moon went by and summer had swiftly turned into fall. We made day trips to go out and pick the last of the summer's grapes and the first of the fall's apples. Soon, it would be time for Puh and me to select a bee hive to rob for another year's supply of honey. Although we knew how to harvest honeycomb without arousing the wrath of the bees, it was still a tricky chore and I hoped that Puh was up to the job.

One day, Rooph and Raena suddenly began to bark and they looked expectantly toward the path to the west of our family compound. It was not long before I heard men's voices and the enthusiastic high-pitched yelps of young pups answering the deeper woofs of the older dogs. I knew that it would be Aunt Vee's sons, finally arriving with the puppies they had acquired from Gray Elk.

Aunt Vee was nearly beside herself with happiness as Bror, Dor, and Lor strode onto the compound. All three men were weighted down with heavy packs. Between their packs and all the gear they toted, they probably carried the equivalent their own weight on their backs. After each son had hugged and kissed his mother, they turned to greet us as well. Ru hung back, but I saw her peek out the doorway before withdrawing from sight. Bror spoke to Morning Star and me, wrapping a brawny arm around each of us.

"I was so very sorry to hear about Awna." Bror hesitated as we nodded to acknowledge his sympathy. "But I must say that both of you are looking very well. Especially you, Morning Star. You are positively glowing! Prospective motherhood certainly becomes you!"

"Why, thank you, Bror," Morning Star replied as she clasped her expanding belly. "Most times I feel as though I have water bag tied around my waist, but otherwise I feel fine."

"Your gown hides your condition." Bror looked Morning Star up and down. "No one would think that you are concealing any water bags under your clothing."

Morning Star was dressed as was usual for a woman during the cool early fall weather, her feet still bare, but wearing a shapeless garment that hung on her like a sack. I was standing behind Morning Star and I embraced her.

Now that my arms were around her middle, it was much more obvious that Morning Star was indeed quite pregnant. Bror's eyebrows raised.

"Ah," he said, "now I can see it. Not a water bag, maybe, but there is definitely a little bundle under there!" Bror paused and then asked, "Where is Ru?"

"Ru is indoors," I replied, motioned over my shoulder.

"Come, I will take you to her," Morning Star offered.

Morning Star and Bror departed, while the other brothers, who also expressed an interest in seeing Ru, followed them. I shook my head. That was an unfortunate turn of events for Bror. He would not get a moment alone with Ru. Aunt Vee must have thought the same thing. She shook her head.

"Bror is so smitten with Ru." Aunt Vee mused.

"Bror is a good man," Puh remarked vaguely before he turned to walk away. Aunt Vee watched Puh stroll off.

"Your Puh is still so lost," she said. "I was hoping that he would start to come around by now. He does not take care of himself; his hair and his beard are a mess. I have offered to help him with them, but he refuses any suggestions of assistance."

"He will find himself again," I stated. It was true that Puh looked as though he had been on the trail for many moons. Unable to make the traditional corded coils of the Old Ones by himself, he simply plaited his hair into a rough braid. Puh had not trimmed his beard since the last time Muh had cut it during the spring, so these days it was rather long and scraggily. And his beard was now noticeably whiter than it had been previously.

"I hope so. He has been through so much. When his father and oldest brother were killed, he and Mror had to provide for their family…they were still so young. I had just met Mror about that time." Aunt Vee smiled at the recollection. "Mror was such a strapping young man! He was 16 winters old but he was already the head of his household. When Mror and I paired, your father, at 14 and about to become paired himself, was left to take over." Aunt Vee paused and sighed. "Never would I have guessed that one day Mror would be gone and I would be here at his childhood home, helping to raise his brother's children."

"It is very good of you to stay here and help us." I touched Aunt Vee's hand. "I am sorry that you have to be away from your own home and your sons for so long."

"It is no hardship on me." Aunt Vee smiled again. "I love the children. And I would do anything for your Puh."

* * *

The three brothers had arrived with packs laden with smoked and dried meats. As they explained, they had a surplus due to the passing of Aunt Vee's parents earlier in the year. Supplies for six people had been stockpiled the previous fall, but what with fewer to feed, they had decided to donate some of the excess to us to help nourish our families.

I felt that this was a kind but unnecessary gesture. I had been bringing in a deer every few days and Morning Star and I carried at least half the venison from each deer to the household down the hill. Thus far, we had ample stores and we were steadily adding to our winter food cache.

When Puh was up to it, we would hunt more deer after rutting season commenced in earnest. The larger breeds of deer and the elk start their mating seasons earlier than the smaller ones, and I had seen plenty of signs that they had already begun the preliminaries. Trees and brush showed where the bucks had rubbed their antlers, tearing off small branches or stripping away layers of bark.

I had to take care where I stepped because the bucks also pawed the ground or, depending on the species, used their front hooves to dig shallow trenches in which they then urinated. They were usually quite pleased by the resulting puddle and would pause to enthusiastically splash in it, coating their fronts with a muddy mix of dirt and musky urine. It was not a spot to accidentally place your feet, unless one also wanted to attract enraged bucks to your person, who might mistake you for a rival—or chance a meeting with an amorous doe—the potential results of which were too ridiculous to bear thinking upon. All the same, it was still early fall and the bucks had just begun to engage in sparring. The serious battling would come later, when the stags' resounding cries would echo throughout the woodlands and open fields for all to hear.

Bror, Lor, and Dor were determined to stay for at least a short while to visit with their mother and assist however they could. Bror's great strength was a boon as we continued to hew firewood. The green wood was heavy and even though there were few men I would hesitate to tackle, moving the sections of tree trunks was a formidable task and Bror proved that he was even stronger than I. I highly suspected that Bror was eager to flex his muscles in front of Ru, but it did not seem to matter what Bror did or how kind he was to Ru, she mostly ignored him. I hoped to smooth the way for Bror by mentioning his high regard for her. When I came down the hill to bring yet another batch of smoked deer meat to the main family compound I found Ru outside, scraping a pegged-out deer hide that I had given her the day before. Ru and I were alone, for once.

"Where is everyone?" I asked.

"Aunt Vee is inside," Ru spoke without looking up, "making honey seed cakes, so she has a rapt audience as our younger siblings eagerly await the fruits of her labors. Aunt Vee's sons have gone hunting. Great Gran has left to bring Puh something to eat and drink."

I sighed to hear that Great Gran was delivering food and drink to Puh. That meant that he was at the burial ground again.

"I have brought smoked venison," I told Ru.

She nodded.

"How are the food stores looking for this coming winter?" I inquired as I cast about for a topic of conversation.

Ru brushed a few stray strands of hair from her face and sat back on her heels for a moment.

"We still need more. If we are lucky, we will have enough to see us through. It does not help that we have those three men staying with us now. They eat more than anyone else I have ever seen. Even you."

I was surprised at this. Not only because I had thought that our supplies were sufficient, but because it seemed an incredibly ungracious thing to say after our cousins had worked so hard to add to the family's stockpile of food, hides, and firewood.

"I think that they contribute a lot more than they consume," I said. "We do not get to see our cousins very often. It is pleasant to spend time with them."

Ru replied with a non-committal noise.

"Bror is very fond of you." I hoped that this would spark some kind of womanly reaction from Ru.

"Bror is simply looking for a mate," Ru said flatly. "The same as his brothers."

"But Bror truly cares for you."

Ru shrugged.

"He would be a very fine provider," I added.

"He is old," Ru stated. "He will be 20 winters this year."

There was no arguing that Bror was not older than the typical man of the Old Ones is at his pairing. Even I was older than usual when Morning Star and I paired after the winter I had turned 17.

"Besides," Ru continued, "I do not want to have a mate. I have enough to do already. And I certainly do not want to get pregnant and bleed to death like Muh."

At last, I realized why Ru was shunning the company of her cousins and especially taking pains to avoid Bror.

"Oh, Ru," I began, "any of us could die on any day. You cannot live your life afraid of something that might never happen."

"Spoken like a true big brother." Ru went back to scraping the hide. "And someone who will never have to worry about being pregnant!"

I was about to heatedly respond that I certainly had to worry about Morning Star's pregnancy, but at that moment Black Wolf, carrying Baby Mi, and Little Fawn, toting Dewdrop, followed by their string of offspring, came up the path. This brought about a lot of barking, as our two dogs, the cousin's two pups, and Black Wolf's numerous dogs set up a clamor that almost drowned out our words of greeting.

"More mouths to feed," Ru grumbled.

I was pleased to have an excuse to leave Ru's acerbic company and welcomed our guests heartily. Baby Mi soon set eyes on Ru.

"*Ru-Ru!*" she exclaimed, reaching for her sister with arms outstretched.

Ru brushed off her hands and rose to her feet. She nodded at Black Wolf and Little Fawn and wordlessly took Mi from Black Wolf's grasp. Ru snuggled the baby tenderly, rubbing her check against Mi's soft curls as she walked away.

"Ru misses her mother," Little Fawn noted.

"We all do," I agreed.

"Where is your Puh?" Black Wolf inquired.

"At the burying ground," I answered. "He stays out there almost any time he is not actively involved in some task. Sometimes he even sleeps there."

* * *

Later that evening, Ru was further exasperated when more relatives made an appearance. My Puh's brothers Kror and Zor and their grown sons—Kror's Sevek and Whot, and Zor's Krenk—unexpectedly stepped off the trail and stood in the middle of the family compound, looking around with interest whilst the many dogs frantically barked at them. Kror and Zor had not visited their boyhood stomping grounds in a very long time. Puh's brothers were not more than a few winters younger than he, and likewise, my newly arrived cousins were slightly younger than I. Like Puh, Kror and Zor were of average height, but their physiques varied somewhere in between my late Uncle Mror's remarkably robust build and Puh's muscular, but lean frame.

Morning Star had come down from our little dwelling to catch up with her parents and siblings, and she was helping the other women prepare food for the crowd of people who now filled the clearing in front of the main house. We had all been chatting amicably, but a silence fell over the group as my uncles and cousins looked over the assembly. They did not seem pleased.

Puh still behaved in a rather subdued manner as of late, but he actually seemed happy to see his brothers and nephews. He embraced each one, smiling at them broadly. The men knew Black Wolf and Little Fawn, but they needed to be acquainted with all the younger children, and Morning Star, whom I proudly introduced as my mate. They traded uneasy glances. I wondered about the significance of this. Uncle Zor briefly mentioned that they had heard some sort of story that I had gained a mate under unusual circumstances.

When they inquired as to the whereabouts of their brother Mror and my Muh, I quickly explained that both Uncle Mror and my Muh had passed. Very formal condolences were extended, especially to Puh and Aunt Vee. They were polite, but I could not help noticing that they seemed unusually agitated.

"It is good to see you all," Puh finally said, "but you have traveled quite a distance. What has brought about this long journey?"

The men again exchanged looks. I noticed that they particularly seemed nervous when they glanced at Black Wolf.

Kror cleared his throat and hesitated for a moment before speaking.

"First, I would like to say in advance I want Black Wolf to know we realize this has nothing to do with him and we mean no offense. But there has been a lot of trouble in the lands we settled back when Zor and I left to find new hunting grounds, land where we could provide for our families without competing with you or Mror for resources."

"I will take no offense then," Black Wolf said. "I will sit back and eat my meal and stay out of your business. Just pretend that I am not here."

Kror nodded his thanks.

"What do you mean by *trouble*?" I asked, wondering why Kror was so worried about offending Black Wolf.

"Some of The People from the East have been raiding our homes," Kror answered, speaking passionately, "stealing food and belongings and destroying what they do not take. They only come when we men are away from home and our women and children are defenseless. The fiends have even killed our dogs! They are trying to force us to move further north onto the open tundra where we will have no shelter from the elements. We do not stand a chance if that happens, especially after winter sets in."

"How do you know they are trying to force you to do anything?" I questioned.

"Because they could hunt and procure their own meat and goods. Instead, they steal or destroy ours. Why else would they do that unless they are trying to drive us off?"

This was serious. I had never heard of this kind of behavior before.

"We are here to ask for your help." Kror went on. "We cannot fight them alone. There are too few of us." Kror looked pointedly at Puh for a response. Puh was reluctant to speak.

"You are my family, but members of The People… Black Wolf is my life-long friend. He helped to save my life last spring. Tris is paired with Morning Star. They are my family now, too," Puh spread his arms to indicate Black Wolf and his kin. "We still have to finish getting our winter stores in. Why can we not talk to these People and work out a peaceable agreement?"

Zor was clearly frustrated with Puh's remarks.

"*Work out a peaceable agreement?* While they are taking or ruining the very things we need to survive? Tor, I know you are grieving and you are not in your right mind at this time. But do you not understand? If we are driven out of our homes and our hunting grounds with winter fast approaching, it means certain death! Do you not care what happens to us? We are on the verge of being wiped-out!"

Puh looked wearily at the group of men.

"Of course I care," he spoke quietly.

Zor's son Krenk looked furiously from Puh to me.

"You do not want to help us because Tris's mate is a woman of The People!" Krenk said in a seething voice he choked out the words. "Those females are spindly, weak, and useless!" Krenk turned to me angrily. "And I hear that they are cold as a winter's night!" Krenk looked accusingly at Morning Star.

"That is why you hesitate; you do not want to give your mate any reason to refuse you!"

I crossed the space between Krenk and me in an instant and threw my closed fist at his head, just the same as Black Wolf had taught me last spring when I had to fight a man of The People to win the right to be paired with Morning Star. Krenk never saw the blow coming and he fell to the ground, landing on his back, arms and legs splayed. He did not move. This created an immediate uproar amongst the families and the dogs began to bark once more.

I was still so enraged that I shook as I stood over him, hands clenched, waiting to see if he would get up. I had never been so incredibly incensed in all my life, and yet I was pained at the same time, to hear him talk about Morning Star in that way. My beautiful mate, my good-hearted, hard-working, and above all, loving Morning Star, who had heard every word that he said. She came up to me and clasped my right arm.

I looked down at Morning Star and noted her frightened expression and my mood suddenly softened. I pulled her to me and put an arm around her waist. As I thought of Morning Star's freely given kisses, her welcoming arms, and all the day to day toil that she did with never a word's complaint, I became angry all over again.

"I will not let him speak of you that way," I told Morning Star.

"Tris, it matters not," she said to me. "Please do not fight."

Krenk was starting to move a little. His eyes opened. He looked bewildered. By now, everyone except Black Wolf, who had remained seated in the shadows at the edge of the grouping during this altercation, stood around Krenk, who sat up with help from his cousin Whot. He could not seem to focus his eyes and he appeared to be confused. Zor knelt before his son.

"Krenk! Do you ken?"

Krenk looked at his father for a long moment. He swallowed and surveyed the faces that surrounded him; finally his eyes came to rest on mine.

"Tris… what… what did you hit me with?"

I was still so furious that I could barely answer him.

"I hit you with my hand. And you will *never* speak of Morning Star that way again, or the next time it will be far worse for you!"

"Tris, *please!*" Morning Star whispered, looking at me earnestly. "Please, Tris! No more fighting!"

"No one will ever disparage you within my hearing," I insisted, but her worried expression made me want to comfort her momentarily. "It will be all right," I assured her.

I turned to Krenk again who was slowly gathering his wits.

"I had forgotten," Krenk began, "that you had won your mate with your fists."

"You also show how little you know about The People, their women in particular. I could not want a more perfect mate than my Morning Star. She is a tireless worker and as full of love as I could want!" Without thinking, I pulled at the back of Morning Star's gown so that the deer skin material tightened over her blossoming figure and plainly showed that she was pregnant. "She bears the proof within her body. She carries my child."

Morning Star was clearly embarrassed, especially in front of this group of staring men. Even Puh showed more interest in the sight than he had in anything else in the last few months. He sat up straight and blinked as he looked at her.

"Tris, please!" She said again, tugging at her dress in an attempt to make her newly voluptuous form less conspicuous.

Black Wolf at last rose to his feet and came to the center of the gathering. My uncles and cousins drew back at the sight of his dark and forbidding countenance. But Black Wolf, although he was a man with a volatile temperament, struggled to put his feelings aside and he managed to force a sociable smile.

"I have a suggestion," Black Wolf told a rapt audience. "There is to be a Gathering of The People later this fall. We should all attend and you could make them understand what has been happening."

"They would kill us!" Zor was incredulous at the very thought.

Black Wolf shook his head.

"They would do no such thing. These are not savages. They would be very upset to hear that some of The People have been behaving in such a dishonorable fashion. I believe that they can put enough pressure on the culprits to make the raids stop."

"Do they allow Old Ones to attend these gatherings?" Kror seemed thoughtful.

This caused Black Wolf to stop and consider for a moment.

"I have never seen any Old Ones there, but…"

"We will be killed!" Zor said again.

"No," Black Wolf insisted. "I will go with you and make sure that you are heard."

"You will help to negotiate for us?" Kror pressed.

"Yes. I will," Black Wolf said with a nod.

Chapter Five

I am exploring a wooded area that is unfamiliar to me. I can hear the rush of moving water nearby. Suddenly, something is on my back; it is clawing at me...

Morning Star was shaking me by the shoulder and calling my name.

"Tris! Tris! Wake up! Wake up, Tris!"

I looked at her in a daze and realized that I had been Dreaming.

"Tris, you were flailing around as though something had attacked you," Morning Star told me. "Were you Dreaming? What were you Dreaming about?"

Morning Star seemed truly alarmed.

"It was nothing," I replied. "Just a dream... I think I dreamt that a lynx or some or animal had jumped on my back and I was trying to get it off of me. It was just a dream..."

"You and your Dreams! Sometimes they frighten me," Morning Star said as she nestled up against me.

"Sometimes they frighten me, too," I admitted. "Very often I wish that I did not have them. But I cannot really wish for that; after all, my first Dream helped me to find Puh when he needed me last spring. And you and I would most likely not be paired if that adventure had not taken place. That would be tragic, because I cannot imagine my life without you, my sweet."

I kissed Morning Star with warmth and she melted into my embrace. Morning Star managed to make every bad Dream a mere afterthought. It was soon all but erased from my memory.

* * *

Sometime later, Morning Star and I were eating a leisurely breakfast of dried fish and berries when my Uncles Kror and Zor and their sons approached our dwelling. Morning Star stiffened and drew back at their approach.

"A pleasant day to you all," I welcomed them somewhat warily. Morning Star moved to stand behind me, but after the men returned my greetings, Krenk went around me, smiling at us sheepishly. He was sporting a large livid bruise on his left cheek that disappeared into his hairline. Keeping an eye on Krenk, I turned my body to face him as he nodded a greeting to Morning Star. I was then surprised to see him pick up her left hand. Morning Star appeared bewildered as well.

"I fear, Morning Star, that I was inexcusably rude to you last night." Krenk bent his head humbly, eyes closed, and placed the outside of Morning Star's hand against his forehead. "I hope you will forgive the ravings of an overly excited and distressed young man."

Morning Star's guarded expression softened to a smile.

"Of course I will forgive you," she said simply.

Krenk removed her hand from his forehead, but continued to hold it as he looked up and met her eyes.

"Many thanks for being so gracious." Krenk patted her hand and let it go, and then turned to me. "I wish to beg your pardon, too, Tris. I deserved the crack on the head you gave me. It will remind me for many moons to come to control my tongue and my emotions."

Krenk touched the side of his head gingerly. He was so sincere and so clearly in discomfort that he now had my sympathy.

"I understand that you were speaking under duress," I said. "I believe that you also came to understand me."

Krenk gave me a pained grin.

"I most assuredly do. That will teach me not to antagonize an older and much larger cousin who knows how to throw his fists."

My uncles and cousins laughed soundlessly.

"Yes," Kror added, "we heard various stories about how you won your mate. We did not realize that she was the daughter of Black Wolf, of course; we only heard that you fought a man of The People and that you beat him…and that he whined piteously about it afterward. He stated that men of the Old Ones should not be allowed in the Challenge Circle because of their great strength. And after I saw you wallop Krenk, I must say the man may have had a valid point. You must have pummeled that man into the ground!"

I shook my head.

"Actually, I scarcely knew what to do. Black Wolf showed me how the men of The People fight, but I only had one very brief training session. Snow Leopard may have complained about the Challenge when it was over, but he was a tough adversary."

"The scar on Tris's brow is from that fight. It was terrible to watch," Morning Star joined in. "My poor dear Tris took so many hits. I never want to witness anything like that ever again."

"Snow Leopard was a little taller than I, so he had longer arms and could reach me more often than I could reach him," I added. "Mostly, I was trying to avoid his fists and figure out how to disable him as quickly as possible. During the entire length of the bout, I only had the presence of mind to throw one blow toward Snow Leopard and it was a poor one, at that. The rest of the time, I fought as we Old Ones do. Luckily, it was enough to accomplish the task." I put an arm around Morning Star's waist and smiled down at her lovingly as she looked up and also put her arms around me.

"So the bash that met with my skull was only the second punch you have ever landed?" Krenk asked. "Oh, my aching head! I am glad you did not get more practice!"

"We are setting out for home," Zor said, changing the subject. "We dare not leave our families for any longer than necessary. They are hiding in a new home Krenk and I built in the thick of the forest, but I do not count on the remoteness to protect us forever."

"Did you speak with Puh and Black Wolf before you came up here?" I inquired.

"Black Wolf only," Kror replied. "We could not find your father."

"That means he was at the burial ground," I informed them. "Puh has trouble sleeping. He says he can only sleep if he goes to the burial ground and lies by Muh's grave."

"So that is where he slept. He gave us his home in which to shelter for the night. We thought he went into the house and wondered where he would sleep there, what with all the people who were already packed into the place." Kror shook his head. "Poor Tor. I can only imagine the devastation he must feel.

He was so wildly in love with Awna from the start. When he started carving those ivory sticks for her, we had no idea what he was doing and we teased him that if he was making toothpicks from walrus tusks, he was going the long way about it."

"I hope that time eases his grief. Soon." Zor commented. "Before the snow flies, or he will freeze to death out there."

We all nodded in agreement.

"What did Black Wolf say?" I prodded Uncle Kror to continue.

"He said that The Gathering starts at the next full moon. It takes place at the convergence of the White River and the River of the Bears. He promised to meet us there the day before it begins. Will you come too, Tris? And bring your Puh? The more Old Ones we can get to accompany us, the more weight will be behind our voices."

"Of course I will," I said. "I am sure that Puh will, too. Maybe it will help him to be away from here for a while."

"I do not like to mention this, but it must be said," Kror began. "We have to do this. This is not only about us," he said as he motioned to his brother and their sons, "but your homes and supplies may be threatened next. We are all in danger until this issue is resolved."

The Dreamer II: THE GATHERING

Before long, my uncles and cousins departed and commenced their lengthy trek homeward.

* * *

In the meantime, we still had a lot of food to bring in for the winter. Bror and his brothers returned to their own household to finish their seasonal preparations as well, although they too agreed to meet with Black Wolf at The Gathering on the day before the full moon. Aunt Vee's sons would need every day between now and then to make their way home, bring down as many deer and elk as possible, process the meat, and then hike all the way out to the Gathering. Most years, they journeyed all the way out to the vast plains on the other side of the mountains where they could hunt the migrating reindeer, but there was no time for that this autumn. Since they could not take their new pups on this long excursion, they left the pair of lively young dogs at our family compound, to be cared for in their absence.

* * *

Fall was in full swing now. Any foliage left on the trees was at its height of color. At times, there were so many migrating birds and fowl winging across the skies that the day temporarily darkened as though storm clouds had blown in. Like us, all other forms of life were readying for another long winter. They were either moving to warmer climes or stuffing themselves with great quantities of food so as to fatten up before they settled in to hibernate.

We were busily collecting tubers, onions, leeks, nuts, and grains. The last of the fall's apples were also harvested. They nearly rock-hard at this point but would be soft and wrinkly by spring.

The next chore was to go after honey. Puh was still wavering between occasional episodes of lucidity and periods of despair and apathy. I had found a promising bee hive that was located in a nearby tree, and luckily, it was not too high up off the ground. The bees had managed to fill the tree's cavity with honeycomb and then continued to build free-form combs outside the main hive which were suspended from a large branch. These could be sliced off at their tops and carefully placed upright in a sack, so that a minimum of honey would leak out of the comb.

Puh and I discussed the procedure.

"This is good weather to collect honey comb," I said to Puh. "It is too cool for sweating."

Puh nodded. It was important that Puh was ready to participate, because he was smaller and lighter than I, so he was the logical choice to climb the tree. Although Puh and I had done this every year since my boyhood, this was not a common undertaking amongst those of the Old Ones or The People.

It was by good fortune that some ancestor had discovered that the bees would ignore almost anything we did as long so we let smoke saturate the surrounding area and made sure that our bodies bore no animal scent.

Although the bees could be soothed with smoke, the few things that could bring them out of their hive in full attack mode were movements that would shake the tree or anything that might resemble an animal in a fur coat or a human dressed in animal skins. Puh would have to ascend and descend the tree slowly and carefully so as not to raise their ire. And we would have to be unclothed. Even the sack I would use to hold the honey comb would be made of woven grasses. The blade used to sever the combs was knapped from stone and carried in a sheath made of plant fibers.

"You have your knife?" I asked Puh.

Again he nodded.

"Good," I said as I picked up the woven sacks. "Let us get started."

A short distance from where we were talking, Aunt Vee stood in the entryway of the house.

"Is today the day you will gather honey?" Aunt Vee asked.

"Yes," I answered.

"Will you go far?"

"No," I responded, "it will not be far. You may smell smoke. Do not be alarmed."

"I have never seen honey collected. May I go along?" Aunt Vee continued as she approached. "I have always been fascinated with bees."

"That would not be a good idea," Puh said flatly. "It will take time. We must light smoky fires upwind of the hive and let the smoke drift over the area for some while."

"I do not mind smoke," Aunt Vee assured us.

"While the smoke does its work, Puh and I must go to the stream to wash, because we cannot carry any scent," I informed her. I paused and waited for that information to sink in. She still looked at us blankly. "We cannot give the bees any hint that there might be an animal nearby," I added. "That means that we must leave our animal-skin clothing at the stream…you may see more of Puh and me than you want to." I did not have the heart to tell her that she would have to bathe and be unclothed as well. Aunt Vee suddenly blushed.

"*Oh!*" She turned on her heel and walked back into the house.

I grinned at Puh.

"I guess the thought of seeing you and me unclothed is not that appealing."

He shrugged.

"She might not mind seeing a young man like you. But as for me, I am old. She always says that I need more fat. I must be a pitiful looking man compared to her memory of Mror."

"I would not be so sure of that. I think Aunt Vee is a bit enamored with you," I told Puh. He looked up at me sharply.

"I cannot think that…" Puh stammered. "She could not possibly…even if…I could never pair with the mate of my fallen brother! The brother who sacrificed himself to save me!"

Somehow, I was not surprised by Puh's shocked and appalled reaction.

* * *

The days were becoming distinctly cooler. We men were now wearing heavy long-sleeved elkskin tunics over our loin cloths and leggings, and many-layered boots on our feet. The women returned to donning an extra apron-like garment over the dress that covered them from shoulder to mid-calf and the tall boots that helped to pad and protect their knees while they were kneeling, as they often did to prepare food at the fireplace, work hides, tend to children, make clothing, or produce other household items.

Frequent frosts meant that Puh no longer slept at the burial grounds. I was relieved to see that he was spending less time there now. It may have been because we had so much work to do before we left to meet my uncles and cousins at The Gathering just prior to the next full moon, but I hoped it also meant that he was coming to terms with Muh's death. He still would not allow anyone to touch his hair or beard so he continued to look disheveled, but at least he seemed to be more his old self. The only time I saw him once again look significantly stricken was when Black Wolf and Little Fawn arrived with Baby Mi and their own children, and it occurred to all of us that Baby Mi was no longer a baby. She was nearing her second winter and she had gone from a tot who took a few occasional and hesitant steps to a toddler who could walk easily and comfortably on her own. And she was now speaking in broken sentences.

"Awna would be so disappointed to miss this," Puh said to us. "Her dear Baby Mi is growing into a child."

* * *

While Black Wolf and his family visited, Puh, Black Wolf, and I prepared to leave on our annual fall hunting trip, one of the few that took us away from the family compound for an extended period. This would be the first time that I would be away from Morning Star for more than a morning or afternoon since our pairing last spring. I did not like the thought of being separated from her, especially while she was pregnant, but there was no helping it. I had to go.

We had gathered up our gear and loaded the travois sled at sunup, and now we were ready to leave. The frost was thick on the ground and each spoken word was accompanied by a puff of white vapor. Morning Star insisted on walking down to see us off, even though she would normally still be up in our little hillside home, warm and cozy by the fire. She stood by patiently as we finished the last few tasks and then, when I realized that all was ready, I turned to Morning Star, pulling her to me.

"I must leave now," I said to her regretfully.

"I know," she replied.

"I will be back as quickly as I can. It should not take but a day or so to bring down enough animals to fill the sled with meat."

"I know," Morning Star repeated, trying to smile but somehow managing to look unhappy just the same. "I will miss you while you are gone."

I held her tighter and leaned down to rest my forehead against hers. Our exhalations merged into one cloud of misty fog. I kissed Morning Star's face several times.

"I will think of you always while I am gone."

She nodded.

"I will be thinking of you, as well."

Black Wolf was fidgeting. He cleared his throat loudly and Puh shuffled from foot to foot, anxious to hit the trail.

"I have to go now." I kissed Morning Star's lips long and hard. It did not seem to be quite enough so I kissed her some more. "I have to go. I love you."

"Yes. I know. I love you, too," Morning Star kissed me, as well. "Be safe. And come home to me soon."

Black Wolf cleared his throat again, louder this time.

We engaged in another long kiss.

"I will be safe. And I will come back to you as quickly as I can," and then I released Morning Star, but still held one of her hands. She walked along side of me toward the sled.

"Let us go, now." Black Wolf said, becoming increasingly impatient. He approached his daughter and hastily bussed her cheek. Morning Star reached for Puh to give him a quick hug and kiss.

Raena was at our feet, so I ruffled the fur on the top of her head as I said to Morning Star, "One more kiss." As our lips met, I heard Black Wolf groan.

"Enough, already!" He turned to Puh. "Have you ever seen such a drawn-out sendoff?!"

"Yes," Puh replied.

Black Wolf sighed heavily.

Finally, after one more round of I-love-yous and more kisses, I had to let Morning Star go. I stepped into the sled harness and began to pull the sled away, but turned back to look at Morning Star before we entered the path and lost sight of the family compound.

Morning Star was still standing there with Raena. I was glad to see that Raena was sticking close by her. It was comforting to know that Morning Star would have the dog for company and protection while I was away, so that even when Morning Star was home by herself, she would not be truly alone. Morning Star waved farewell to me, moving just her fingertips.

I smiled at this gesture and raised my hand in response.

"Tris, you are going to walk into a tree," Puh warned me quietly.

"Oh!" I said. "Many thanks, Puh."

I returned my attention to the trail. I glanced back one more time, but the trees blocked my view of home. My beloved Morning Star was gone from sight.

* * *

This excursion would take us to a place that was nearly a day's hike away. An early start would get us to the wood and meadowlands frequented by many different species of deer during the rut, where dominant bucks gathered and jealously guarded their harems. While we walked through the slanting rays of morning sunlight, we strode amidst the colorful falling leaves as they floated earthward from their lofty perches. The sled was laden only with our wisent cloaks, my pack, lengths of rope, extra spears, a couple of large axes, empty sacks, and several hide tarpaulins, so it was still fairly light and easy to pull. I was glad to have something to take my mind off Morning Star. I had to keep the travois sled poles in the ruts made by many previous trips to prevent it from getting caught up in tree roots or from going off the edge of the trail. All the same, my thoughts often returned to her. I had to convince myself over and over again that she would be fine in my absence. The other women were just down the hill if Morning Star needed help. In fact, I guessed that while I was away she would probably spend most of her time at the family compound.

We had been traveling for some while when Black Wolf spoke.

"Let me take a turn at pulling the sled, Tris."

My shoulders were starting to become quite sore, so I gratefully stepped out of the harness and picked up my pack from the sled. Black Wolf filled the void left by my pack with his own and took his place at the head of the sled. Puh, Black Wolf, and I would switch roles between puller and pedestrian several times before evening.

"It is too bad my dogs are of no help when hunting deer," Black Wolf commented, "because they surely would have been helpful in pulling this sled!"

We sometimes made use of Black Wolf's many dogs when we were hunting boars, since they kept the boar or sow's attention focused away from us while we approached from the rear, but when it came to deer they were problematic. Then, the *bark at the front end of the animal* mentality of these dogs was extremely awkward, as mostly it served to make the deer run away.

At this time of year, the larger deer, such as the giant deer, elks, and many of the red deer, were nearly done with their breeding season. The lead bucks were thin and worn out from breeding the does in their harem and fending off challengers. Late in the day we came to an expanse of open field, where we saw a giant deer herd that was defended by a stag who must have been a very impressive animal just a few short moons ago. He was huge, with an enormous spread of antlers that were each nearly as long as I was tall. Now, he was becoming emaciated and his step was slow and deliberate.

Another buck approached. This one was younger and his antlers were somewhat smaller, but he looked well fed and strong. He appeared to be sizing up the stag. As if guessing what might be running through the other buck's mind, the stag turned to face the interloper and bellowed mightily. The younger buck bellowed back. The sound of their voices was incredibly loud. Their cries must have carried for a great distance. We stopped to watch them as they continued to bawl vociferously at one another. Finally, the younger buck decided to make his move and galloped toward the stag with an earth-trembling gait. The stag let the buck come close before he ran the last few steps to meet him, head lowered. The terrible collision of these two massive animals was almost beyond description. My head and neck hurt just thinking about the force behind it.

They drew back and re-engaged countless times. Even though we were far enough away to watch undetected, we could hear their grunts and panting as they locked antlers and tried to push one another around. The younger buck had some success at shoving the older stag until his neck was bent at an uncomfortable angle and his side was exposed. If the younger buck had been able to swiftly untangle his antlers, he then would have been able to gore his opponent, but he could not disengage quickly enough to accomplish this.

The stag was obviously tiring. He could not straighten his neck and the younger buck, powerful legs and shoulders straining, held him in place. Finally, the stag's legs collapsed beneath him and their antlers dislodged. At that moment, the older animal forced himself back up onto his feet and he took off at a slow trot. He was spent and he knew it. The triumphant young buck bellowed at the stag's retreating form and he then cantered joyfully amongst his new harem. Most of the does had already been bred by now, but he would still have an opportunity to mate with any of the yearling does who were late coming into season, or the mature does who had not yet conceived during previous matings.

Puh smiled at me and put a hand on my shoulder.

"Watching that made me think of you and Snow Leopard," he said. "You were the younger, stronger challenger and you beat the tough older buck!"

"And, like the deer, I rammed Snow Leopard with my head several times," I said, grinning back at Puh.

The Dreamer II: THE GATHERING

* * *

As of now, the larger deer and the elk were either settling down after all the excitement and pandemonium of the breeding season, or else they were exhausted past caring about potential predators. But the smaller roe and fallow deer were still quite distracted by the procreation process and they, too, had little attention to spare for us. These important factors meant that all the deer were easier to hunt and we intended to use this to our advantage.

If everything went according to plan, we would arrive at our well-used hunting shelter later in the day and probably spend a little time repairing the damage that had occurred since our last stay before bedding down for the night. With luck, during the next day or so we would have ample opportunities to bring down a sufficient number of deer to fill the sled with meat. The temperatures were cold enough to allow the raw meat sit for the day or two it would take to make our way home again. Because predators would be attracted to a sled laden with fresh meat, we would have to be very alert during the trek home and all three of us would pull the sled at once so that we could move at the fastest possible pace.

Much as we had expected, our shelter had suffered during its period of vacancy and we needed to patch up the spots where the fir bough thatching had thinned or fallen through. The floor also needed to be renewed with more fresh fir boughs and dried grasses in order to keep us up off the cold ground. Because of the fir trees' sap, the repairs were a sticky project, but it did not take long to make the hut more or less restored. We then set about building a fire and finally sat down to eat and drink, chatting quietly about our hopes to get through the next day with no misadventures. Darkness came quickly, and with it, the biting cold returned.

Black Wolf pulled his wisent cloak around his shoulders more snugly. He then looked skywards, where the waning moon illuminated white clouds as they scudded across a star-studded firmament.

"This night is freezing. We will get another heavy frost," he predicted.

Puh also gazed up through the tree limbs overhead.

"Yes. It will not be long before we receive our first snow."

"I am ready for sleep," Black Wolf announced. "I will see you both again in the morning."

We nodded our response to him. Black Wolf was swallowed by the dark interior of the little shelter and we heard him situating himself for the night. Soon, the sounds of his snores drifted to our ears, easily heard over the sighs of the wind and the occasional vocalizations of creatures that were lurking somewhere in the vicinity. Puh and I smiled at one another.

"Shall I tell him to roll over?" I asked Puh. He waved my remark aside.

"Let him sleep. At this rate, he will wake and turn himself over. Then you can go in and get a little rest."

"What about you?" I inquired. Puh shook his head.

"I do not sleep. Not very much, anyways. I will sit out here by the fire. Maybe I will drowse a little."

"Puh, you must sleep sometime."

But gauging by Puh's appearance since Muh had passed, Puh truly did not sleep much. I wondered how long he could carry on this way, but then I realized that he had slowly returned to eating and he had managed to become fully coherent again; surely, normal sleep would eventually follow.

Puh shrugged but put a hand on my shoulder.

"Why do you not go and lie down, yourself? The next few days will be long ones."

"No. I would not get any rest anyway, what with Black Wolf making so much noise."

"All right, then…" Puh said with a grin, "tell him to roll over."

I shook my head.

"I think I will stay out here for a while. Besides, it does not feel right to go to bed without Morning Star. I do not know that I can sleep without her next to me."

Puh looked at me solemnly for several moments.

"Yes, I know what you mean."

* * *

The next morning I was roused by Black Wolf's rumbling bass uttering the words *Take away your hand.*

"What?" I opened my eyes and found that I was lying next to Black Wolf on the floor of the hut. In my sleep, I had placed my hand on top of his arm. "Oh."

I withdrew my hand and slowly sat up. Black Wolf momentarily glowered at me darkly, looking bigger than ever in the close confines of our shelter. He scratched at his head, snorted a little to clear his nose, and then yawned, showing a set of strong teeth in the midst of the copious plaited facial hair. Now that I was used to beginning each new day with the sight of my lovely naked delectable Morning Star, feeling her soft touch and kisses on my lips, this was indeed a rude awakening.

Black Wolf suddenly grinned.

"Did you forget where you were?" he asked.

"Yes," I replied, still rubbing the sleep from my eyes.

I looked out the entrance to the shelter and saw that Puh was already standing by the fire with an armload of gathered deadwood, patiently placing each piece of timber in just the right place to allow the fire to breathe as it also increased in size and strength. The sky was starting to brighten. As Black Wolf had foretold, a thick coat of frost blanketed the world under a fragile white crust. The air was quite frigid.

The Dreamer II: THE GATHERING

We had slept with our water bags positioned between us in the hut to keep the contents from freezing during the night. I wondered if Puh had come in to escape the chill temperatures. If he did, he had managed to do so without disturbing my sleep and had left again before Black Wolf and I had awakened.

Black Wolf and I exited the shelter and each went to find a place to relieve our bladders near the edge of the shadowy woodlands before returning to the warmth and light of the fire to eat, slake our thirst, and discuss strategy. I was pleased to see that Puh appeared alert and strong. His eyes were sunken with lack of sleep, but he seemed ready to take on whatever the day may hold.

We were steadily filling our stomachs as we talked. It was important to be well-fueled before we set out. We stuffed ourselves with dried meats, several of the hard little apples, handfuls of roasted shelled nuts, and Aunt Vee's honey seedcakes. Leaving the sled and most of our gear at the shelter, we soon departed for the trails that led to open grasslands.

The sun was still quite low in the sky, but its golden radiance was captured in the rising mists that were swirling in the air just above the ground. Our breaths came in little clouds. We tread slowly and carefully as we made our way down the trail, trying to make as little noise as possible what with so many crunchy leaves and sticks underfoot.

The deer were beginning to stir, leaving the places where they had bedded down for the night and soon they started to trek toward their daytime meadow haunts. It was not long ere we heard the sounds of animals crashing through the brush. Suddenly, several fallow does appeared as if from nowhere and leapt across the path. They did not notice us. The commotion continued and a moment later, a fallow buck charged out of the forest in pursuit of the does. He also did not perceive our presence. The noise of his chase carried on for some time before the relative quiet returned to the woods and all we heard was the cheerful morning songs of the birds.

"If we had been a little closer, we might have had one of those does," Black Wolf spoke with evident disappointment.

"That is what the buck is thinking," Puh said with a nod.

Black Wolf gave Puh a long look.

"You *are* coming back to life."

Puh did not respond; he simply kept walking. But Black Wolf and I exchanged small grins. This was a good sign. Puh was regaining his sense of humor.

We had not gone much farther when we saw a single file procession of does and adolescent fawns winding through the brush. They were walking at a steady but easy pace. Taking care not to make any sudden movements, we broke from the trail. Each of us took a position behind a tree and there, we froze in place. The trees did not completely shield us from the view of the deer, but they did help to disguise our forms. Our plan was to simply stay still and hope that the deer would come close enough to strike at least one of them. These were fallow deer and relatively small as deer go; the does, for example, were scarcely more than one-tenth the weight of a giant deer doe. However, several of these animals would still provide a significant amount of meat and we needed to bring down as many as possible in a short period of time. Therefore, we were not going to pass up any opportunities simply because the deer were of a smaller species.

As luck would have it, the deer stayed on the path, each hoof-fall making a delicate crunch as it landed on the leaf-strewn trail. We hardly dared to breathe as they neared. We could hear their exhalations and the clicks of the older does' arthritic joints. *Closer…closer…*

We let the first few does pass us before we burst into their midst. Each of us thrust his spear into the side of a deer, aiming for the area behind the foreleg, where we might hit the heart or lungs, habitually twisting the shaft of the weapon as it was inserted to widen the wound.

The deer took to a panicked flight, bounding off in all directions. The three injured does attempted to follow their companions, but foundered within a short distance. Puh, Black Wolf, and I each located one, sliced its throat and hung it upside down from a tree to allow it to bleed out before we butchered it. Leaving all three does suspended from their trees, we moved on to find our next likely prospects. The sun had not yet reached its zenith and we still had a lot of daylight left before we would have to return to our shelter.

Does were our targets at this time of year because the rutting bucks were exceedingly gamey and therefore poor eating. However, when a giant deer stag came into view, we stopped and traded glances. The rut was largely over for the giant deer at this point. Maybe this buck would not be too musky. He was thinner than many of the bucks and his neck no longer carried the extra bulk that many of the stags had during the fall. I wondered if this was one of the bucks who had lost his harem to a fresh stag that had not been worn down by the constant mating and battling.

I could see that Puh and Black Wolf were weighing our options as well. Although this stag's meat was apt to be a bit tough and possibly somewhat gamey, if we killed this animal, we would have all the meat we needed to fill the sled. That said, even a tired giant deer was still a formidable beast. We would have to strike with great force to penetrate the tough hide and work our spears in such a way that we would create the largest possible wounds. It would not be like our attack on the fallow does; this buck had antlers with a span nearly as wide as Black Wolf and Puh were tall, if they were to lie on the ground end to end. That meant that he would be passing through wide openings between trees and we would not have the advantage of lunging out from cover at close quarters. We would have to let the stag pass us by, run up from behind, and thrust our spears into him. Following that exercise, we would need to seek refuge in the trees, either amidst a stand that was too tightly packed to let him get at us or up the tree's trunk and out of the enraged animal's reach until he finally expired.

We looked at one another, not speaking. Finally, Puh nodded. I did, too. Black Wolf smiled and nodded as well.

The giant deer was now up ahead of us. We were downwind, so he was unaware of our presence. We stealthily crept from behind him as he absently nibbled acorns from the ground. I had already selected a safe place of escape: a grouping of young trees the stag would not be able to enter. I could see that Puh and Black Wolf had also looked around and settled on their own sanctuaries. When we were within a few running steps, we once again nodded to one another and then commenced our attack.

This was by far the largest animal I had ever encountered at close range. I stabbed my weapon into his thick skin, bracing my legs and using my arms and shoulders to twist the shaft of the spear when it snapped with a loud crack. The stag's wound was almost at face-height for me and his blood spurted across my upper body.

Puh and Black Wolf had inflicted their own lacerations and at first, the stag did not know which way to turn, but we did not wait for him to make up his mind. We each fled in a separate direction, Puh and Black Wolf both ascended a tree and I ran to my grove. The stag was wheezing and making a peculiar cry.

He looked around in shock. Puh and Black Wolf were out of his line of sight so he did not see them, but I was plainly in view as I stood amongst the trees. Head down, the buck staggered a few steps in my direction. I wondered whether this meant that he was failing and about to drop, but then the stag blew a stream of blood from his nose and antlers lowered, galloped toward me at a full run.

Suddenly, the surrounding trees did not look as tightly packed as I had hoped, nor as sturdy. Wide-eyed, I watched the giant deer close the gap between us, his cloven hooves thundering and kicking up clumps of turf as they impacted the ground. I involuntarily—and uselessly—held out the remains of my broken spear, vaguely aware that Puh had come down from his perch and was chasing the stag.

"Tris! Up a tree! *Up a tree!*" Puh shouted.

At that moment, the stag's head dropped and he stumbled, causing one of his huge antlers to snag in the earth, and violently jerking his skull to one side. The animal toppled over, landing heavily only a few steps from where I stood.

Puh reached me first, with Black Wolf on his heels. The stag was still alive, panting and bleeding profusely from his snout and the three slashes to his body. He groaned and snorted, crimson bubbles appearing at his nostrils. The buck's legs were still wheeling as though he was trying to outrun his fate. Puh unsheathed his knife and he slowly moved nearer the great beast's throat. With a brisk stroke, he made his cut. The giant deer soon passed.

Puh put a hand on my shoulder and gazed into my face.

"Tris, you are drenched."

I looked down and saw that from the waist up, I was splashed with a brilliant scarlet splattering. My face was actually dripping with the buck's blood.

"You for sure have red hair now," Black Wolf said with a grin.

 **Chapter Six** 

It is on my back, striking and clawing at me. I cannot shake it loose. There is pressure against my throat, cutting off my windpipe.

I had expected that I would dream about the giant deer, but instead, just before sunrise I woke up choking. I was relieved to open my eyes and find that I was lying between Puh and Black Wolf in the little hut. So Puh had come in tonight. I was glad to know he was safe and warm, and almost as importantly, that he was sound asleep.

I stroked my throat to ease the sensation of constriction that remained after the Dream, and swallowed several times. Searching in the dim interior of our shelter, I found my water bag and took a good swig. Finally, my throat felt fairly normal again. Puh was awakened by my movements. He propped himself up on one elbow and then peered out the entrance of our shelter.

"The sun is still below the horizon, but the first light is showing," he observed. "We need to get going as soon as possible."

I nodded. Puh paused to look at me.

"Are you all right?" he asked.

"Yes," I answered. "I had a Dream. I have been Dreaming about a lynx, I think. It jumps on my back and scratches me."

"That does not sound good," Puh remarked.

"It is a little unnerving," I admitted.

Black Wolf began to stir, making bear-like growling noises in his semi-awake state. Puh and I both turned toward him.

"Speaking of unnerving," Puh said with a grin.

"Huh?" Black Wolf rolled over to face us. "Ack! It is not even light out yet! What are you two yammering about at this time of night?"

"It is no longer night," Puh informed him. "The sun is rising. We need to rise, as well."

"At least I do not wake up to Tris rubbing my arm again. Ack! Last morning I was sleeping and I felt a touch on my arm. I think it is Little Fawn, and, well, she has not looked for my attentions in many years so I was actually happy until it began to cross my mind that I was not at home and it could not possibly be Little Fawn. I opened my eyes and I cannot tell you how disappointed I was to see that it was my daughter's bearded big mate! Ack!"

"If it is any consolation to you," I started, "you were not the only one who was dismayed."

* * *

There was much to be done. Yesterday's hunt had been extremely fortuitous, what with bringing down four deer before midday. The giant deer was far too big to hang up and bleed as we had the fallow does, so we had butchered him on the spot, cutting the meat into slabs and bagging it in sacks, which we then hung in a number of trees some distance from the carcass. Black Wolf wanted the antlers, so using an axe, he removed them from the skull. The enormous hide was also bagged and suspended from a tree branch. The fallow does were similarly treated, except that they had no antlers to harvest. This arrangement was designed to prevent as much loss of our hard-won meat as possible, since there was no single cache for animals to raid. And the carcasses that might attract predators were distributed over a large area, none near us nor the sacks of venison that awaited us from their various locations throughout the forest.

Much like the day before, everything outside was white with frost. We built a small fire to warm ourselves while we ate our breakfast before setting out to reap the rewards of our previous day's labors. We had numerous sacks of frozen deer meat and hides to collect, so as soon as we had filled our bellies, we put out the fire and placed our few belongings on the sled.

The Dreamer II: THE GATHERING

We loaded the giant deer meat and hide first, putting those heavy items at the bottom of the vehicle. Then, one by one, we stopped where each doe's meat and hide had been stowed and added their yield to the heap. By now, the sled was quite densely packed and it was a ponderous burden to pull back to the trail where, thankfully, the going was much smoother. We each toted our pack on our back and carried our spears with extreme care, as it would be only too easy to accidentally poke a harnessmate since the three of us were now working as one to pull the sled down the path.

Black Wolf was in between Puh and me, but just slightly ahead of us and, as usual when we were not trying to hide our presence as we trekked, Black Wolf sang. The hard work of pulling this weighty load meant that we all panted with effort, so his songs were now in a booming if somewhat breathless bass.

> *Oh, there was a big old wolf, his color it was black*
> *And there was no animal in the forest that he could not track*
> *He and his fellow hunters stalked a monstrous beast*
> *In hopes that they could kill it and it would soon provide a feast*
> *As luck would have it, the creature, it did fall*
> *And now down the trail, his heavy ass we do haul…*

Black Wolf's songs, when they were not traditional

songs of The People, were sometimes his own invention, made up as we hiked along. His theory was that his loud singing would frighten away anything that might intend to do us harm. We of the Old Ones do not sing so we had never tested this philosophy. But thus far, it did seem to be effective; we only saw an assortment of birds as they flitted through the brush, and a few squirrels who scolded us thoroughly as we passed.

I had been particularly concerned about attracting predators, since I had been well-dowsed with the giant deer's blood. After we had butchered all the deer, we stopped at a near-by stream to renew our water bags and wash. But even though I had scrubbed my hair and upper body well, and attempted to clean my now darkly stained elkskin tunic in the near-freezing waters, I was sure that I still carried plenty of blood-scent.

* * *

The sun had begun its descent toward the west when I sensed that something was not right. The forest was strangely quiet. Black Wolf had tired of singing, but it was more than the absence of his songs. I glanced at Puh. He had noticed, as well. He looked around and sniffed. I, too, drew the air in through my nose, but I did not detect any odors other than the smell of our own sweaty smoke-scented bodies.

"Black Wolf, stop for a moment." Puh spoke quietly.

Black Wolf slowed his pace for a step or two, as did we, and the sled ground to a halt.

"I am ready for a brief rest," Black Wolf said. Then he noted our facial expressions. "What is wrong?"

"I think we are being followed," Puh replied. He stepped out of the sled harness. Black Wolf and I did the same. We did not want to be hampered by the sled if we had to defend ourselves. The three of us took positions around the sled and looked into the woods, spears at the ready. Puh, still facing out towards and scanning the brush at the sides of the trail, loosened our spare spears and the big axes from the places where they were lashed down on the load.

Then I saw movement between the trees. A gray furry body.

"There," I pointed.

"And there!" Black Wolf indicated the trees behind us. "Wolves!"

There was no use getting back into the harness and trying to outrun them to save the contents of the sled. Even if we had been unencumbered, there was no way we could have gained any distance on these fleet-footed animals. In fact, almost any wolf was capable of running down even the swiftest man within a very short period of time. Our best strategy was to stand our ground and try to discourage them from actively attacking us. It could be that they were simply in the area and had been drawn toward the curious spectacle of three men dragging a meat-laden vehicle down the path, and that they would chose to move on without engaging us.

Or, they might try their luck. Which was what I expected. There seemed to be maybe nine or ten animals, all healthy-looking adults. As soon as a wolf made eye contact with one of us, we would raise our arms, shout as forcefully as possible, and shake our spears threateningly at them. The wolves continued to pace around us, keeping out of reach. But I guessed that sooner or later, one or more would dart in closer. This was part of their hunting pattern. Sometimes, if we had enough men, we employed this technique ourselves. Working together, some of the party would distract the quarry by feigning a charge while others attacked from a different direction. But like us, the wolves did not want to risk serious injury. If we could demonstrate that we could indeed inflict significant harm upon them, we might be able to drive them off even though they outnumbered us.

Puh took control of the situation and made the first move. He waited until one of the harrying wolves came near and then leapt toward it with a fierce cry and, plunging his spear into the canine's side, gave the weapon's shaft a vicious twist. The wolf yelped in pain and quickly ran away, but it was likely mortally wounded. Following Puh's lead, Black Wolf and I chose our victims and also dealt our own blows. The wolves then seemed somewhat more cautious, but they were still undeterred. All the same, I thought we were doing rather well until I heard Black Wolf's warning.

"Tris! Behind you!"

Suddenly, I felt something impact my lower back. One of the wolves had managed to get behind me when I stepped forward to lance one of its comrades and it had lunged upward and latched onto my pack. Wolves are large animals—some of them nearly outweigh me—and this wolf was clearly determined to pull me down. If he succeeded in pulling me off my feet, I would be in a very dangerous situation; the other wolves would be upon me in a flash and they would do their best to rip out my throat. As I tried to jab my spear backwards toward the wolf, another came up behind me from the other side and grabbed onto my right ankle with its teeth.

I was not sure how long I could remain standing with both animals trying to tug me off balance but Puh quickly came to my rescue, spear in one hand and one of the big axes in the other. He crashed the axe onto the skull of the wolf at my ankle, slaying it with one mighty stroke. I then succeeded in stabbing the other wolf, which had let go and backed away at the sight of his ally's demise. I was so excited at this time that I unthinkingly let my spear pass through the entire body of the wolf and it was completely impaled through the ribs. The wolf let out a sharp, high-pitched bark, reeling in shock for an instant before it took off running, my spear still lodged in its side. As I watched the fleeing animal, I had a brief moment in which I realized with considerable consternation that I had just lost my favorite spear.

I quickly took up another spear and Puh and I ran over to assist Black Wolf, who was fending off two more wolves. Luckily, these last canines scattered as soon as they faced the three of us. After the whispers of their leaf-rustling footfalls receded, all was quiet, except the sounds of sucking-in air as we struggled to recover our collective breaths.

While Black Wolf kept watch in case the wolves should regain their confidence and return for another assault, Puh knelt at my feet, feeling my booted ankle.

"Tris, take off your boot," Puh said.

I sat down at the side of the trail and with shaking fingers, unlaced the straps that held my boots to my lower legs. Puh patted my shoulder soothingly.

"Take a rest first, if you want. You seem a little unnerved."

"I am, but that is all right. I can do this." I pulled off the outer boot; the torn elkskin material clearly showed evidence of the bite. The inner boot, the liner, was made of thick reindeer fur. I removed it and ran my fingers along the ankle section, revealing a few small holes which were weeping blood where sharp teeth had penetrated the two layers. An inspection of my ankle revealed three minor nicks.

"You are very lucky, Tris," Puh flexed the injured joint. "Does this hurt?"

"No, not much," I replied, "I can walk."

"The bruising will be worse than the bite," Puh observed.

I nodded and reassembled my boot, taking care to first make sure that the two foot-shaped cutouts that cushioned the inside of the boot liner were properly situated before donning it. I then checked my pack for damage. It had a gaping opening at one corner, so I repacked the contents so that my food bag sealed the fissure and then I was ready to resume our trek home.

* * *

We arrived at my family compound just before dark. It was a relief to see the fire pit's cheerful flames through the deep shadows of evening and to take in the pleasing scent of cooking food. Our numerous dogs barked in greeting, the sounds of their woofs bringing out the rest of our family members. As I anticipated, Morning Star was at the main household. She rushed out the doorway and threw her arms around my neck.

"Oh, you are home! You are home!" Morning Star held me tightly and covered my face in kisses. "I missed you so much!"

I kissed her many times, too, and snuggled my face up against hers.

"Yes, I am home. I missed you, as well. I am so glad to be back." I stepped out of the sled's harness and twisted my body to flex my stiff shoulders and back.

"Come inside and eat," Morning Star ordered, pulling me toward the opening of the domicile. "We have plenty of hot food on hand."

I looked toward Puh and Black Wolf, who were also abandoning the sled where it sat. We could unpack it later. We were very hungry, thirsty, and tired, and more than ready to devour a big meal.

"That sounds wonderful," I said with a nod. "I am ravenous!"

I could see that a smoked deer haunch was already roasting over the outdoor fire pit and, indoors, more food was being prepared at the fireplace.

When at last I was in the warm and welcoming room, Morning Star's facial expression abruptly changed.

"Tris! What happened?"

Now that I was standing in a space brightened by seal oil lamps, she had noted my blood-stained tunic and my torn boot and pack. Everyone went silent and stared at me. I did not want to worry Morning Star. I smiled and shrugged.

"It was nothing," I assured her. Morning Star looked at me doubtfully. "Really. It was nothing. The blood came from a deer; it was a foolish mistake on my part to let the deer bleed all over me." I grinned at Morning Star lightheartedly, hoping she was convinced.

Great Gran approached and she, too, looked me up and down.

"Stand back next time," she said, smiling. She knew. She always knew. Standing back would have been useless, but Gran knowingly aided my deception.

* * *

As Puh had predicted, my ankle became sorer over the next few days and more colorful as well, as the bruises blossomed. Even though the teeth punctures were slight, the force behind the bite had been considerable. I did not want to alarm Morning Star and I tried not to limp, but it was impossible to hide the contusions. Normally, she was a surprisingly agreeable mate, that is, *surprising* considering how spirited she had been throughout most of her life before our pairing. But now her old spunk came back and she insisted that I stay off my feet as much as possible. I was amused that my petite Morning Star had no qualms about pushing me to a sitting position and adamantly demanding that I *stay there!* while she worked around me. Finally, I had to gently but resolutely return to my chores. Fortunately, I could truthfully tell my devoted mate that the ankle no longer bothered me.

It was vital that I returned to my work as quickly as possible because we had much to do before we left for the Gathering. We had to process the venison that was brought in, all of which needed to be made into cuts of meat that would be smoke-cured under the chimney hole atop the fireplace, or sliced thinly and smoked on racks over outdoor fires. Sometimes, Black Wolf and his family would return to their own home and prepare their share of the meat there, but since they usually stayed at our compound any time we men were away, most often we all participated in the task. This turned it into more of a social function. Besides smoking the venison, we also had to clean and cure the hides. Black Wolf had decided to turn the two giant deer antlers into shovels, as Puh and I had done with several of the shed antlers that we had picked up in the forest. Once properly trimmed and shaped, the huge antlers easily lent themselves to digging, as long as you did not attempt to put too much leverage on the shaft or hit too many rocks that might chip the blade. Plus, the removed tines could also be worked into handles for tools like knives, chisels or awls.

It was pleasant to spend this time with our friends. Besides enjoying their company, their presence meant that Mi could be with her own kin for a prolonged period and that Morning Star also had the comfort of having her parents and siblings nearby. This was particularly important to me as she entered the last few moons of her pregnancy.

* * *

The Dreamer II: THE GATHERING

One evening Morning Star and I were for once alone in our own home. I had been hafting new spearheads to shafts and Morning Star was finishing a new pair of boots for me, but now it was time to put away these things and settle in for the evening.

"I will need to make a new tunic for you, next," Morning Star said.

"Why?" I asked. "I have two."

"One is rather ragged and the other has a big dark stain on it."

I was a little confused.

"But I still have two…"

"You cannot wear either one of those tunics when you go to the Gathering. You will be representing your people. You will need to look your best."

This had never occurred to me.

"Yes, I suppose that is true. Will men of The People be dressed in their finest clothes as well?" I inquired.

"I do not know," Morning Star responded. "I have never been to a Gathering. It is only for men to attend. But I would think they will be well-clad. After all, they will be meeting with all the other men in this region and all the elders will be there. The Head Elder, too. So I will start cutting a new tunic for you tomorrow. It will not take long to make."

"Many thanks." I pulled Morning Star to me and hugged her, kissing her forehead. "I am so lucky to have such a smart mate. And one who takes such good care of me."

Morning Star's answering smile beamed up at me.

"And I am so lucky to have such a big strong mate who also takes such good care of me."

We then sat down near the fireplace to soak up the warmth from the blaze. Morning Star seated herself between my legs, as she often did, and leaned back against me. Raena moved to sit by us, resting her head on my right thigh. She wagged her tail as I briefly petted her. Then I put my arms around Morning Star, leaving the flat of my hands on her round belly. I very much enjoyed this because I reveled in feeling the movements of our baby beneath her garment and taut skin. The baby gave a good lurch and Morning Star stifled a cry.

"Ooh," she said. "This is an exceedingly vigorous baby!" She rubbed her stomach. "I have been considering names for it."

"Oh?" I was not sure how to respond. She and I might have very different ideas on that particular topic.

The People named their children for things: birds, animals, trees, landmarks. We of the Old Ones were given "real" names: my Puh was Tor, my brother was Ty, my oldest sister, Ru, and so on. I was not really looking forward to this discussion and dreaded the list of possible names I might be given to consider.

Morning Star nodded.

The Dreamer II: THE GATHERING

"We will need to think of a boy's name and a girl's name."

"Yes," I agreed, fervently hoping that she was not going to suggest something like Spotted Frog or Honey Buzzard.

"Which names would you like to use?"

The only name that came to mind also came to my lips.

"Awna," I said. "If it is a girl, I would like to name her Awna, for my Muh."

Morning Star turned to gaze at me, gently caressing my arms as they encircled her.

"Oh, Tris! That is a lovely idea! Do you know what I would like to name our son?"

I shook my head.

"I have no notion."

"I would like to name him Fox. Especially if he has your red hair."

This was a great improvement over the sorts of names I had expected her to propose which were, unfortunately, not very profound or noble.

"I like that name," I admitted. "My hair has been compared to the color of red fox fur for as long as I can remember. I have always felt a special affinity for that animal."

* * *

The day of our departure for the Gathering came all too soon. I hated to be separated from Morning

Star again but, as with the hunt, there was no way around this. The only good thing was that this time we were not burdened with the sled. We only brought what we could carry in our hands and on our backs.

Morning Star had carefully arranged my hair into the neatly coiled cords of the Old Ones and I wore the new tunic over my best leggings and loin cloth. The boots she had made were on my feet and I had to concede I was glad she had gone to all the extra trouble. The fresh footwear felt wonderfully comfortable. Morning Star had also taken pains to make sure that my wisent cloak, which was also relatively new, was well shaken-out.

Black Wolf was also bedecked in what passed for his finery. His many braids, sometimes mirthfully referred to as his *spider hat* since they gave the appearance of an enormous spider on the top of his head, shone with grease, and his whiskers were recently plaited into the intricate plaits the men of The People usually wore in their long beards.

Puh, on the other hand, had made no effort to improve his appearance. His untidy hair was straggling out of a single braid that fell the length of his spine. His beard still had not been trimmed since last spring and now it was nearly as long as Black Wolf's. He at least seemed to keep it untangled and clean, but it did nothing to flatter him. And his clothes were markedly well-worn. Muh would have been aghast if she had seen him looking like this. Muh had taken great pride in the care of her family and she made sure that all of us were as presentable as possible at all times.

As the days passed and we carried on with our journey, I wondered if Puh had not been the wisest of us all in deciding not to bother about his outward looks. After all, it was a lengthy trudge to the Gathering. Following a five days' long hike and sleeping in a hastily erected lean-to each night, we all appeared a bit bedraggled and smelled strongly of campfire smoke since we always slept near the fire at the front of the lean-to. Even with the flames so close, we took turns sleeping in the middle of the shelter, as that was the warmest and most coveted spot.

Although we arrived at the Gathering the day before it was officially to begin, the area surrounding the meeting place was already well populated with the lean-tos of the attendees. I had never seen so many people in all my life. There must have been at least twice as many people here as there were at the village not far from our woodland home. Our family members—Puh's brothers Kror and Zor and their sons, plus Aunt Vee's sons Bror, Dor and Lor—were not yet present, so we strolled up the main path that ended at what must have been the entrance to the largest manmade structure in existence. The building was long and narrow, almost log-like in shape. It seemed to be constructed from bent young trees and thatched with whatever materials could be collected in the vicinity: smaller branches, grasses, reeds, and mud or clay. Smoke drifted from multiple chimney holes in the roof.

As Puh, Black Wolf, and I advanced toward this peculiar scene, we saw that some of the lean-tos were larger than others and appeared to be inhabited by men who were trading for goods. Some had food-stuffs, some had knapped stone, some had goods made from cured hides, but there was one that stopped us in our tracks. This man had a large collection of dolls. Or at least, that is what my youngest sisters would have called them. They were figurines of some sort, but they did not resemble Saree's beloved Hork in the least. To begin with, they had no hair.

Black Wolf lifted one and held it out for our inspection. "She has no feet," he pointed out. "She must have lost them in a sad misadventure like Fast Otter when he was attacked by a lion while he was sleeping in his lean-to. The lion managed to mangle Fast Otter's feet before his companions could save him."

The sculpted piece of sandstone was obviously meant to portray a woman—a naked woman—but she was like no female I had ever seen. She was well endowed, both front and back, and decorated with many carved horizontal lines and zig-zags. And she was enormously fat, like a bear that had been feasting on salmon in preparation for winter's hibernation. The only woman I have ever known to carry any extra weight was Black Wolf's Little Fawn, but even she was positively svelte in comparison to this figure.

Puh responded incredulously to Black Wolf's remarks.

"You look at *that* physique and all you notice is that she has no feet?"

"That *is* a lot of woman." Black Wolf shrugged, scrutinizing the creation as he slowly turned it in his hands. "It would take the skins of many deer to clothe her. There is no way I would ever lie with a woman like this. I do admit that I prefer a woman with an ample amount of flesh to cover her bones, but it is possible to take a good thing too far." Black Wolf shook his head. "Hmmm…too far."

Puh stared in pure amazement, still pondering the outlandish sculpture.

"It has been long enough that she looks pretty good to me," he said finally.

For a moment, I thought there was something vaguely recognizable about her. But that was preposterous; surely I did not know anyone who resembled this woman.

Black Wolf picked up another figurine.

"This one has no feet *and* no head. Ack! What…how…with private parts like this, it looks as though she has endured the longest pregnancy ever and eventually given birth to a fully formed six or seven winters-old child." He was thoughtful for a time. "A man could put his whole head up inside her and take look around as if to be sure it would be a good place to house a future infant, much like a badger inspecting a hole in the ground as a potential home."

The proprietor of these works of art now hovered at Black Wolf's elbow.

"Ah, I see you are a fellow with a good eye for the feminine form," he said to Black Wolf. "I will trade you that piece in exchange for pelts, food, or what have you."

Towering over him, Black Wolf looked down at him indignantly.

"Thank you, but I have a mate at home who has a much finer build than this…lady…if I should want to look at a *feminine form*."

"Well, you are a lucky man." The trader shrugged and turned to speak with another person who might be more likely to be interested in making a deal. Puh and I had been given a quick glance, but other than that, we were completely ignored. Such was the way of it. Some of The People, like Black Wolf and his kin, embraced us; others were wary or simply curious at our differences in appearance and traditions. Still others were outright hostile.

As we continued our way to the grand building that would house the Gathering, a stranger came up from behind us and tapped Black Wolf on the shoulder. Black Wolf turned and frowned.

"Good day to you, Fish Hawk," he said stiffly. When Black Wolf was very formal with someone, it usually indicated that he was not happy to see them.

Fish Hawk nodded in return. He was perhaps 25 winters old, a tall, sharp-featured man with dark braids and a plaited beard. He looked at me and Puh, seeming to regard me for a long moment.

"I know you must wonder where my allegiances lie, after my brothers' behavior last spring," Fish Hawk said. "I want you to know that I did not agree with what they did. And I especially want to apologize to Tris for their actions." He turned to me. "You are Tris, are you not?" Speechless, I nodded. He laid a hand on my forearm as he introduced himself, "I am Fish Hawk, brother to Snow Leopard and Badger Boar. I had hoped that I would someday get to meet you so I could tell you how sorry I am for my brothers' reprehensible conduct, particularly Snow Leopard. I understood the Challenge. You both wanted the same woman. I was surprised when I heard that there was a man who was willing to get into the Challenge Circle with Snow Leopard. He was renowned as not only the finest hunter but also the finest fighter amongst The People. And he was also tough. You could have taken off his leg and he would not have flinched or made a sound. But I saw you fight with him and I could not help but admire how you stood up to all his blows, no matter where or how hard he hit you. In fact, he later said that you caused him a great deal of distress because he could not see that any of his hits had any effect."

I finally was moved to find my tongue.

"Well, they surely had their effect. That was why I did all I could to stop them."

Fish Hawk smiled.

"I have heard that you Old Ones are quiet and understated. Yes. You certainly did all you could to stop them; you broke many of his teeth, probably cracked his ribs and his jaw as well. No one but Snow Leopard could have kept going with all those injuries and, within a relatively short time, gone after your woman and stolen her from your pairing ceremony. That was when I parted company from my brothers. You won your mate fairly. Stealing her was unconscionable. Again, I am sorry. I am glad that you were able to successfully retrieve your woman. I hope you and your mate will have many happy years together and that you will accept me as your friend. It would mean much to me."

I touched Fish Hawks forearm, too, and returned his smile.

"Many thanks. Morning Star and I are very happy. We will soon have our first child."

"That is truly great news," Fish Hawk said with a grin.

By now, Black Wolf had lost his guarded demeanor and was smiling as well.

"Fish Hawk, you have not yet met Tris's father. This is Tor. He has been my closest friend since we were boys."

Puh and Fish Hawk grasped forearms and nodded to one another to show that they were pleased to meet.

"I do not mean to pry," Fish Hawk said, "but I have never noted that Old Ones have come to our Gatherings in the past. Do you come as Black Wolf's guests? I must forewarn you, some of The People may not be very receptive. I will stand with you, of course, but know that you may face some…some…well… rudeness."

"We are expecting that," Black Wolf admitted. "We are also expecting a few more Old Ones…ah…here they come, now. These men are Tor's brothers and nephews. They have come to address the Elder and ask for assistance against the men of The People who are raiding their homes."

"The men are doing *what*?" Fish Hawk's eye brows flew up in surprise. "I have never heard of such a thing! A man's home is his sanctuary! No one would dare disturb a man's home!"

"Well, some men are. And we need to put an end to these crimes as quickly as possible."

Fish Hawk was fully in agreement. My uncles and cousins then joined us, and Fish Hawk was presented to the newcomers. At this point, Fish Hawk motioned for us to accompany him a little ways from the throng of people.

"I will do all I can to help, but you should know that the Head Elder died a few days ago, so there is a massive power struggle going on at this moment. And to add to the confusion, his daughter wants to rule in his place."

"His daughter?" Black Wolf repeated. "I heard about his daughter a few years ago. Her name was Willow-something. She was known for being quite clever. She had a mate. I would think that she has enough on her hands without taking on anything else."

Fish Hawk shook his head.

"Her mate passed last winter. Killed by a bear during a hunt. They never had any children. Therefore she has no family and *nothing on her hands*, as you put it. In fact, rumor has it that she is anxious to produce an heir who will eventually follow her as Elder. Willow Woman was the only surviving child of her parents, so it is up to her to continue the line of eldership that has been passed through Standing Oak's kin for many generations. It may be that she is looking for a mate at this Gathering. If the gossip is accurate, she will definitely have plenty of men from which to choose."

We all chuckled. She would be the only woman attending this function, so this was undoubtedly true.

* * *

The Dreamer II: THE GATHERING

Fish Hawk escorted us into the huge, torch-lit structure. Torches were a new thing to me and their acrid smoke stung my eyes and made me cough. Some of The People spoke with odd accents and sometimes I could not understand their words. But my keen hearing allowed me to catch occasional bits and pieces of conversations. Sometimes I just heard the words: *Old Ones!* or Snow Leopard's name uttered in hushed tones. I also heard a man say, *Old Ones! But at least those barking-mad Bone Crunchers did not come to our Gathering!*

I leaned toward Puh.

"Who are the Bone Crunchers?"

"I do not know," Puh answered, looking around calmly, but alertly.

Many men recognized Black Wolf on sight. He was nearly a head taller than the tallest man present, so he was conspicuous no matter where he went.

There seemed to be some sort of a staging area at the back of the long room, heaped with what appeared to be sacks, baskets and assorted supplies. Men continually added to the pile of sacks, arranging them carefully so that they were neatly stacked. I guessed that this was where they stored foods needed to feed the many men at this Gathering.

"Where are the other Elders?" Black Wolf asked, referring to the minor elders who headed various clans. Fish Hawk now had to shout to be heard over the din of voices.

"They are dispersed about the room, trying to drum up support in their bid to become the next Head Elder."

"What about Willow-whatever? Where is she?"

"I will try to find out." Fish Hawk left us, elbowing his way through the crowd, but soon returned. "Willow Woman arrived not long ago and wanted to rest after her long journey. She was last seen sleeping at the rear of the building while she waited for her lodgings to be made ready. Let us work our way back there and see if she has awakened by now. Even though the Gathering has not officially started yet, I think she should know what has been happening. If she is of the same mind as her father, or any decent person, she would be very unhappy to hear what some men of The People have been doing."

What with the various elders competing with one another and the men of The People who were simply resentful of our attendance at this Gathering, the clamor within this confined space was deafening. Some of the men assumed that it was Fish Hawk who had brought us here and he was drawn into heated arguments regarding the validity of our presence. Fish Hawk, undaunted by conflicting opinions, spoke passionately on our behalf. Black Wolf attempted to reason with some of the more vocal opponents while Kror listened carefully and added details to Black Wolf's narrative about the attacks they had suffered.

The Dreamer II: THE GATHERING

Even the staid Bror quietly put in a few words. Puh simply watched the spectacle, silently standing by us.

The men quarreled loudly about the lack of game, especially the large game needed to feed the growing numbers of The People moving onto these lands. Some of The People staunchly rejected our presence, declaring that the Old Ones should have no say at the Gathering.

"We cannot say that the Old Ones do not belong here," Black Wolf said adamantly. "They have lived on these lands since times untold and they have as much right to be at this Gathering as any man does! Fighting amongst ourselves is useless and, worse, it is counter-productive. We should be combining our strengths, not picking away at each other's weaknesses. The People and the Old Ones could accomplish much if we would only work together."

The hot noisy smoky closely-packed room made me feel lightheaded. I felt the need to gain some breathing room, so I edged a short distance from the others in my group toward the storage area at the rear of the structure. There, I noticed that some of the sacks on the platform were adorned with odd markings. Upon closer observation, I noticed that they somehow seemed familiar. Suddenly, a pile of lumpy "sacks" on the platform moved, and dark eyes popped open, boring into mine with incredible intensity. As this creature sat up, I saw it was a woman. A very large woman. She was scantily clad in what would be summer attire for women of the Old Ones. Her braided hair wrapped around her head and the undulating rolls of soft brown flesh were covered with blue-black lines, much like the footless figurine Black Wolf had first brought forward for our consideration at the trader's lean-to. She looked me up and down and smiled broadly.

"Ah! A big red buck! You are the biggest man of the Old Ones I have ever seen! So well built and fair of face!"

I was taken aback at this forthright assessment of my person. Puh and Black Wolf had come over to stand on either side of me, closely followed by Fish Hawk and my uncles and cousins.

"I...I am told that I look like my father," I said, indicating Puh, to my right.

She stared at Puh for a long moment.

"No," she said flatly. Then she scanned Puh more closely. "Maybe, once upon a time," she finally added.

Next, she shifted her attention to Black Wolf, wearing what could only be described as a leering grin.

"And this must be the famous Black Wolf. No one else could be so tall! The broad-shouldered big red buck is ever so tempting, or would be if it were not for that blaze of red hair and skin so pale that it could have come from under a rotting log. But you, Black Wolf, you are a fine specimen of a man!"

I think Black Wolf was actually blushing.

"That is very kind of you to say, but…"

"I have heard all about you," she giggled, "…*and the bears!*"

She giggled some more. We were startled to hear that such a tinkling laugh could come out of someone of her size.

"Um…that is not really true," Black Wolf began. Due to the fact that Black Wolf had chosen to live in the wilds instead of a village like most of The People, it was insinuated by some that Black Wolf was a big hairy savage who mated with bears. While he was indeed quite big and hairy, the rest was fanciful invention.

"Oh, I like a man with an adventurous spirit!" she assured him. "Come and sit by me! I am Willow Woman. My father, Standing Oak, passed a short time ago, and I am here to oversee this Gathering. I will continue as Head Elder in my father's stead."

By now, the others in the crowd had stopped speaking and Willow Woman had everyone's attention.

"The Gathering does not start until tomorrow," she went on, "but since we already have so many of The People on hand, and a number of Old Ones who have come here to voice their concerns, I will open the Gathering now. Right now. There will be no discussion as to the possibility of any of you clan-level elders replacing my father. He said that he wanted me to take up his seat and lead this Gathering as Head Elder."

An anonymous voice spoke.

"*A girl?*"

Willow Woman smiled.

"I am no young girl." Her resounding speech was clearly heard by everyone. "And especially after listening to all of your pointless bickering just now, I know that none of you are capable of governing our people." Then she gave Black Wolf a side-long glance. "You might be the exception," she whispered to him.

Black Wolf did not seem to know how to react to this. He smiled unsurely and slowly took a backward step.

One of the braver men approached.

"I wish to pay my respects to you, Willow Woman," he said.

She nodded imperiously and waited for him to go on.

"I also wish to say how I regret Standing Oak's passing. He was a man the like of which we will never see again."

"My father was a great man, but there will be another even greater. I speak of my son."

All eyes were drawn to her immense girth, wondering if some of that bulk might be due to a pregnancy. It seemed unlikely, especially since Fish

Hawk had already spoken of a rumor regarding her wish to conceive an heir.

"I do wonder, though," the man tentatively began again, "if we are wise to include the Old Ones in this Gathering." He turned hastily to us. "I mean no disrespect," he continued. "I have always been treated well by any of the Old Ones I have met. But this is a Gathering of The People. And it has always been a Gathering of The People. Why should they have a voice at our Gathering?"

Willow Woman appeared to think this over. Black Wolf took a few steps forward.

"These Old Ones are dear friends to me," he said quietly to her. "They are good men. Some of them have had their homes attacked by men of The People. They just want to tell their story. I ask that you hear them." Black Wolf paused. "I would be very appreciative if you heard them," he added.

Willow Woman smiled broadly at Black Wolf.

"I know of a way to settle this dispute," she announced. "Each man gets a rock. Those who agree to let the Old Ones take part in this Gathering will pile their rocks here, on the right, and those who do not will place their stones here, on the left. The rocks will tell us which opinion is the most popular and we will go with that decision."

Some of the men went outside and collected baskets of small river stones which were dispersed to all in the crowd except for we men of the Old Ones. Each man then came up to Willow Woman and placed his rock on the corresponding pile of his choice. As some approached the pile to the right, they nodded and smiled at us encouragingly, but many of those who opted for the one on the left openly scowled at us. Finally, the stones were counted. And counted again. But the number of rocks in each pile was exactly the same.

"How you will decide?" Black Wolf asked Willow Woman. He leaned to whisper. "I implore you to consider listening to my friends."

Willow Woman beamed at him and stood up, displaying a stone in the palm of her hand.

"I also have a rock," she said, wearing a self-satisfied smile. "I will agree to cast my stone with the Old Ones if you will…um…help to provide me with an heir *and* if all the other Old Ones in the territory agree to come to this Gathering before it closes and tell of their experiences, if they should have any. I want to hear if these raids are widespread and who the perpetrators are. I will add to you, Black Wolf, that I do not seek a mate. I only seek the man who will father my son."

Black Wolf, the man whom I have seen fearlessly rush a boar head-on and take down many a foe, visibly quailed. Swallowing hard, Black Wolf nodded. Willow Woman grinned triumphantly and sauntered over toward the two piles of rocks with a fluid jiggling waddle. Affecting great aplomb, she placed her stone on top of the others in the pile in support of our plight. There was an uproar amongst the men of The People; some were pleased, and some not. Willow Woman left the room without stopping to converse with anyone.

"Well, old friend," Puh turned to Black Wolf, "I do not know whether to congratulate you on this honor or not."

Personally, I thought not.

"Ha-ha. That is *very* funny!" Black Wolf said and turned to me. "Do not be too amused, Tris. She had her eyes on *you* for a moment! If it were not for the fact that I could not bear to risk breaking my daughter's heart if she were ever to find out that you were chosen to service this woman, I might have encouraged her to go for the much younger Big Red Buck instead of me. As it is, if her proposed scenario comes to pass, I will spend the rest of my life worrying that Little Fawn will find out and slash my throat in my sleep. That is, if I am lucky, it will be my throat!"

Chapter Seven

"It would appear that Willow Woman likes tall men," Bror said, looking back and forth between Black Wolf and me. It always surprised me to be referred to as "tall" when standing next to Black Wolf. I was tall for a man of the Old Ones, but I was nowhere near his height.

"I am tall and she did not give me a second look," Fish Hawk said with a grin. "I do not know whether to be offended or relieved."

Zor shrugged resignedly.

"After the flame-colored hair and rotting-log skin comments, I did not expect to be considered at all."

Black Wolf wore a pained expression on his face.

"You men can joke all you want, but you had better appreciate what I am going to go through on your behalf!" He paused in thought. "Maybe I can escape from any physical obligations by offering to use my hunting skills to harvest meat for her."

Puh shook his head.

"You do not beget an heir by going hunting."

Black Wolf groaned.

"I do hope I live through this!"

"A word of advice," Kror said solemnly to Black Wolf. "Be sure to be the one on top. Better yet, mount her from behind like a she-bear."

This was an unfortunate analogy in view of the bear stories that circulated around Black Wolf. Black Wolf glared sulkily at Kror.

"I have fathered six children! I know what to do! Just make sure you all return as quickly as you can with your fellow people and rescue me from this ridiculous predicament!"

"We will," Kror promised. "And Black Wolf, we are very aware of the great…um… *personal sacrifice* you are making for us. I cannot tell you how much it means to us that you are willing to go to such…um…*extraordinary lengths* to help us. We Old Ones will be indebted to you always." Kror grasped Black Wolf's arm earnestly as he spoke.

"She is an uncommonly large woman and those markings on her skin do give one pause, but she is not unattractive. I do not think it would be such an unpleasant undertaking," Kror's son Whot chimed in. "I would be happy to be asked to father an heir.'"

"If I am to die trying, I will be sure to first recommend you as my replacement," Black Wolf said dryly.

I was somewhat surprised at Black Wolf's reticence. I was well aware that most pairings were not bonded by love or considered to be strictly monogamous. Nothing was sure in life and one never knew when one might be killed or crippled, so very few men abstained from an opportunity to lay with a woman. Black Wolf and Little Fawn's pairing had been particularly contentious and I had heard bits of conversation which led me to believe that Black Wolf was not always a faithful mate. While this was by no means unusual, I was troubled by the thought. To my knowledge, my own parents had been unfailingly loyal to one another and in my pairing with Morning Star, I could not imagine being with anyone but her. In fact, Great Gran had once smilingly observed that my beautiful Morning Star had spoiled me for anyone else. Puh never said anything when Black Wolf hinted at his romantic adventures, but his silence was more eloquent than any words could be. I guessed that while Puh may disapprove of Black Wolf's behavior, he could not bring himself to admonish so steadfast a friend. Or divulge his secrets.

* * *

Several men of The People came up to us. One of them addressed Black Wolf.

"Willow Woman has asked that you join her. She is readying for her evening meal and she would like your company."

Black Wolf nodded politely.

"Of course." As Willow Woman's men turned to lead the way, Black Wolf looked over his shoulder and whispered harshly, "*hurry back!*"

* * *

The remaining two men were on a different errand.

"Willow Woman wishes that you return with as many Old Ones as you can before this Gathering closes one moon from now. Do you think you can accomplish this task?"

"We will most assuredly be back here before the next full moon with as many of our people as we can find," Bror told him.

"Then we will wish you a safe journey and see you upon your return."

"Many thanks," we each replied. The men left us and disappeared as they were absorbed into the mob of moving bodies.

We exited the structure to find a quieter place in which to confer. We were hungry, thirsty, and craving a good rest.

"Tor, do you know where Awna's family moved?" Kror asked Puh.

"I have only a vague idea. As you know, they did not approve of our relationship and they never spoke to either Awna or me again after we were paired," Puh replied.

"Well then," Kror said shaking his head, "you are not the one to go out and request their support. My sons and I will go. I think I know where they are. Last spring I heard they had gone to a place near the Great Lake."

"Kror and I are paired with sisters. Krenk and I will venture out to their kin and speak with them," Zor offered.

"Our Muh has relatives who reside not far from our home," Bror stated. "My brothers and I will seek them out and bring them here. We should be back by the new moon."

"What about Puh and me?" I asked. I did not know of any other Old Ones in this region.

"What happened to Awna's half-brother Bakkae?" Kror asked. "He was always sort of a hermit; he had no interaction with his own clan or anyone else, for that matter. That is, except for the woman he took in. Every few years, someone will report seeing them in the distance, but no one ever seems to have talked with them."

"If Bakkae is still alive, he would be in his mid-forties by now," Puh responded. "He was Awna's older brother by her father's previous mate. I only met him once. Do you know where he settled?"

"Yes, well, I have a rough idea, at any rate. He seemed to be based near the White River. I think that if you and Tris are willing to go after them and follow the river, you would eventually find them," Kror answered. "What was his woman's name? Reeka?"

"No, it was Ria," Zor said. "They are not known for being social, so do not expect much from this couple. I do not think anyone has happened upon them since the summer of the drought."

"Awna's family was like that," Puh said. Poor Puh looked aggrieved. I wished they would stop talking about Muh and Muh's clan.

"Bakkae, even more so," Kror told us. "He was a strange man. I think the only reason he found a woman who would put up with him was because he came upon her when she was barely more than a child. The story goes that while he was out hunting he discovered a mammoth that had fallen through the ice of a swampy pond. The mammoth appeared to be dead, so he went up to investigate and found that a young girl was there, and that she had fallen through the ice as well. She had become separated from her people and was starving. Seeing the dead mammoth, she tried to make her way onto the ice to carve out some meat but she, too, broke through and was suspended in the waters from her armpits down. Bakkae, like most of Awna's kin, was quite tall. His legs were long enough to leap onto the mammoth's body and stand on it in order to rescue the child. She was nearly unconscious with cold so he carried her home. And she has been with him ever since."

"I heard something about that as well," Bror said. "That took place a long time ago. I was a boy when my Puh told me that story and it was old news, even then."

"All right," Puh said, "we will set out to find Bakkae and return with him if at all possible. But, I think it would be a good idea to camp here for the night and leave at first light. It is too late to make much distance before dark."

* * *

We made our camp a little ways from the Gathering, erecting our lean-tos near the edge of the forest. We built a fire to warm ourselves before going to sleep and arose early the next morning, packing quickly while simultaneously chewing pieces of dried meat.

Before we departed, Bror spoke to me.

"I have not had a chance to ask you yet, but the thought is never far from my mind. How is Ru? She is well, I hope?"

I smiled at Bror. He seemed so serious about his query.

"Ru was quite well when I left home," I replied.

"Good," Bror said with a smile, "I worry that she works too hard. Ru needs someone to take care of her."

I did not think it was likely Ru needed anyone to take care of her or that she would accept any help from him, but I nodded just the same.

"She does work hard."

"When you next see her, will you tell her that I send my regards?" Bror asked.

"I will, Cousin," I promised.

"Many thanks. We go now. Safe journey to you."

"Safe journey to you," I responded.

We split up to embark on our independent missions. Puh and I walked to the White River and hiked along its stony banks. The river's waters moved swiftly, the resulting turbulence creating the ivory-colored riffles that gave the body of running water its name. The skies were clear but the wind was biting, thus we donned our cloaks to retain as much body heat as we could.

As nightfall neared, we realized that our lean-to could not possibly withstand the blasts of wind, so we found a grove of small birch trees where we could make a shelter. Selecting an opening in the grove where we could bend the tops of the young trees over to meet at the center of the little clearing, Puh held the bent saplings in place as I lashed their upper branches together. This formed a rough frame for a little hut. We then cut fir boughs to thatch the outer walls and line the floor. The tarpaulin hide used to cover our lean-to was now spread out over the fir bough floor to keep us up off the sticky sap that still leaked from the floor's branches. Our hastily built structure was not completely weatherproof, but it did cut most of the wind and allowed Puh and me to sleep in relative comfort.

It is behind me. I feel its claws tear into the skin on my face. I cannot get it off. I am choking.

"Tris! Tris!" Puh called my name.

I awoke with a start, gasping for breath. Puh was staring into my face with deep concern.

"Are you all right?" he asked. I nodded, still in a sleep-fogged stupor. "Was it the lynx Dream again? You seemed to be wrestling with something."

I nodded once more and rubbed my throat. It took a moment before the choking sensation eased enough to speak.

"Yes. I am starting to really dislike that Dream."

We had no time to dwell on my night visions. Puh and I did not bother to make a fire that morning; we simply gathered our belongings and wrapping our cloaks around us, set out once again into the gale, keeping the rushing waters to our left. The land seemed to be continually rising, as though we were climbing one very long hill. The terrain was still quite rocky and we often had to skirt large boulders. At midday, we came to what appeared to be a fork in the trail. It seemed well used. For the first time, Puh and I could see fresh human foot prints. We had seen other larger tracks in the rare muddy patches on the path, but they were older. These were crisp, as though they had just been imprinted into the soil. Puh and I decided to break from the main trail and follow this path in hopes that it might lead to Bakkae's lodgings. Judging by the number of new foot marks, it was certain that someone lived nearby.

When the narrow trail ended, we were somewhat discouraged to find ourselves at what appeared to be a pile of rubble that may have once been a home. Puh and I set down our packs and opened them to seek food and drink. As we consumed our repast, Puh and I scanned the area.

"This heap does not look like much but I see signs of occupancy," Puh said. "Someone must reside at this place. There must be some way to get into this…dwelling. You go around that way, and I will go this way. One of us will be sure to locate the entryway."

"Yes, Puh." I walked the perimeter of the wreckage, noting indications of inhabitation: small footprints, smoking embers in the fire pit, a knife laying on the outdoor hearth, and stacks of foraged wood. I paused as I found what appeared to be children's toys. They seemed to be small spears and there was also a long strip of wood that had a short length of gut cord hanging from it. I was curious about this stick and the attached cord, which had a loop at both ends. One loop kept the cord affixed to the piece of wood; the other hung free. I then noticed that the little spears were notched at their base. Maybe the notch was fitted to the free loop and it somehow launched the spears? I had heard of something called an *atlatl*, a stick that threw spears, and I wondered if I now held a toy version of that tool in my grasp. I leaned my spear up against the ruins of the structure to unburden my hands and then placed the butt of a tiny spear into the loop and pulled back on the cord to see if it would indeed throw the spear, but it only dropped to the ground with a feeble clatter.

Just as I remembered I was supposed to be looking for a doorway where we could summon the occupants of this domicile, a slight scuffling sound reached my ears. I opened my mouth to call out *Is anyone here?* when I felt a sudden weight collide with my upper back. The lynx! But it was not paws that clawed at my face, it was small rough hands. I could not see or reach the person on my back, but the diminutive dirty hands led me to believe that they belonged to a boy. The child seemed to abandon the idea of scratching me to death. Instead, he leaned over my shoulders and seized the ends of the long wooden strip I still held in my grasp. His knees firmly planted in my back, the boy braced with his legs and jerked backwards on the stick with impressive strength, so that the wood was now tight against my throat. Although the child was quite strong, I was able to push the stick away from my neck. I then lifted the stick and boy into the air, holding them away from me. I gazed upon the fierce creature, dressed in a bewildering combination of odd clothing. His eyes are wild with hate but I did not want him to let go of the wood, drop down, and run away before I could question him, so I shifted my hold to his ragged tunic.

This brought about a flurry of action from the boy, whose hands immediately began to pummel me. His legs thrashed energetically. One of the flailing legs kicked me forcefully in the groin. *I think I will die.* I involuntarily threw this wrathful being away from me and I was doubled over in pain when Puh appeared at the far side of the wrecked home. Puh had not witnessed the altercation but, without a doubt he had heard the blows.

Puh looked at me, stunned.

"Are you all right?" he asked.

Clearly, I was *not* all right. I ignored the question other than to groan in reply. The boy lay motionless where he had landed face-first in the rubble of his home. Although I was in agony almost to the point of vomiting, I was horrified at what I had done. This child might possibly be my own cousin.

"Is he dead?" I gasped.

Puh turned his attention to the prone figure lying amidst the ruins. He did not respond for a moment while he approached my attacker. As Puh gained a closer perspective, he was looking at the person with his head cocked to one side, one eyebrow raised and wearing an oddly silly grin the like of which I have never before seen on his face.

"Um…*she*. No, *she* is not dead."

She had landed tunic awry, presenting an undignified view that is usually reserved for a woman's mate and Puh must have seen that she was most definitely female.

Puh seemed a little hesitant to touch her, but he stepped forward to rearrange the back of her tunic so that she was decently covered.

I hobbled slowly to Puh's side and we exchanged puzzled glances. She has been knocked senseless and was bleeding copiously from her nose. I had already made up my mind that I was not going to get too near, but Puh stood behind her and lifted her by the shoulders, supporting her head with his right hand so that the blood which was saturated her hair and pooled on one side of her tunic could run onto the ground instead. Then, using his left hand, he reached around and applied pressure to either side of her nose in an attempt to stem the flow of blood.

Moments later, still thus propped in Puh's arms, she began to regain her wits. Choking on blood, she uttered these words in a soft and strangely accented husky voice: "Do not take my bow."

The Dreamer II: THE GATHERING

"Are you Ria?" Puh asked. She nodded in reply, quickly pulling off her boots before any blood could drip on them. "Do not fear us," Puh continued. "We will not take anything from you."

Her eyes rested on each of us in turn, as if weighing our trustworthiness. She did not comment right away, but leaned forward, pinching the bridge of her nose in attempt to quell the stream of red fluid. But whenever the backflow built up and caused her to choke again, she let up on her grip and the torrent gushed alarmingly once more. I glanced at Puh. We were both uneasy and unsure of what we should do. Seeing all this blood brought back the horrible memories of Muh's death, and Puh and I were both disconcerted at the sight. But Ria remained completely calm and eventually the bleeding slowed and then stopped.

Ria was one of the smallest adult women I had ever seen, no taller than my Aunt Vee but she was considerably leaner. Even without all of the blood from the abrasion on her forehead and her rapidly swelling nose, she would still not be an attractive person. Her braided hair, which she pulled back at the nape of her neck, was a dull, muddy, red-orange, and it was well flecked with stands of silver. She had the weathered complexion of someone who spent a lot of time outdoors. Her build, at least while hidden under an over-sized man's tunic, was indeterminate; the only exceptional thing about her appearance was her expressive tilted green eyes. I was perplexed. Why was she wearing a man's tunic, which was now torn thanks to our brief fracas, instead of the usual long garment that most women wore? Granted, this tunic came down to just above her knees and her tall boots came up over her knees, so her legs were protected from the elements, but this was without question an unusual choice of attire.

"Who are you? Why are you here?" Ria finally spoke.

"I am Tor," Puh said. "My mate was Bakkae's half-sister. This is my son Tris. We are here to talk with your man."

Ria studied Puh for a moment and then gently asked about Muh.

"Your mate *was* Bakkae's half-sister? Did she pass?"

Puh hesitated and then answered in a strangled voice.

"Yes."

"You loved her," Ria stated matter-of-factly.

"Yes, I loved her very much," Puh affirmed. I noticed glints of dew-like moisture develop in the corners of his eyes and Puh visibly swallowed as if to force down his grief.

Ria looked at Puh with sympathy, as if she empathized with the depth of his anguish.

"That is nice. I mean to say, I am very sorry that she has passed, but it is nice that you so loved her."

Bakkae was obviously not here.

"Are you expecting Bakkae to come home soon?" I asked.

Ria suddenly looked away and she was silent for a long moment. She seemed to take a little time to compose herself.

"I do not know," she finally answered. "He has been gone a long while."

Puh and I looked at one another. We could not afford a lengthy wait for Bakkae's return.

"How long?" I asked.

"Four years, as of next spring."

Puh and I were shocked at this news.

"Have you been out here alone for nearly four years?" Puh said, voicing my own thoughts.

"Well, almost alone," Ria began. "I have been visited by men of The People—when I am not at home, of course—but I know it is them because of their shallow narrow footprints. No man of the Old Ones leaves tracks like that. They consistently steal everything they can carry away. When I saw you," Ria said, pointing at me, "and you were holding my bow, I was afraid that you were going to take the last thing I had with which to hunt for food. Bakkae made that bow. I do not know how to make another one. If I lose it, I will starve. But if those vile men keep stealing all the supplies I put away for the winter, I may starve anyway."

Ria leaned forward once more and rubbed her head gingerly.

"I did not mean to…um…damage you," she said, twisting her neck slightly to face me, "It is just that someone my size has to use all methods at her disposal to even the odds against people who are much larger and…you *are* quite big." Ria seemed genuinely remorseful for hurting me, but appeared to hold no grudge about the injuries that I had given her, philosophically accepting them as her due.

I nodded in response. I was still in considerable discomfort but I was sure, or at least hopeful, that I would soon recover.

Puh looked at the destruction all around us.

"Did those men destroy your home?"

Ria shook her head, wincing at the motion.

"No. That happened last winter. As you must recall, it was unusually snowy. During a particularly bad snow storm, the roof collapsed one night. I was sound asleep when it happened, wrapped in many fur blankets for warmth, but I had one of Bakkae's tunics in bed with me. It always comforted me to have his scent near me while I slept. That is why I am dressed this way. I was only able to recover my boots, this tunic, and a few odds and ends, like this bow, a knife, and the bedding I was wrapped in. Almost everything else is buried in that heap of debris," she said, motioning toward the remains of her home.

"Do you still live in there?" Puh inquired.

"Yes. I can squeeze through an opening to take shelter," Ria said as she rose to her feet to show Puh the entry, but she reeled as she stood upright and Puh reached out to steady her. For the first time since we had encountered Ria, she surrendered a small smile.

"Many thanks," she said to Puh.

"Maybe you should remain seated for a while. You took quite a bad blow to the head," Puh suggested.

I wanted to point out that Ria was not the only one who was suffering, but I decided to leave my ailments out of the conversation.

"I am all right," Ria insisted. "I will need to move eventually anyway. I must go down to the river to clean myself soon. The blood will be much harder to remove after it has dried."

Ria led us to the tiny chasm that allowed her to still make use of at least a small section of her house. I could now envision what had taken place on that blustery winter's night. The weight of the snow had overloaded the wooden frames of the small wood, stone, and mud structure, bringing it down around Ria. She was exceptionally lucky to have escaped unscathed, even if she had lost most of her stores and belongings in the event. The opening was just large enough for

Ria to scramble in and out, so we were not able to go inside, but we could see by peering through the entryway that the chamber was scarcely larger than the average bear's den.

Ria was determined to go down to the river to wash, so Puh and I went with her. She made her way with a tottering walk, holding her head to one side with a hand cupping her forehead and fingers clamping her nose to prevent further bleeding. Despite her efforts, a little blood began to leak from her nose, but she doggedly continued. Puh and I were concerned for her, but I was not willing to get close enough to actually be of assistance. Puh, on the other hand, took Ria's arm to steady and guide her toward the river. The rocky gravel shore must have been very cold on Ria's bare feet, but she was undeterred. As Puh released his grip on her arm, Ria waded into the rushing waters, still clothed in the torn and bloody tunic.

I stooped at the river's edge to wash the blood off my face and Puh also knelt to clean his red-stained hands. Puh kept an eye on Ria in case she should founder in the waist-deep, rapidly moving waters. Ria loosened her hair to scrub it and rinsed the blood from her face, arms, and hands. She made a fruitless attempt to remove the stains from the tunic and soon gave up, discouraged by the frigid waters and lack of improvement. Ria waded back to the shore. As she emerged from the river, Ria looked so pathetic and miserable that my heart went out to her. Puh must have been similarly affected.

"Your tunic is beyond help," he said. "I will give you mine. I can use my cloak to stay warm."

"Many thanks," she responded, her lips quivering and nearly blue with cold.

Without hesitation, Ria stripped off her wet clothing and now stood naked and shivering before our widened eyes. She waited patiently for Puh, who stared with surprise for a moment. Then, as her teeth begin to chatter and she hugged her arms over her body for warmth, Puh quickly recovered and removed his tunic. Ria pulled the heavy garment over her head. It was not as long as Bakkae's had been but it was more than adequate to cover her and, it was at least intact and dry. Despite the fact that Ria's injured face was particularly unattractive just then, I had noted with some appreciation that she had a lithe, well-muscled little body that appeared to be soft and round in all the places where a woman should be soft and round. All the same, I could not help comparing this awkward person with my lovely Morning Star and the memory of my beautiful mother. I had never met anyone even remotely like this barely civilized female.

Ria sank to her knees and searched amongst the smooth river stones at the water's edge. Selecting a few, Ria held the cold stones to various places on her face, particularly her forehead and nose. I realized that this was probably the most effective way to reduce the swelling that was becoming more and more apparent as time went by.

Now that Puh was bare-chested, he was soon shivering as well.

"Tris, go up and revive that fire. We will need to get her warm."

"And you, too," I added.

"Yes, me too," Puh agreed. "I will stay here until she is ready to go back and then we can get her settled for the evening. She cannot be left alone in this state."

* * *

Later that night, after we had seen that Ria was asleep inside her tiny hovel, Puh and I chatted quietly by the outdoor fire pit. We had set up our lean-to in the sheltered area near the fire so we could take advantage of the heat source on this chill night.

"If Bakkae has been away for almost four years, he is most likely dead," Puh said. "He must have died or been killed while he was on a hunt. We will have to return to the Gathering without him." Puh paused. "We cannot leave Ria here, injured and alone in a broken-down house where she will starve and freeze to death this winter. She no cache of food stores or firewood. The men who robbed her even stole her blankets. We must convince her to leave with us."

"But even if she leaves with us, where will she go?" I asked.

Puh shrugged.

"We will ask her where she wants to go. Maybe she has some idea of where her clan is and she would like to be restored to her own kin."

"If that was her wish, would not Bakkae have done that already?" I questioned. "She must have been frantic to find her family."

"I do not know. As Kror said, Bakkae was an odd man. I would not put it past him to have kept Ria away from her clan so that he would have a mate to share his life. He would have been in his early 20's when he found Ria and he was still unpaired. That is almost unheard of. He must have been desperate for a woman at that point. So I can believe that he would do his best to hold onto a lost girl-child if he came upon one. Of course, had he found a boy that would have been different. That youngster would have found himself back in the bosom of his family very quickly." Puh seemed to be thinking. "There is something else to consider. It is becoming much colder. I want to go home and retrieve our winter clothing. We could be there in four days, leave Ria with our kin if she has no other plans, and then return to the Gathering."

I was not sure about the wisdom of bringing Ria to our home, but I had to acknowledge that we owed it to Black Wolf to get back to the Gathering with all possible speed. And there was one other thing we had to take into account.

"What if Ria is too unwell to travel? She could hardly walk to the river," I pointed out.

"Yes," Puh concurred, "you must have thrown her very hard. What possessed you to do such a thing to a woman? I can see that she must have scratched and hit your face…did she surprise you? Did you mistake her for a man at first?"

"At first, I thought she was the lynx from my Dreams. Then I thought she was a boy. I was not too bothered by her assault until she kicked me…then all thoughts of decorum went straight out of my head," I replied.

Puh gave me a long look.

"So that is why you were doubled-over. Now I see. Well, if Ria is unable to travel right away, we will have to wait here for a few days until she has sufficiently recuperated." Puh added more foraged wood to the fire. "One thing is for sure," he continued. "She is a feisty woman. And tough. I do not know how she has managed to survive for so long by herself."

"She is rather clever, too. I admired how she used those rocks at the river. I was nearly inspired to do the same thing, but I could not quite bring myself to load up my loin cloth with cold stones."

* * *

The next morning, the wind had mercifully lessened and the bright sunshine was indeed welcome.

The Dreamer II: THE GATHERING

Ria's nose was now a grotesque sight and her forehead and the skin around her eyes were also quite bruised and swollen. She continued to use cold stones to relieve the pain and swelling. Her voice had a naturally low timber, but now it had a definite nasal tone. The blocked passages of her nose also made mealtimes a challenge since it was difficult to try to breathe through her mouth and eat at the same time.

Puh broached the subject of abandoning her home.

"Ria, I would like to talk with you about leaving this place. You must know that you cannot make it through another winter here."

Ria looked up abruptly at Puh.

"I would like to leave, but what if Bakkae should come home and find it deserted? How would he know where to find me?"

Puh gazed at Ria with compassion.

"Ria," he began gently, "if he has not come home after all this time, he is not coming home. Nothing but death would keep a man from his mate for so long. We will take you wherever you want to go, but you must leave this place. Do you know where your clan is at this time of year?"

Ria shook her head as tears formed in her eyes.

"No. Bakkae might still be alive. Besides, I have nowhere to go. My family was trekking to a distant place unknown to me when I became lost. Bakkae was all I had, especially since no babies ever came from our union. I cannot give up on him."

"Then you can come home with us," Puh said. If you want to cherish a hope that Bakkae might be alive, you can do it from there. But, in the unlikely event he is still living, he would be very unhappy to know that the woman with whom he was paired had perished under such conditions while she awaited his return."

Ria was silent.

"We were never paired," she said at last. "There was no one to give me to him. I just stayed with him."

Puh hesitated, evidently searching for an appropriate response.

"That does not matter right now," he said. "What matters is that you are somewhere safe. If these raids continue, you will not be able to accumulate any winter stores. Tris and I live in a location not yet affected by the raids, so you will be secure with my family."

"*Not yet affected by the raids?* Do you mean I am not the only one who has been robbed?" Ria questioned.

"Yes. That is why we wanted to speak with Bakkae. Many of the Old Ones are attending The People's Gathering to tell the Head Elder what has been occurring and we were instructed to get the support of other Old Ones to bolster our cause. We came here to ask Bakkae to return to the Gathering with us," Puh informed Ria.

"Bakkae would never have agreed to accompany you. He could not abide the company of others. Most particularly the men of The People. And after their most recent behavior, I am starting to share his opinion." Ria stated.

"I understand why you feel the way you do, but many of my good friends are men of The People. Most of them are very honorable. Do not pass judgment on an entire race based on the actions of a few miscreants," Puh said softly.

Ria stared into Puh's eyes and slowly nodded.

"I will leave with you."

Chapter Eight

The good weather held. We stayed three days at Ria's home, abandoning our drafty lean-to for a hastily erected shelter Puh and I had constructed. Although the deep purple bruises on Ria's face made her look worse than ever, Ria could at least breathe through her nose again. After those three days had passed she claimed that she felt able to begin the journey back to our family compound. It took less time for Ria to collect her belongings than Puh and I needed to gather and arrange our gear in our packs. Ria had a container that carried all her little spears and her restrung bow slung over her left shoulder. She tied a belt around her hips into which she tucked her knife. These few items were all she had left.

We found that Ria was a strong and tireless hiker. She must have been in considerable pain, but she never so much as uttered a single whimper. When I fell slightly behind Ria and Puh, I was amused to see them walking side by side ahead of me, Ria looking much like a smaller version of Puh except that he was clad in his wisent cloak. Both wore their hair in a single long braid, which swung freely with each step. My corded coils had come undone so my hair now hung in a single plait as well. I could have asked Puh to help me coil and bind my hair, but since he and Ria had no interest fixing their own coiffures, it seemed somehow inappropriate to show an interest in mine.

Although the daytime temperatures were fairly mild and physical activity helped to warm us, the nights were well below freezing. Our lean-to did not provide enough protection from the elements to keep us comfortable. This was especially true for Puh and Ria, since they were under-dressed. So we stopped early each evening to build a new hut. Puh and I had often shared a hut in this way while we were on the trail, and Black Wolf, too, when he was with us, but it felt odd to have this comparative stranger and a woman, at that, within our midst. Ria appeared to feel a little ill at ease too, but Puh seemed to have no qualms about her presence. After we finished our evening meal and retired to the cozy interior of the shelter, I laid down under my cloak with my back toward the center of the structure. I was taking no chances that one of Ria's feet might accidentally kick me again in the middle of the night. Puh took the opposite side and Ria settled in the spot between us.

As always when I awakened, I peered out the opening of the shelter to assess the day's weather. The sky was already beginning to brighten to a pale shade of blue. We had slept much later than was usual on the trail. I looked at Puh and Ria. Puh had placed half of his cloak over Ria and he was curled around her small body. Seeing them like this gave me a momentary pang as I remembered the countless time I had seen Puh with his arms around my Muh, but the sight of Puh's contented expression over-rode any misgivings. Poor Puh had suffered acutely since Muh's passing and I was gratified at the thought that he might take pleasure in anything again. Ria also looked completely serene as she lay with her head on Puh's shoulder.

The scene made me miss Morning Star more than ever. I longed to have her near me, to be wrapped around her the same way Puh embraced Ria. I was heartened to know I would be with her again soon, but it could not be soon enough for me.

I should awaken Puh, but he was deeply asleep and seemed to be more at peace than I had seen him in many moons. I did not have the heart to disturb him. However, I did not feel at all at peace. Besides yearning for my beloved mate, my throat was parched, my stomach was empty, and my bladder was full. And, not having the benefit of an extra body's heat under my cloak, I was also cold.

Taking care to move slowly and quietly, I exited the hut. After purging my bladder of its contents, I stirred the dying coals from last night's fire and patiently rebuilt the flames. Before long, the day's light and the songs of the birds roused Puh and Ria from their slumbers and we were on the trail again.

We did not converse frequently, so we were left to think our own thoughts as we hiked along, taking in the beauty of the late fall countryside. Most of the trees had shed their leaves by now. The strong winds of a few days ago had stripped away a good portion of the remaining colorful foliage and now the pathway was strewn with a thick layer of rustling leaves. Soft breezes occasionally wafted these many-hued bits of ground cover aloft, making them look like little birds suddenly taking flight.

Sometime after midday, we startled a brown bear as he stepped out from behind a tree and into the center of the trail. The bear sported a thick coat of lustrous fur and he was well-padded with plenty of fat. He was a sizable creature, but he wanted no truck with us. He paused for an instant as he looked our way, but then continued to cross the path and disappeared into the brush. We could hear his movements as he pushed his way through the naked bushes and the sounds of his footfalls as the brittle leaves crunched under his massive feet, but we saw no more of him.

The bear's sudden appearance made me think of Black Wolf and I wondered how he was faring. I was profoundly grateful to our old friend for his willingness to help us, but I worried for him. While it was true that most men did not shy away from making love to a woman, the thought of romancing Willow Woman was a daunting prospect. But it was not necessarily just her appearance that made her seem so formidable. She had an imposing presence that caused people to freeze in place like a scared rabbit and simply stare at her. When Willow Woman spoke, people listened as though mesmerized and they were helpless to oppose her. How would Black Wolf deal with such an incredibly unconventional and powerful woman? And, what would happen following his return home? Little Fawn was a warm and caring parent and friend, but like Black Wolf, she had a volatile temper. While people might turn a blind eye to the infidelities of others—as long as they did not flaunt it—mates did not usually take kindly to the news that their partner had found comfort elsewhere. Black Wolf had good reason to be concerned; particularly since Willow Woman was a well known person and people were bound to gossip about a prominent entanglement such as this.

* * *

Another night and another hut was constructed by the side of the trail. In only two more days I would be with my sweet Morning Star again. The thought made me smile. Visions of her filled my dreams and I was nearly beside myself to be with her again. I had never been away from Morning Star for so long and by now, the journey seemed interminable. We would probably stay home only briefly before setting out again, but that time would be keenly savored while it lasted.

* * *

The next morning dawned clear and cold. In the early light, I could see that Puh was already awake. With Ria nestled against him, he lay motionless and gazed pensively at her sleeping form and battered face. Puh seemed to sense my scrutiny and he glanced up to meet my eyes, but he did not speak.

Later, after we had downed a quick morning meal of dried meats and berries, and roasted shelled nuts, we resumed our trek homeward. This day was bitterly cold and I silently speculated that Puh may have regretted offering his tunic to Ria, especially as clouds gradually rolled in and a fine snow started to drift down from the gray skies. A dusting soon covered the trail, making it a little slippery in places. But the soft, powdery carpet had its advantages: it clearly showed the tracks of animals that had recently visited this area. We saw deer hoof prints, sets of hare paw-marks where one of those long-eared creatures had hopped down the side of the trail for some time, assorted squirrel tracks, and evidence of where a fox had trotted through. But then we noted large canine foot prints and paused to investigate them.

"They are ahead of us," Puh said.

"Not as many as the last time," I agreed. "Maybe six or so?"

Puh nodded.

"*Last time?*" Ria echoed.

"Last time there were about ten wolves," Puh informed her. "We had a sled-load of fresh meat and they were quite interested. Intrigued enough to be more persistent than is usual."

"And I had been dowsed with the blood of a giant deer the day before, so I am sure that I attracted their attention as well," I added.

Ria looked down at the blood-free tunic Puh had given her.

"Now I am more grateful than ever to benefit from your generosity, Tor," she smiled at him. It occurred to me that even if the upper part of her face was still discolored and disfigured, she did at least have an attractive smile. "I know that you must be very cold," she continued. "I am so sorry that you are suffering on my account."

Puh touched her arm briefly.

"You have to be thoroughly chilled in this frigid weather as well. But it will only be until tomorrow. We will be home before long."

A lone howl suddenly rent the air. It was from a source very close by and soon was followed by a chorus of cries and yips. The sounds of crackling brush came to our ears, followed by little woofs and growling. I was not too alarmed as of yet. Although hungry wolves will attempt to kill any living thing they think they can tackle, this time it was a smaller pack and they had nothing like the incentive shared by those earlier wolves.

Puh and I moved to stand on either side of Ria so that she would be sheltered between us. She was so small that it would be easy for even a single wolf to take her down.

The wolves were moving in on us, as before, taking care to assess the situation first by circling the area around us, their mottled gray, buff, and white bodies weaving smoothly amongst the tree trunks and undergrowth. We could hear their panting and the excited huffs, barks, and ominous rumbles that issued from their throats.

Puh and I waited for a wolf to come close enough that we could dart out with our weapons for a jab, but before we could do anything, Ria stepped in front of us, her bow armed with a tiny spear and several of the little spears tucked between the fingers of her right hand.

I watched in complete amazement as she took her aim at one of the wolves and, pulling back on the bow's cord, let the miniature spear fly. It hit the animal in the side, causing it to leap and emit a high-pitched yelp. Almost instantly, another spear flew through the air, striking a second wolf in the shoulder. She had a third spear poised for flight, but the wolves decided they had had enough and fled.

Puh and I stared open-mouthed at Ria, who was watching the wolves depart with the rapt focus of an avid hunter. When Ria was satisfied that they were really gone, she returned the remaining little spears to their container, slung her bow over her shoulder again, and calmly proceeded down the path once more. Puh and I looked at one another in disbelief, but there was no time to stand there flummoxed. Ria was steadily hiking away from us, so we hastened our pace to catch up with her. My thoughts, however, remained centered on the astounding scene that we had just witnessed. After what had taken place the last time I had shown an interest in her bow, I was reluctant to ask her about it but I was anxious to learn how to use the bow and tiny spears.

By the time we were prepared to make camp for the night, the snow had slowed to an occasional earthward-tumbling flake. As usual, we looked for a grouping of small trees that we could use to make a rudimentary frame for a hut. While Puh and I constructed our night's lodgings, Ria foraged for firewood, collecting several armloads.

As darkness overtook the land, a waning moon rose and gave off just enough light to brighten the snow-whitened landscape. The freezing temperature made the heat from our fire welcome indeed. We sat as close to the flames as we could, shifting a bit now and then to warm new spots on our bodies, much like a roasting slab of meat is turned to ensure that it is evenly cooked. A pair of owls hooted back and forth to one another from nearby trees, but we were too weary to be kept awake by their calls. We settled ourselves to go to sleep as soon as we had finished our meal of dried foods.

* * *

The moon was still high when I was awakened. In my dazed and still exhausted state, I at first thought that a bear might be shuffling around outside our hut, but then it dawned on me that these were not bear noises and they were coming from inside the shelter. As I heard a soft prolonged feminine sigh, a notion began to formulate in my mind. My suspicions were confirmed when I was bumped by an arm and then by the miscellaneous articles of clothing that were apparently being cast-off by their owners.

I was utterly flabbergasted. Had Puh and Ria forgotten I was here?

A quick peek outside the hut showed that it was snowing again and the fire was almost out. I really did not want to go out-of-doors at this time of night so I opted to attempt to ignore them and hope that, with luck, I might be able to go back to sleep. I did not begrudge Puh the affection that he had been missing for so long; I just did not want to be present while he was receiving it. Then the subtle sounds of breathing and long, drawn-out kisses turned into a smothered cry and the breathy sighs became gasps. It brought back vague childhood memories. I had not realized what I was hearing at that time; it was not until I became paired myself that I knew it was the muffled sounds of my parents' lovemaking in the other earthen room. But especially now that I have been paired with Morning Star for some moons and knew exactly what lovers experienced, I found that the same situation going on just at my back was intolerable.

I involuntarily clamped my hands over my ears, but I could still hear the relentless sounds. Again, I peered outside but it was still snowing. I soon recognized the guttural groans of climaxing. *Oh, good. It is over.*

But then I realized that it was not over, but only the end of the first session.

"Yes, yes, yes, yes..." Ria whispered as the movements started again.

I cringed inwardly, my mind shouting *No, no, no, no...!*

I was disconcerted to view my Puh as a highly passionate lustful being. Did older men like Puh still love with the same physical vigor that I was used to as a newly paired man of not yet 18 winters? I did not want to lay there long enough to find out.

Still half-asleep and in disbelief at what was occurring between Puh and Ria, I wrapped my cloak around me and went outside to spend the rest of the night by the fire. I poked the red hot coals to bring the flames back to life and slowly rebuilt the fire, stick by stick.

It was bracingly cold. I tugged my braid out from under my cloak and wrapped it around my neck for extra warmth. I then drew my cloak up around my head and surrounded myself with its great bulk, my arms around my knees, drawn up in front of me. I could distinguish the gentle piffs as the individual snowflakes landed on me.

I hoped I could get a little sleep this way, but it was difficult to ignore the faint noises escaping from the shelter that still reached my ears. I just wanted to be home with my mate. I wanted to feel her in my arms and kiss her and make love to her and never leave her side again. I managed to doze now and then, but I awakened chilled each time the fire died down, so I was forced to continually add wood to keep it alight. Morning was painfully slow to arrive.

* * *

The sun was still low in the sky when I felt a hand on my shoulder. As I removed the cloak from my head and peered bleary-eyed out of my cocoon, the snow that had accumulated on it slid off and made a powdery ring around me as it landed on the ground. Puh looked into my face with concern. He was wearing only his loin cloth, leggings, and boots. The snowflakes that came to rest on Puh's warm naked torso immediately melted, but the snow that fell on his hair remained as a fine white dust.

"Are you all right?" Puh asked.

I nodded sleepily.

"Yes," I replied, brushing the still-falling snow from my face.

"I am sorry if we…if we…disturbed your slumbers last night. It was not something I looked for to happen. It was just that I awoke to find her hands on me and then my hands were on her…I had almost forgotten what it is to breathe in the aroma of a woman. And then it was like an avalanche that was not going to be stopped until it reached its conclusion."

I thought to myself that I had heard more than just one avalanche. Then I considered his statement about the delicious scent that only women carried.

"It is true that women do have a different smell than we men."

"Yes," Puh smiled, "they smell better than we do."

I thought that this was highly probable but then I wondered aloud.

"Morning Star has never complained…"

"No, she is not a complainer. Besides, as I recall, your Muh often said that she actually liked my body odor. The appreciation must lie within the owner of the nose, because I would think that a man who reeks of sweat and smoke from fires and whatever addit-

-ional scents we are carrying around on that day would not be very appealing."

"Puh, you must be freezing."

He had begun to shiver.

"It is cold," Puh said as he reached for more wood to add to the fire.

"If you are going to stand out here and talk, sit next to me and wrap half my cloak around you," I offered. Puh readily agreed.

He sank to the ground and placed a section of cloak around himself.

"Many thanks. Ria has just fallen asleep, so I left her snuggled under mine. I will let her rest and wake her before we are ready to leave."

"I understand that you had not anticipated…what happened," I said. "There is no need to be sorry. If it was pleasant for you, I am glad."

"*Pleasant?*" Puh repeated. "It was much more than that! She is someone I truly care about. My heart is touched. I have never known a woman to be at all like her. It is strange; I have never been with any women other than your Muh and I could not have found one who was more different than she."

I nodded. That was certainly true.

"I will never stop loving your Muh, but somehow my heart has made room to also love another." Puh went on, "When we return to the Gathering, I want to ask around to see if any of our fellow Old Ones have any information regarding Ria's people. If I can find them, I intend to ask for her."

"You will ask for her?" I was startled at his announcement.

"Does that sound so unreasonable?" Puh asked. "I knew from the moment I had laid eyes on your Muh that I loved her. Even though my first view of Ria was quite memorable and more than enough to get any man's attention, it was not quite as instantaneous this time. Still, I know. If Ria is agreeable, I want to be paired with her."

"So you have not yet said anything to her?" I inquired.

"No, I want to give her a little more time to get to become acquainted with me," Puh answered. "But I plan to speak with her before too long. I sense that she is also developing feelings for me. At least, I hope she is."

* * *

Even with a late start, we still managed to arrive at the family compound well before nightfall. As usual, we were greeted by the throng of barking dogs. Raena reached us ahead of her companions; she leapt up to put her paws on my chest and strained forward to lick my face. Even though Raena was a large dog, she could not quite make contact, so I stooped and let her give me a few quick brushes with her tongue before I hastened onward to find Morning Star. Old Rooph limped up too, and I also paused for a moment to pat him, but I had eyes for only one person.

Morning Star was the first one out of the door. I ran up to her as she also flew toward me, holding her bulging stomach to help support the heavy load she was carrying. I wanted to pick her up off her feet, but I did not dare for fear of hurting her or our baby. I held her tightly and kissed her over and over again as we breathlessly told another, "I missed you so much!"

Puh, with Ria by the hand, caught up with us. By now, everyone in both of our families had emptied the main dwelling to welcome us.

I noted that most wore curious expressions when they saw Ria, who clung to Puh unsurely amid all these strangers. I had to acknowledge that she likely had not seen so many people together in one place during the entire span of her lifetime. Not to mention that the group included Morning Star and her family—who were of The People from the East tribes— whose errant members had been stealing from her recently.

The cold became more ruthless than ever as the sun dropped closer to the horizon, so we did not spend much time outdoors rejoicing at our homecoming. We retreated to the warmth of the house and Puh, his arm around Ria, introduced her.

"This is Ria. She will be staying with us for as long as she has want or need."

Now that I was standing in a room lighted with oil lamps, Morning Star stared at my scratched and still slightly bruised visage. She looked back and forth between Ria and her obvious injuries and me, with my slighter ones.

"Tris, your face is scratched and bumped," Morning Star said.

"Yes," I nodded. "Do you remember my lynx Dreams? Well, it was not actually a lynx, but I did get a few small scrapes."

"I am afraid that I was the lynx," Ria spoke shyly. "I did not know that the stranger did not mean me any harm and I attacked him. I am very sorry for it," she admitted.

"Tris, you did not hit her, did you?" Ru asked accusingly.

Ria responded before I could say anything.

"No, he did not. He merely threw me to rid himself of me after I jumped on him."

"And I am very sorry for my part in our altercation, as well," I said to Ria.

Little Fawn appeared to be looking past us, as though she was hoping Black Wolf might still arrive.

"Where is Black Wolf?" she asked, sounding somewhat alarmed. "Did he not accompany you home?"

Ria stared at Little Fawn, who stood hunched under the low ceiling, bringing to mind a cow elk standing under a low tree branch with her head hung low.

"No," Puh started. "Black Wolf volunteered to stay and…negotiate." Puh could not seem to mask his guilt at this deception, but I believe that I was the only one who noticed it. "We had some success in addressing the new Head Elder, but we are tasked with returning to the Gathering with as many Old Ones as we can muster. Tris and I were sent to find Awna's half-brother, but we found Ria instead." Puh smiled and looked down on Ria. She returned his smile. "We have stopped at home to obtain warmer clothing so that we will be properly dressed in the increasingly frigid weather. Black Wolf will join us again when we make our final trip homeward."

"My dear Black Wolf," Little Fawn wrung her hands. "He might be impossible at times, but oh, he is a conscientious man; he has always been so noble!"

Little Fawn did not often refer to Black Wolf in such glowing terms. Now it was my turn to attempt to control my facial expression as I recalled the numerous times Black Wolf and Little Fawn had feuded fiercely over some matter, sometimes for days or even moons on end. I could only guess that she must be missing him.

Ria was given the names of everyone in the room. She nodded somewhat bashfully at each person in response, softly repeating each name to herself.

"She talks funny!" Saree piped up, whispering loudly as only a three-winters-old child can.

Puh lifted Saree into his arms and hugged her. "Ria does not talk funny, she just talks differently. She comes from a place many days' hike from here and the people who live there speak with a distinctive accent. We must make Ria feel welcome while she is so far from her home."

Saree looked closely at Ria, seeming a little puzzled as to how she could improve upon Ria's reception to our clan. Finally, she seemed to have an epiphany. Saree brought forth Hork and held her out to Ria.

"This is my Hork."

Ria gawked at Hork for a moment before she recovered and said gently, "How nice."

Puh set Saree down and she ambled off, cradling Hork like an infant. Ria leaned nearer Puh and asked quietly,

"What is a *Hork*?"

"Hork is Saree's doll," Puh replied. Puh was still busily embracing and kissing all his children but he took a moment to request, "Ru, see if we have any clothing that will fit Ria. She lost most of her belongings when her house caved in and she will freeze if she stays dressed like this."

"Yes, Puh." Ru was cheerful for a change. "I will go and sort through our stores of assorted clothes and bring out some things that Ria may choose from."

Puh gave Ru another hug and kiss.

"Many thanks, Pretty One." Then Puh seemed to have a second thought. Possibly, he recalled that Ria had no sense of modesty and might opt to change into her fresh clothing whilst standing amongst all her new acquaintances. "Take Ria into the storage area with you."

Ru nodded and lifted one of the seal oil lamps from its shelf to bring light to the storage chamber while they looked through the piles of used clothing.

"Yes, Puh. Come with me, Ria."

I was still absorbed in kissing Morning Star and telling her how much I loved and had missed her, when I slowly became aware that our homecoming was not a happy occasion for one person. Aunt Vee looked stricken. She alone had not come up to meet Ria and had glared at her resentfully from the time we entered the room.

* * *

Ru not only found clothing that fit Ria, she also insisted on combing out Ria's hair with her fingers and fashioning it into the traditional coiled cords of the Old Ones, fastening the cords up as most women did. Ria's face was still a ruin, but on the whole she looked much better. Ria held Puh's tunic and placed it in his hands.

"Many thanks for the loan of your tunic, Tor," she said.

Puh pulled the garment over his head.

"Many thanks for keeping it warm for me. It feels especially nice to don an article of clothing that still carries your body heat."

Ru, now next to Morning Star and me, looked quite pleased with her handiwork.

"You seem to be in very good spirits," I said to Ru.

Ru shrugged.

"I am so thrilled to see Puh happy again. Ria is a funny little thing but she seems sweet."

Sweet? The wolf-slaying woman who was capable of bringing a grown man to his knees? But then I remembered that I was supposed to pass on Bror's message.

"While we were away, I saw Bror and he asked me to give you his regards."

Ru shrugged again.

"That sounds like something Bror would say."

We all settled down onto the mats that covered the floor of the main room and when the evening meal was ready, we enjoyed a festive repast. But as agreeable as this meal was, both Puh and I looked forward to other delights. We soon left our family and friends for our respective homes and go to bed early.

* * *

As I had expected, Puh and I could only stay for a short period of time before we had to go back to the Gathering. During our brief respite, we not only made up for lost time with our families, but we also brought in more firewood to feed the constant flames that burned in our fire places. The many downed trees from last summer's storm provided us with a great quantity of easily accessible wood.

Puh and I were toting yet another large log back to the compound when Puh spoke.

"Tris, if I am able to find out where Ria's kin are, will you go with me to ask for her?"

"Of course I will, Puh," I answered. "Have you spoken to Ria yet?"

"Many thanks, Tris. No, I have not talked to her yet. But I plan to do it today, if the timing seems right. She has been busily working to turn my little house into a home. Ria seems to like it here. She has been warmly received by almost everyone."

"Almost," I nodded.

"Yes," Puh sighed. "Vee does not seem to like Ria. I do not know what Vee could possibly have against her. Ria has been quite amiable during her stay. Everyone else seems to have taken to her without any hesitation."

"It may be because Aunt Vee had her own aspirations for you," I said.

Puh shook his head.

"Vee has never let on and I have never given any indication that I was interested in her. I told you once before, do you not remember? I could never even consider…never feel that way… about my brother's mate."

"I know, Puh. I am sad for Aunt Vee, but I am pleased for you, if you are happy."

Puh grinned broadly.

"Yes, I am very happy." Puh suddenly became serious. "I had assumed that I would be alone for the rest of my life." Puh admitted. He paused deep in thought for a few moments before going on, "I still grieve for Awna. I miss her every day. Sometimes I even think I hear her, hear the movement of her clothes as she walks, hear her voice, or her sighs. I will never completely get over her loss. But Ria has brought me joy again."

"I am glad, Puh. Truly." We stopped to rest prior to hauling the wood the rest of the way home. "I feel a little guilty to be here at home while Black Wolf is left…um…negotiating…at the Gathering. We should be leaving soon, should we not?"

"Yes, we should. But I do not want to leave too soon, because if Willow Woman is determined to produce an heir, it may take a little time." Puh said.

I was confused.

"*A little time*? Morning Star and I were able to make a baby right away."

"But you and Morning Star are still young. When you are young, the babies come once a year or something close to that. As people grow older, both parents are less fertile and it may be harder to conceive…despite all efforts," Puh stated.

"Oh. I did not know that."

* * *

That night, a severe cold descended upon the land so quickly that fall abruptly came to an end and the season turned to brutal winter. Puh and I were very grateful for the warmer clothing upon which our survival would depend. I hoped that the other members of our family had the presence of mind to also venture to their homes at some point to re-outfit themselves for the rest of their journey. Little Fawn fretted that Black Wolf would be cold, but I felt assured that at least for now, he was probably staying quite warm. There was also every probability that he could procure warmer clothes from one of the vendors at the Gathering.

Puh was in an elated mood as we prepared to leave once more. Ria had accepted him and he was cautiously confident that someone would be able to tell him where to find Ria's clan. Ria, too, was walking around as though on a cloud. Little by little, her face was healing and the colorful bruises were diminishing. Everyone except poor Aunt Vee was so pleased for them. She was further aggrieved when she saw that Puh's beard was at long last trimmed and his hair was once again coiled and bound into a thick rope that hung down his back. Aunt Vee must have offered to help him with his hair and beard at least once every moon, but he would not allow anyone to attend to the task that Muh alone had handled. However, now that Puh had let Ria handle the chore, Aunt Vee was both injured and incensed.

* * *

On the evening before our planned departure, we were all gathered at the main household for our nightly meal. Puh and I had been eating as much as we could since our homecoming to make up for the many days of dried trail foods we had consumed and also to fuel up before we departed on our next long journey. Mi sat in Puh's lap, as always, and Ria was snuggled up against him as they ate.

"How long do you expect to be gone?" Little Fawn asked.

"I do not know," Puh replied. "If all goes well and we find out where Ria's family is, we will go to them before we come home. It may not be until another moon has passed, but hopefully we will return before then."

"Yes, I hope so," Morning Star said, looking at me. "Our baby will come at about that time. I would wish that you could be here for that, Tris."

"I wish it as well," I said as I nuzzled her and then kissed her cheek.

"I have a reason to want to come home as quickly as possible, too," Puh said, smiling at Ria. "To be with you. Then, in the spring, or whenever you like, I can take you to your family and be paired with you."

Ria's mouth dropped open in surprise.

"But I am going with you!" she exclaimed.

"Ria, my love, the Gathering is only for men," Puh told her.

"Put her back in those men's clothes and they will be none the wiser," Aunt Vee muttered.

Puh looked at Aunt Vee sharply. I think the only reason he did not respond was because Aunt Vee had so selflessly taken care of his family for so long that he could not berate her for speaking out against his chosen one. But his wordless look of reproach was seen and made it understood that such remarks would not be tolerated.

Aunt Vee's gaze dropped to her hands in her lap and she was silent.

Ria, however, brightened at the idea.

"Yes, I can dress the part for the Gathering. I will need to wear something appropriate to get through the snow, anyway," she pointed out. "And, after all, if they are seeking Old Ones to tell their stories about being raided, do I not have my story to tell?"

Puh still seemed undecided.

"Tor, I beg of you," Ria implored, gripping his arm earnestly. "I beg you to take me with you. I could not bear to wait here, always wondering if you were coming back to me."

Puh now grasped the reason why Ria was so desperate to accompany us. He gazed lovingly at Ria and tenderly placed a hand on the side of her face.

"All right," Puh said. "I will not make you wait for me. We will find suitable winter clothing for you and you will leave with Tris and me in the morning."

 **Chapter Nine** 

Ria was so pleased at Puh's change of heart that she threw her arms around his neck and covered his face with kisses, causing many of us to chuckle at her exuberance.

Ria was still hugging Puh tightly, when Ru rose to her feet and stood by Ria and Puh, waiting to be acknowledged. When at last Ria looked at Ru, she spoke.

"Come, I will take you back to the storage area and we will seek some things to appropriately outfit you while you are on the trip back to the Gathering. I think that you will be able to wear some of Ty's old clothing."

"Many thanks, Ru," Ria replied, rising to join her. "Will you have boots to fit me? My boots are not treated with birch tar. I was able to bring down enough small deer to keep me supplied with boots, but they never lasted long because the skins were too thin and I could not make birch tar."

"You hunt?" Ru asked incredulously.

"I had to hunt," Ria answered. "I was on my own. I could not bring down animals of any size because I only had my little bow and arrows, but I could kill rodents, small deer, and other manageable animals like that. Although I tried to learn how to make birch tar and birch oil to help preserve and waterproof my tanned hides, I never mastered the technique, so I was lucky to get even a moon's use out of a pair of boots. The soles were soon worn through and I could only replace them so often before the numerous restitchings ruined the topsides of the boots, too."

The room was absolutely silent except for the crackling of the fire. Everyone looked at Ria with a new appreciation for what she must have gone through. Puh gazed at Ria proudly. He stood, too, and wrapped his arms around her.

"Birch tar or no, you are an amazing woman," Puh told her.

"Many thanks, Tor, but the birch tar would have been a very handy thing to have! As it was, every hide I was able to procure had to be used to make boots or to replace the grips on my bow or finish the rehafting of my knife handle," Ria said softly.

"We must search for the other necessities you will need on our journey, too: such as snowshoes and a small pack." Puh then brought a lamp down off a shelf and he led the way to the double-hung, elkskin doorway to the storage area.

Ty leaned toward me. "What are those things—*bows and arrows*—that Ria spoke of?" he asked. "If they allowed her to make kills by herself, we must try to make our own!"

"I have been thinking the same thing," I admitted. "I am not sure about the arrows, they might be the tiny spears I saw, but her bow is a long slender stick with a cord attached to both ends. It throws those little spears with enough force to pierce the skin of a modest-sized animal. But do not ask her about it! She may seem like a complacent little person right now, but if you touch her bow she turns into a rabid beast!"

"She does?" Ty drew back, aghast.

"Yes! Take my word for it, do not test her!" I then noted that Morning Star was looking at me as though I had taken leave of my senses. I could well understand Morning Star's skepticism. I was nearly twice Ria's weight and yet here I was, warning Ty not to tangle with her. I turned to Morning Star. "It is true!" I exclaimed. "You would not believe the hurt she can inflict on an unsuspecting victim…even a much larger victim! She lived by herself for nearly four years prior to our arrival. The only way she could have survived for so long, especially after her home was destroyed and she was repeatedly robbed of her essentials, was because she was so tough and resourceful. We will have to ask Puh to inquire for us."

Ty nodded. "Good idea."

Little Fawn changed the subject.

"When they return, I will tell Black Wolf that he must build us a home nearer to here. I have been thinking that Morning Star will soon have her baby and I cannot bear to be a half-day's hike from her and our new grandchild. Our home is really too small for our family, anyway." Little Fawn then addressed Morning Star and me. "You would not mind if we lived somewhere nearby, would you?"

"Of course not," I assured Little Fawn. "I would welcome it. I will help with the construction. But we will probably have to wait until late spring to begin."

"Oh, yes! It would be so nice to have you in the area!" Morning Star agreed.

I noticed that Aunt Vee seemed to be lost in thought. Just then, Puh, Ria, and Ru emerged from behind the hides that curtained the chilly storage chambers from the living quarters.

Puh had heard the end of the conversation.

"I would very much like it if you and Black Wolf moved your family closer, as well," Puh stated cheerfully. "I also will help Black Wolf build your new home."

"Thank you!" Little Fawn smiled with appreciation. "Thank you both!"

Aunt Vee cleared her throat before speaking.

"That makes me feel easier about my decision," Aunt Vee began. "Tor, I would like to ask that you bring my sons with you when you return. I can see that you will have plenty of help and I will not be needed anymore. So I would like my sons to come for me and take me home. That is, if you do not mind passing on the message."

"Yes, Vee, I will take the message to them," Puh said. "You certainly have sacrificed much to stay here and care for my children, and I will never be able to adequately express my gratitude nor repay your many kindnesses."

Aunt Vee smiled a little.

"Just to hear those words is payment enough. I love your children almost as I love my own. With luck, you will be gone long enough that I will still be here when Tris and Morning Star's baby is born so that I will be able to cuddle the new infant before I leave."

* * *

The dawn came all too soon, and then it was time to go away from my sweet Morning Star once more. The worst of it was, I did not know when I would return. If Puh, Ria, and I set out to find Ria's kin after the Gathering closed, we might be gone for a moon cycle or even longer.

Morning Star was well aware of this, too. She did not accompany me down to see us off this time. The sun was still low in the sky and it was bitterly cold. I asked her to stay home, warm in bed, and she did not try to convince me otherwise. She only nodded, tears welling at the corners of her eyes as she hugged me tightly.

"Take care of yourself and the baby. I will be back as quickly as I can," I promised. "I will miss you so much. I hate being away from you…especially now." I caressed Morning Star's taut round belly and kissed it.

Morning Star stroked my hair as I was bent over her bulging stomach.

"I know you will come home when you can. I will miss you, too… I will miss you terribly." Morning Star sniffled a little. "Be safe. That is all that matters." Morning Star smiled a bit, "also, I should add that I would like my Da and your Puh and Ria to be safe as well. I envy that Ria will go with you. How I wish that I could go, too."

"Yes, that would be nice," I kissed Morning Star's lips. "But be glad you are staying here where you will be comfortable. Besides, you would not want to be traveling with Puh and Ria. At least, I know that I am not looking forward to it."

"Why ever not?" Morning Star asked.

I grinned at her.

"They are not ideal sleeping mates. Well, they are for each other, but it is one of those situations where three people in a shelter is one too many."

Morning Star giggled.

"Oh, Tris! You cannot be serious!"

The Dreamer II: THE GATHERING

I gazed lovingly into Morning Star's face as I held her in my arms.

"I cannot say as I blame them. After all, if you were with me, I would want to do the same thing. Then we would need separate huts," I said lightly. "That would be a lot of extra construction to take on at the end of every day on the trail. But it would be worth it."

"It sounds as though you still might want separate huts," Morning Star said with a laugh. "Oh, I am glad you have brightened my mood. I was so sad at the thought of your going away for so long. And I am still unhappy, but at least you have made me smile before your departure."

"I will keep that smile in my mind's eye and in my heart until I am home, again," I told her.

* * *

As it turned out, the two-hut joke became a reality. Puh, Ria, and I had set out in the cold and blustery early morning air and hiked down a snow-dusted trail for most of the day when we came upon my cousins Bror, Dor, and Lor.

The cousins were a little confused at Ria's presence, but a brief explanation put that to rights. The men had already begun to build their shelter for the night and they had a started a fire. Their hut was not big enough to accommodate three more people, so we still needed to erect our own.

But even at that, as we all pitched in to finish the last final steps that would complete our shared campsite, I whispered to Bror.

"May I join you and your brothers in your shelter?"

"Yes, of course. But why would you want to? My brothers snore like bears and for all I know, so do I," Bror replied.

"I can put up with sleeping amongst snoring bears better than I can put up with sleeping next to a newly love-struck couple."

"Oh," Bror said quietly. But then a thought seemed to cross his mind. "*Oh!*" he said again. "Ah, I see. Well, lucky Tor and Ria. Now I am hoping that Dor and Lor will be snoring *very* loudly indeed because I do not want to have any notion of what may be going on next door."

"Neither do I," I agreed.

* * *

Our journey back to the Gathering was lengthy and unseasonably frigid, but at least the persistent snow did not accumulate on the earth's surface. The minute flakes swirled about as they were carried on the icy blasts of wind, but never appeared to be much more than a fine dusting on the ground.

While the extreme cold and heavily gusting winds may have made for harsh conditions, at least we did not have to slog along through deep snow with clumsy snowshoes strapped on our feet.

The shorter daylight hours meant that we needed an extra day to arrive at the Gathering. We were surprised to find that even though the event was nearing its end, it was still well attended.

The countless lean-tos were replaced by an assortment of sturdier shelters. Most of the structures gave the appearance of being hastily constructed, but solid enough to protect its inhabitants from the elements.

The edge of the forest had been trimmed back quite some way as men hewed trees for building materials and firewood. We probably would have to make our camp some distance away to find any foraged wood for our own fire.

Fish Hawk must have been waiting for us. Soon after our arrival he came out to meet us.

"Welcome!" he said, turning to grasp each of our forearms in greeting.

"Many thanks," we responded.

"I heard some men say that more Old Ones were coming up the path and I hoped that they had seen you," Fish Hawk said to us. "Kror had no luck in convincing Awna's family to make the trip, but the rest of your kin have already rejoined us. They have spoken with Willow Woman. She seems to be earnestly thinking on their plight, but it will help if you have brought others to tell their tales."

"My relatives will be here in a day or so," Bror spoke first. "They are quite willing to share their experiences. They did not realize that anyone else had been raided. They needed to finish replacing the last of their stolen stores before they came to the Gathering but they promised that they would be here."

Fish Hawk nodded.

"That is good." He glanced curiously at Ria from time to time, but evidently he was too polite to ask her identity. It must have crossed his mind that she could not possibly be the statuesque Bakkae whom we had been sent to retrieve.

Evidently, Puh did not wish to deceive our friend.

"Fish Hawk, this is Ria," he said.

Only Ria's wide eyes could be seen amid all the clothing that swathed her small frame.

Fish Hawk and Ria exchanged shy nods.

"Bakkae's Ria?" Fish Hawk asked in a hushed voice.

"Yes," Puh and Ria replied at the same time.

Fish Hawk seemed a little troubled. He took a moment to ponder the situation.

"Ria, I am sure you know that the Gathering is only for men," Fish Hawk said gently.

"Yes," she answered simply. "I will not make myself conspicuous."

Fish Hawk smiled.

"That is good. Let us go in. The cold is brutal and I am sure that you all would like to get inside where it is warm…a bit hot, even."

"How is Black Wolf?" Puh asked as Fish Hawk ushered us indoors.

"Black Wolf is…well, you will see soon enough. Let us find a place to stow your gear."

We followed Fish Hawk inside the long narrow building where our sense of smell was immediately assaulted by the fetid smoky air. Despite the thick atmosphere that made my eyes water and irritated my throat, I was once again agog at the number of men in this crowded room. Many men stood or sat in groups, absorbed in spirited discourse. Although most of the Gathering's business had already been concluded, these men stayed to catch up on news, make trades, or arrange future pairings. I looked for the familiar faces of Black Wolf and my uncles and cousins, but I did not see them. We traversed the length of the room and came to the back wall which was still occupied by the diminishing heaps of supplies. I was startled to see Fish Hawk take hold of a section of the wall and swing it ajar, thus exposing an opening. Fish Hawk motioned us through.

"Come! You may leave your packs and other gear in here," he said.

We accompanied Fish Hawk into the chamber and had just barely laid down our spears and packs when

Black Wolf burst through another of the odd doorways at the far end of the room. He was smiling broadly as he joyously embraced each one of us, even Ria, who seemed rather taken aback at the sudden show of enthusiastic affection from the great bearded giant with wild braids protruding from his head.

I was relieved to see Black Wolf looking so well. I had expected that he would be pleased to see us, but I had also expected that he would seem more desperate to be removed from his situation. It seemed that all my concern for him during our absence was for naught.

As Fish Hawk had said, it was decidedly hot inside the edifice that housed the Gathering, so those of us who were still clothed for our long journey began to peel off our outer layers of apparel. Ria was dressed in my younger brother's cast-offs, and when she removed the fur pelt that wrapped around her lower face and Ty's hooded winter coat, Black Wolf's jaw dropped with surprise.

"Who is this?" he asked. Unlike Fish Hawk, he had no compunction about making pointed inquiries about strangers. "At first, I thought that you had brought Ty along with you and I was thinking that it would be good thing for him to experience one of our Gatherings, but then I noted that Ty would be taller."

"This is Ria," Puh said as he took Ria by the hand. "She will be telling of the raids that have occurred at her home. And while we are here, I hope to garner information regarding the whereabouts of her family so that I may ask for her."

Black Wolf's eyebrows were high on his forehead. "This is a bit sudden," Black Wolf said, but then his expression softened. "But if you are happy, old friend, then I am glad for you both." Black Wolf clapped a hand on Puh's shoulder. "We will be eating soon. Let us withdraw to Willow Woman's compartment and await the feast."

"*Feast?*" Bror repeated. "I am exceedingly hungry!"

Actually, we were all ravenous.

"That would be agreeable, indeed. Many thanks!" I said. The thought of eating jolted me from my dumbstruck and dazzled state. "What does this feast honor?"

Black Wolf shrugged.

"Nothing that I know of. It is simply mealtime." And Black Wolf turned away from us to dislodge another one of those mobile sections of wall that once again revealed a new chamber.

This space was the grandest accommodation I had ever seen. It rivaled even Black Wolf's cousin Gray Elk's spectacular cave dwelling that was decorated with the skulls and antlers of giant deer and elks. It was nowhere near the size of the huge room where most of the men were now socializing, but it was still quite commodious.

The walls of Willow Woman's compartment were bestrewn with an array of fine pelts, all artfully displayed. There were several raised platforms, upon which more furs were heaped, and the floor was covered with layers of woven reed matting. The space was lighted by several of the smoky torches and warmed by a fire that burned under a chimney hole in the great structure's ceiling.

Willow Woman lounged comfortably on one of the platforms, lightly clad, seemingly to show off the odd, charcoal-colored lines and markings that adorned her skin, but she got to her feet as we entered her lodgings. Willow Woman immediately focused on Ria.

My respect for Ria grew immensely as she stood her ground even as the gargantuan female approached. Ria's eyes were round, but she returned Willow Woman's steady gaze unflinchingly. Puh, on the other hand, seemed concerned for Ria. Stepping closer, he put an arm around her waist and drew her nearer. Before Willow Woman could address Ria, she squared her shoulders and began to speak.

"I am Ria. I am here to tell of the thieving that has occurred at my former home."

Willow Woman paused as she regarded each of us, nodding to acknowledge our presence. Then her attention settled back on Ria once more.

"At first I thought you were a boy, but you fill out your clothing somewhat differently than would a boy.

You mention your former home. Have you been driven from your house?"

Ria shook her head.

"No. I left voluntarily. It was destroyed when the roof caved in last winter. I had nowhere else to go until Tor and Tris found me and took me away with them."

"Who are Tor and Tris?" Willow Woman asked.

Ria indicated Puh and me.

"This is Tor. This is his son, Tris."

"Ah, the Big Red Buck. I remember you." Willow Woman looked me up and down, the same way she had when we had met. Then she peered at Ria. "What has happened to your face?"

"I fell," Ria stated flatly.

Willow Woman wore a dubious expression, but she did not pursue the subject. Instead, she waddled back to her comfortable seat amongst the many luxurious furs where she had previously reclined.

"We will be eating momentarily, so please sit. Find a spot wherever you would like," Willow Woman invited. "We will talk after we have enjoyed our repast."

I had ample opportunity to observe Black Wolf while we ate. He sat next to Willow Woman, the two frequently leaning against one another, laughing and speaking animatedly with obvious fondness. This was a startling turnaround from Black Wolf's all too apparent initial revulsion at the prospect of sharing any sort of intimacy with Willow Woman. Just as I was bewildered about the attraction between Puh and Ria, I also could not understand what must have transpired between Black Wolf and Willow Woman. I could only guess that both women must have some charms which were not immediately evident to the casual observer.

At the conclusion of the meal, Willow Woman prompted Ria.

"So, little Ria. Tell me what happened."

Ria sat primly upright, very close to Puh, who clasped her hand. She seemed to be composing her thoughts. We all waited for Ria to speak.

"It happened several times," Ria told us. "Starting last spring. About once each moon and always when I was not at home. When I would return, I found that the foods I had left to dry or smoke outdoors, any hides I was curing, any tools or utensils that were lying around, all were gone."

"Who do you think took them?" Willow Woman asked.

"Judging by the footprints left by the culprits, which were shallower and narrower than those of the Old Ones, I can only guess that it was men of The People."

Willow Woman appeared to be thinking.

"You never saw them?"

"No," Ria replied.

The Dreamer II: THE GATHERING

Again, Willow Woman seemed to be lost in thought. Finally she spoke. "This is my problem. No one who has come here to testify has actually seen the men who have committed these acts. The rhyming brothers…"

"Kror and Zor," Black Wolf supplied.

"Thank you, my dear Black Wolf," Willow Woman patted his knee and smiled at him. "They said that their mates saw the men, but they did not bring them here. I have no direct accounts of the supposed crimes." She paused and then continued. "Black Wolf has assured me that his friends are as reliable as the sun and the moon, so I believe that these tales I hear are true, but it is difficult to go after the perpetrators if no one can tell me who they are."

"My relatives will be here in a few days," Bror spoke up. "Perhaps they can supply us with more detailed information."

Willow Woman nodded. "I hope so. Otherwise, I am at a loss as to how to move forward."

* * *

When Bror's kin arrived and told their story, their narration was very similar to Ria's and Kror and Zor's: goods were taken or destroyed, and dogs were killed. But they could not provide a physical description of the men who had attacked their homes. The only productive aspects of the Gathering were that we had been able to glean a few important facts. First, one of the men attending was able to confirm that Bakkae, or someone who had borne a remarkable physical resemblance to him, had perished years back, found dead in an open meadow. The man who had discovered him did not know any Old Ones, so he did not know to whom he should report this death. But when he saw us he was eager to tell us about it, unasked, in hopes that we might know of his family. He seemed to be a kind, good-hearted fellow. He had buried Bakkae to keep the predators away from his body and marked the grave with a shed deer antler, stuck firmly into the ground.

The second useful bit of information had to do with Ria's family. It seemed that her two brothers were last known to be living near the Great Lake. Coincidentally, that was also close to where my mother's family had resettled.

Shortly before the closing of the Gathering, a winter storm raged outside, shaking the walls of the huge structure and causing the smoke to periodically blow back down the chimney holes in dense clouds that made us choke. It was early evening and we disliked the thought of venturing out into that weather so that we could find our shelters before dark, but we would soon have to leave. All but Black Wolf and Fish Hawk, that is. We donned our winter layers once more and Black Wolf walked us toward the exit, where we stopped to converse.

"The snow is not deep, but those winds are strong. Do not get blown away on your trek back to your huts!" Black Wolf warned us light-heartedly.

"I just hope that our huts have not blown away," responded the ever practical Bror.

"Our shelters are well protected by a dense grouping of fir trees, so they should be all right," Puh said. He turned to Black Wolf. "Tris, Ria, and I leave in two days to seek her family."

"Us, too!" Bror motioned to his brothers and himself. "We go with you, too, Uncle Tor."

"Am I not invited to join you as well?" Black Wolf asked.

"Of course, old friend. I did not want to make any assumptions about your plans. Also, we have not had a chance to speak before now, without Willow Woman being present, and I did not want to touch on the subject under those circumstances."

Black Wolf laughed.

"While I did not expect to enjoy her company as much as I do, I do not intend to stay with her and she does not desire that I do so. She is a remarkable woman: intelligent, witty, and dare I say, lusty, but I will be all too happy to return to my own home and family."

"Ah, that reminds me," Puh began, "Little Fawn asked me to tell you that she wants to relocate your family to a spot that is closer to her new grandchild."

"Surely, no new grandchild yet exists!" Black Wolf exclaimed.

"No," Puh answered, "not as far as we know. But Tris and I did tell her that we would help you if you would like to build another home."

"I hope that you did not make any promises that we would start before spring?"

"No," Puh said, shaking his head. "Spring will be soon enough. I was also thinking that, with the raid issue still unsolved, we may be safer if we are closer together. We never know if or when those men will expand the scope of their attacks to include our lands."

"That is true," Black Wolf started, "I hope those louts are soon caught."

"What will happen to them after they are brought to Willow Woman?" I inquired.

Black Wolf shrugged. "I have no notion. We have discussed many things, but we have not spoken of what punishment might await the raiders."

"I hope I am given the chance to take my revenge," Ria said quietly but fervently. "I will make a great quantity of arrows and shoot them into those thieves until they resemble giant porcupines."

"What is an arrow?" Black Wolf questioned.

"I will tell you about them later," Puh promised. "For now, we must go before it grows too dark, or we will have a very difficult time finding our shelters."

Black Wolf nodded. "I will wait to hear, then." He thumped Puh's shoulder with a weighty hand. "That is a spunky little woman you have there."

As Ria turned to look up at Black Wolf, he gently patted her cheek and she grinned back at him.

"She is, indeed." Puh agreed.

 **Chapter Ten** 

Although I was eager to leave the Gathering and get on with the next stage of our journey, our departure was sober in nature. Since no one present could identify the raiders, there was no way to know who these men were and therefore, no resolution. For all we knew, they might have been amongst the men who were at the Gathering. In fact, there was every probability that this was so. But on the positive side, when word spread of the injustices that some of our people had suffered, we Old Ones had the sympathy and the full support of almost every man. We were hopeful that this might convince the perpetrators to halt their attacks, but we did not count on it.

When Fish Hawk heard about our mission to find Ria's clan, he asked to join us. It was winter and he had nothing to return to except dull village life where everyone would be doing mundane seasonal chores and sitting around the fire, awaiting spring's warmer weather. Travel through a frozen landscape was no light jaunt, but at least it was something to do.

Bror and his brothers had volunteered to come along for much the same reason. They were in no hurry to fetch their mother and settle in at home for a long winter's hibernation. Kror and Zor, their sons and extended kin, on the other hand, were anxious to return to their families, so they left for home as soon as the storm passed, the day before we planned to embark on our trip.

On the final morning of the Gathering, Black Wolf and Fish Hawk met us at the place where we Old Ones had made our camp. We would have departed a day earlier, except that we had to wait for Black Wolf to be released from his obligations.

Black Wolf appeared before us, resplendent in a new hooded winter coat, boots, mittens, and winter leggings. The sight of him made us stop packing and stare in astonishment.

"Those are the finest garments I have even seen!" my cousin Lor stated.

"Willow Woman had them made for me," Black Wolf admitted with a bashful grin.

"A very generous gift," Puh said. "It would appear that Willow Woman was appreciative of your…services."

"She gave every indication of being quite satisfied," Black Wolf replied. "As long as Little Fawn is not too curious as to how I earned this present, I may actually survive to see my new grandchild."

"And your new son," Puh pointed out.

"*New son?*" Black Wolf repeated.

"Was that not the point of the exercise? Or should I say *exercises?* That Willow Woman plans to have a son who will one day replace her as Head Elder?" Puh asked.

Black Wolf seemed to think on this for a moment.

"I sincerely hope she does have a son on the way," Black Wolf said. "If not, I fear that a second round of servicing would be the end of me."

"No, not you, Black Wolf." Puh laughed.

My cousins and I shared amused grins. Ria was busily stowing items in her pack, trying not to give any attention to the conversation at hand. Soon we were ready to leave. It would take us at least five or six days to hike to the Great Lake region. Maybe longer, if the weather became so hostile that it would be unwise to travel. Luckily, the conditions simply continued to be cold, windy, and prone to frequent snow showers. Normally Black Wolf would have engaged in loudly broadcasting his never-ending repertoire of songs soon after we hit the trail, but the brisk air discouraged him from his usual habit.

Our journey was slightly delayed when on the second day out we came upon fresh elk tracks. Given the fact that there were eight of us, we knew that there would be little trouble in taking down this large animal and that the meat would do much to sustain us during the rest of our excursion. So we opted to pursue the beast and, by the end of the day, were happily consuming his meat and organs.

The next morning we set out once more with full stomachs and packs topped off with slabs of frozen elk meat. One great convenience of winter hikes was that the chilly weather made it easy to keep perishable foods from spoiling while we were traveling. Water, however, was another matter. We had to keep our water bags tucked under our coats to prevent the contents from freezing solid. Finding liquid refreshment was not difficult, since we were following the White River up to the Great Lake. The challenge was in traversing the river's stony, ice-slicked banks to get at the frothy waters. However, by the next full moon, even these raging currents would be frozen to a silent barely discernible presence—just a wide flat expanse that snaked its way between two rocky shores. After that, water would become a more serious issue.

Ria knew the lands around her home quite well but we passed through these areas within the first four days of our journey. The woodlands became sparser, the open grasslands more prevalent. We saw many grazing animals. The most numerous were the great, shaggy wisents, which stood huddled together against the wind and driving snow. A few aurochs and deer were seen as well. It was good to know that there was plenty of meat on the hoof from which to choose.

With a group of men this size, we had many more hunting options open to us than we did when we hunted in twos and threes, and chances were, we would need to bring down at least one more animal before we headed toward home.

On the sixth day, we began to see tracks of men in the light snow that dusted the landscape. Despite the fact that snow was a frequent phenomenon, there was seldom more than a few fingers' breadth of depth on the ground, and in many places the constant gusting winds had scoured the earth bare. But it was also possible that our perception of snowfall was only an illusion. Perhaps it was not actually falling from the sky, but merely propelled into perpetual motion without ever actually hitting the ground.

* * *

Around midday, Black Wolf pointed to the north.

"Look! Mammoths!"

We observed the mountainous beings as they lumbered along, evidently unbothered by the cold or our presence. Although we were some ways off, it was obvious that they had noticed us—maybe even before we had seen them, given that they were viewing us from a higher vantage point. The mammoths faced our direction, eyeing us keenly. Even though it would not be feasible for us, at such a distance, to be of the slightest threat, I heard a low warning rumble that presumably was emitted from the lead mammoth, who then, walking at a leisurely pace, led her small herd away from us.

Puh stared at the retreating mammoths. I patted his shoulder; knowing he was likely reliving the hunt that had cost the life of his oldest brother. Feeling the weight of my hand, Puh turned toward me and his sorrowful countenance confirmed my thoughts.

Everyone, except Fish Hawk and Ria, already knew about that long-ago hunt. Killing a mammoth used to be part of achieving manhood. When the Old Ones were more numerous on these lands, we were able to gather enough hunters to make this onerous task possible. But even so, only the oldest, youngest, and sickest mammoths were targeted. These huge animals were immensely strong and much faster on their feet than one might think. Their herd instincts fostered the preservation of their families; therefore, they were very protective of one another. Especially now that most hunting parties only consisted of a few men, mammoths were usually avoided . That said, occasionally men would happen upon a lone mammoth—usually a bull—and sometimes he would be too ill or maybe trapped in a swampy pond, and too exhausted from trying to extricate himself to stand up to the rigors of fighting off the onslaught of determined hunters. However, even the weakest mammoth still had the potential to easily kill a man—as Puh had witnessed for himself.

* * *

Later, we stopped to rest for a bit to drink a little water and swallow a few mouthfuls of meat. When Ria took down the soft pelt she wore over her lower face and pushed back her coat's hood slightly, I saw that the damage to her nose and forehead was nearly healed. She was still not beautiful or even pretty, but when she smiled at Puh, she did have an agreeable appearance, albeit in an unusual sort of way.

Ria was now flushed with excitement at the thought of being reunited with her family.

"I wonder if they will remember me," Ria said. "My brothers were younger than I. They would have been about eight and ten winters old when I was lost."

"That is old enough to remember," Puh assured her, leaning down to kiss her lips. Ria tip-toed up to meet his kiss, even though small icicles were hanging from his mustache and his beard was coated with frost.

"The tracks on the ground show that this trail is well used," Bror pointed out. "I think we will find your people in a day or so."

Bror smiled at Ria kindly and she nodded hopefully to him. It was too cold to stand in one place for long, and we were soon underway once more. I was thoughtful as we trudged along, following behind Puh and Ria, who were hand in mittened hand. I had long been mystified at what Puh saw in her, but then comprehension finally came to me: he had found a like-minded, resilient, and indomitable spirit, all contained in a woman who loved him with all her being.

* * *

As Bror had predicted, soon after we veered off the riverside trail to explore a well-traveled side path, we found an occupied dwelling. Black Wolf hallooed at the top of his lungs to announce our presence.

The hide-covered doorway cracked open just wide enough to show a face, and it was a rather startled face, at that. Apparently troops of eight people, including one black-bearded giant, did not often present themselves at their domicile.

"We do not have much left!" The man said with a strong accent that resembled Ria's, and his head withdrew from sight.

We exchanged puzzled glances.

"He must think we are here to rob him!" Ria's words were tinged with disappointment. Undoubtedly, she had hoped for a warmer welcome.

"We are not here to cause trouble! We seek the family of Ria," Puh shouted to the unseen residents.

The head resurfaced.

"Who?"

Another head emerged.

"Ria? Ria, our sister?" The owner of the second head now came out to greet us. "Do you have news? Please come inside and warm yourselves by our fire."

As we followed him in, he explained.

"I am sorry for your rude reception. Our home has been plundered several times and although we never saw the culprits, when my brother set eyes upon you, he thought for sure that you must be the same band of thieves, come back to clean us out again."

They had no lamps. The little abode was lighted only by a fire in the fireplace. A thin winter hare was roasting over the coals on one side of the hearth but no other food was evident. This was a meager meal for the six people who would be dining off the small creature.

Ria was quick to expose her face so that her brothers could see her.

"Vosh! Vit! It is I, Ria!" she exclaimed.

They stood opposite Ria, looking at her closely.

"You do not look as I remember you, but your voice is unchanged," the older brother said. He smiled and embraced Ria.

"Well Vosh, your voice and looks are both very different from the last time I saw you, but I still can see traces of the brother from my childhood. And you, too, Vit. Do you remember me at all?" Ria asked.

Vit stared at her doubtfully.

"I do recall that we once had a sister. But then one day she was gone. Are you our sister?"

While the siblings became reacquainted, I further examined this barren room and its inhabitants, which included one woman and three children. The woman was soon introduced to us as Vosh's mate and two of the children belonged to them. The third child was Vit's son, but the boy's mother had perished during the birth of a stillborn sibling a few years ago. The brothers were small and sturdy, like Ria, but the resemblance seemed to end there. It was only a guess, but the allotment of intelligence appeared to decline in the descending order of each birth, with Ria, as the eldest, by far the keenest intellect.

Ria was understandably pleased to be with her brothers. She asked many questions about her parents, who had been deceased for some years now, and she wanted to know what her brothers had been doing since she had last seen them. Vosh and Vit were eager to talk about their lives, how they had built this home so that their families could share it after Vit had lost his mate. The hunting was good, but Vit had injured his foot and he was too lame to walk very much. With only one healthy hunter in their small clan, this had seriously impaired their ability to provide for themselves. Now that they had been regularly victimized by the raiders, they were barely eking out an existence.

When Ria was asked about her circumstances since she had been parted from her family, she skimmed over any hardships and spoke only briefly of her years with Bakkae and her current happiness with Puh.

"Now that we have found Ria's kin, I would like to ask for her," Puh joined in. "I would like to be paired with Ria. I promise you, I will take good care of her. I love her. I want to be with her always."

I was rather surprised at Puh's plea for Ria. Not in the sense that I was surprised by his sentiment, only that it was so different to my own entreaty to Black Wolf. I had asked for Black Wolf's permission *to give my attentions* to Morning Star. It was no wonder that Black Wolf had looked at me as though I had gone daft. Puh spoke of love, care, and wanting to be with Ria always. Was this how a man usually asked for a woman?

As Puh waited for their reply, the brothers looked at one another.

"Let us confer over our evening meal," Vosh finally said. "Then we will answer."

"Many thanks," Puh nodded. "If we may, would it be all right to set up some shelters near here? We will need a place to camp for at least tonight or possibly longer, if that is agreeable."

"Of course," Vosh replied with a smile. "Build your shelters wherever you see fit, but check the clearing by the head of the path and see if it suits."

"Again, many thanks. We had best get to work." Puh took off his pack and removed a bundle containing several large slabs of frozen elk meat, which he partially opened to expose the contents. "In the meantime, please accept these as a token of my sincerity and friendship."

Ria's family gasped at the offering. There was no doubt that it was greatly appreciated.

We vacated the premises immediately and went about finding a place to build our usual three huts for temporary shelters. Vosh's suggested clearing did not contain enough trees, but we soon located a good place for our camp. The three hut set-up seemed to work the best for the eight of us: three snorers in one hut: Black Wolf, Dor, and Lor; Fish Hawk, Bror, and I in another; and Puh and Ria in the third.

Because Ria was not familiar with our style of construction and we were well accustomed to working together in quickly putting up these little shelters, she did not assist us. Instead, she collected tinder and firewood and started a sizable blaze.

By the time our new homes were ready for occupation, she had already begun to cook the elk meat.

It took far longer to cook the meat than it did to consume it. We were finishing our sup when we heard Vosh calling out to us in the dark.

"We have made our decision if you would like to come back to our hearth to hear it."

Puh and Ria looked hopefully to one another.

"Maybe one of your brothers will give you to me tonight," Puh said to Ria, hugging her.

"I would like that," Ria replied.

Puh gave Ria a quick kiss before we started our walk back to the family household. Vosh and Vit were alone in the main room and they received us with polite formality.

"We have made our decision," Vosh said again, looking to Vit, who nodded encouragingly. "We will agree to let our sister Ria pair with you, Tor, if are willing to meet our conditions."

"Of course," Puh started. "I am sure that you want to know that your sister will be well cared-for, and that you will be able to see Ria from time to time. I am more than willing to give any assurance you would like to prove that I will do my best by her."

The brothers seemed a little taken off-guard by this statement. They did not speak as their eyes met.

"That is very well," Vosh said, "but that is not what we had in mind. You see, most of our stores have been stolen or destroyed. The only thing we have in any quantity is firewood, and that is because it was too cumbersome to take away; even after they set fire to our stockpile of wood, we were able to put it out and salvage most of it, undamaged."

"I would be happy to bring in more meat for you while we are here," Puh offered.

"I will help you, Puh," I eagerly chimed in.

"So will I," Black Wolf added, closely followed by the others in our group.

"That would be our condition. We will give Ria to you if you will do just that," Vosh stated. "One large animal ought to be fine."

"But surely you would need more than just one animal to see you through until Vit is able to hunt with you?" Puh questioned. "Even a wisent or an aurochs would not get you through the winter. Let us bring back several animals so that you may smoke the extra meat and then you will have stores you can eat at least until spring. It will not take long, assuming that the weather does not worsen in the near future."

"Actually, one large animal would be ample to get us through the winter…if it was a woolly mammoth." Vosh still wore the same casual smile, as though he had simply asked Puh to bring in a brace of ducks and not one of the most dangerous animals in existence.

Ria broke through the shocked silence before any of us could react.

"That is a ridiculous request!" she shouted. "Tor, let us leave at once! I will not hear of this! A woolly mammoth! Why not ask for a bolt of lightning? Tor, let us go!"

Ria had Puh by the arm and she tugged him toward the door, but Puh was transfixed in place, staring at Vosh and Vit, who stood side by side, still smiling pleasantly.

"You want a mammoth?" Puh said in a low monotone. I had not heard Puh speak this way before, but I could tell that he was seething. In fact, even though he barely showed any outward emotion, I had never seen him so angry.

"Oh yes. My mate just loves mammoth meat and she would dearly love to have the hide. It would make several warm cloaks." Vosh said, clasping his hands before him earnestly.

Puh turned and looked at us.

"Puh, you know I will go with you, whatever you decide," I told him.

"As will I," Black Wolf promised.

Fish Hawk and the cousins nodded vigorously at Puh.

Ria was the only dissenter.

"No! Please, let us go now!" And she again tried to pull Puh toward the door.

"Ria is worth more than a hundred mammoths," Puh said, speaking in the same monotone. "But if that is what you wish, you will have your mammoth."

"*One hundred?*" Vosh repeated. "One will do. We do not want to seem greedy."

Ria was both appalled and horrified. Puh put his arm around her gently and led her toward the door.

"All right, we will go now," Puh said quietly.

"Just kill the animal," Vit called out to us as we filed out the narrow opening. "We will do the butchering."

* * *

Back at our camp, I added more wood to build up our fire. The wind had calmed for once but it was still bitterly cold. Ria pleaded with Puh to pack up and leave for home in the morning.

"Tor, no! It is not worth it! I stayed with Bakkae without being paired; I can stay with you! Any one of you could be hurt or killed!"

"Cloaks from a woolly mammoth hide?" Bror said, shaking his head. "Do they have any notion as to how heavy those hides are?"

"My brothers are clearly not right in their minds," Ria continued. "Please, let us leave in the morning."

Puh looked at Ria for a long moment and then placed both his hands on her shoulders.

"Ria," he said softly, "I will not be reckless. Mammoths are bigger than we are, and although they are smart, we are smarter. We will think this through."

Ria could see that Puh had made up his mind and that he would not be moved to change it. Ria nodded dejectedly with tears in her eyes but she did not otherwise respond.

Now that the wind had calmed, it was actually pleasant to sit at our fire. We bundled our cloaks and placed them under our behinds to pad our bottoms from the cold hard ground. Ria snuggled up against Puh and he draped his arm over her. No one spoke for several moments. We just sat and watched the crackling flames.

"Tor," Black Wolf opened the conversation. "You are the only one amongst us who has been on a mammoth hunt. What do you advise?"

"I would advise that we go out tomorrow and scout the areas that the mammoths use. See where they spend their day, where they water and, if we can, where they shelter at night. We need to see what the terrain is like in those places and what we can use to our advantage."

"We will need every advantage we can get," Fish Hawk agreed.

"Yes," Puh said, "and once we decide where to make our attack, we will have to be sure that we hit our animal in its vulnerable places. A mammoth's skin is about as thick as your first finger joint is long. Their layer of fat will likely be nearly an entire finger length's deep. As you can imagine, this makes it very difficult to mortally wound one of these animals. When confronted, they are apt to charge and sweep their tusks back and forth, thus mowing down anything in front of them. The trick is to approach from the rear and inflict as much damage as we can to…well…its rear. The skin is thinnest near the anus. If we can cause enough blood loss in that way, we can bring the beast down."

"But how do we keep it from turning around and presenting the deadly front end to us while we are trying to focus on its back end?" I asked.

"By making it think that the threat is in front?" Bror suggested.

"That is one way," Puh said. "We will have to wait and see what we find when we go out tomorrow. We only saw that one herd of cows and juveniles on our way here, and we will want to avoid them. We need to find a solitary bull."

"Preferably a very old sick blind bull with a very bad limp," Black Wolf quipped.

"Yes, one so old that his tusks are broken off short and he has become deaf, too," Lor agreed. "He might even be senile, at that."

Puh smiled at the mental image of such a creature.

"That may be a bit much to hope for. I am thinking we will find a young bull that will be confused by the situation. After all, adult mammoths do not really have any predators. No teeth or claws can penetrate their skin and layer of fat, so they are not used to worrying about other animals coming after them. Assuming we don't find an enfeebled decrepit old mammoth, a naïve young bull taken by surprise might be our best bet."

* * *

Fire! The frozen lake is on fire! Dense smoke dirties the clear blue skies over roaring, wind-whipped flames. A resounding crash reaches my ears.

I opened my eyes and found that I was on the floor of my shared hut, lying between Fish Hawk and Bror. Both were snoring lightly. I groggily reflected that this was supposed to be the non-snoring hut, but just the same, I was not going to complain. The cacophony of snorts, snuffles, and wheezes that came from one of the other huts made the gentle sounds from Bror and Fish Hawk seem like whispers by comparison.

As I gathered my sleep-addled thoughts, I considered the Dream. How could a lake be on fire? I had been having rather muddled and chaotic dreams as of late. Dreams of hunting with Puh, dreams of fending off wolves, but mostly, I dreamt of Morning Star and our coming child. I was missing Morning Star badly and I constantly worried for her. She appeared in my sleep every night and although sometimes they were pleasant dreams of her lying in my arms and I was kissing her endlessly, other times I dreamt that she was in labor and I was panicked because I was not there to be with her. I dreamed that our baby was born, but somehow it was not an infant but rather an older child, as though it had skipped its infant stage altogether. But those were regular dreams, vague and misty. This most recent vision, this was a Dream. But a lake aflame…how could it be so?

The sun was just starting to brighten the new day. Last night's snowfall had covered the world outside our hut in a fresh white coating. I appeared to be the first one awake, so I pulled my heavy winter leggings over the lighter versions that covered my lower limbs in milder seasons. After donning my coat, I tugged mittens over my hands and then I went out into the frigid, early morning air. A little smoke still rose from the embers of last night's fire. I picked through our pile of foraged firewood and shook the snow from several small dry branches, using one of them to stir the embers to life. As a few flickering flames leapt up from the coals, I carefully added the sticks, letting the fire catch on each one before placing new wood to the flames. I was breaking up still larger branches when I was joined by Black Wolf, and then Bror. Gradually, everyone was awake and when we had all eventually settled around the blaze, we commenced to plan our day. Our breakfast would be thinly sliced elk meat, roasted over the fire pit. The aromas of cooking meat made it hard for me to concentrate on our conversation, but I forced myself to focus. It seemed that we would set out toward where we had last seen the mammoths and search for their tracks. They had to get their water from somewhere. I thought it was possible that we might be able to ambush an animal as it was going to or from a water source.

* * *

As it happened, we did locate a vast number of mammoth tracks along with innumerable piles of dung.

Mammoths are creatures of habit and they appeared to drink at the river every day, generally first thing in the morning. Each set of tracks told a story: here a mother steadied her calf against the current as it drank, here a big bull had come along at a later time, his larger tracks obliterating many of the smaller ones beneath them.

The terrain was less than ideal for plotting an ambush. The ground was largely flat open meadow, and there were only occasional groups of trees and brush to use for cover. The Great Lake was frozen over for as far as the eye could see, as were several smaller lakes that flanked the immense body of water. It appeared that the mammoths, singly and in herds, retreated to the middle of these frozen lakes each night, using various paths to arrive at their destinations.

I was perplexed as we stood among the hundreds of mammoth foot prints and little hills of manure on the snowy surface of the ice.

"Why would they come here?" I questioned Puh. "It must be bitterly cold out in the middle of a frozen lake at night."

"I suppose they feel safe," Puh answered. "They can see for long distances in every direction and anything sneaking up on them would stand out against the flat white background. Besides, between their long, dense fur and all that fat, they are well insulated from the cold. All they care about is feeling secure so that they may rest without disruption."

I nodded with understanding.

"What do you think we should do?"

Puh did not respond right away. He looked around, his sharp eyes taking in every detail. But he kept looking back toward one of the smaller lakes, where we had noted the tracks of several bulls who must congregate there every evening. My mind drifted back to how Ria had been found when she was little more than a child, trapped in the ice with the dead mammoth. She was incredibly fortunate that Bakkae had come along when he did. No one would have survived for very long under those conditions. Puh's words brought me back to our present conundrum.

"I think we should build a big fire over there," Puh indicated a small lake.

"So the mammoths will be cozy at night?" Black Wolf asked with a laugh.

"No," Puh said. "To weaken the ice."

The fire in last night's Dream came to mind and I caught the gist of his plan immediately. If we could weaken a portion of the ice, the surface would quickly refreeze and the blowing snows would soon cover the evidence of what we had done! The grasslands where the mammoths were now plowing up the frozen soil with their tusks in order to feed on tubers and grass roots were upwind, so they would be oblivious to our trap. Once it was set, our task would then be to drive the mammoth toward this spot—but that would be tricky. How does one convince a mammoth to go anywhere?

"We will need to build a large intense fire. Set it and leave it to burn until it melts the lower reaches of the ice, at which time it will fall through to the water below and put itself out. The surface of the water will skim over with new ice before nightfall and the snows will quickly cover the scar on the lake. If we can get one of the bulls to follow this particular trail and head straight out to that spot, and he falls even partially through the ice, he will be significantly hampered in his efforts to defend himself."

"But how do we make sure he goes down the trail and then walks to that spot?" Bror queried. "From what I have seen, there is not much that makes an impression on a bull mammoth. Except maybe food or a cow mammoth."

"What about using torches?" Fish Hawk suggested. "We could chase them with torches. Most animals will run from fire."

"The mammoth might run from it…or turn toward it to stamp it out," Puh said. "You never know which option it will choose and the second choice would not be favorable for us. But for the time being, let us start the fire on the lake. It will take time to forage enough wood to make the kind of blaze that we need. It must be self-feeding so that it will burn by itself for a long time."

"Yes, burn by itself…it would not do to have to stand beside it to feed the flames with fresh wood and end up falling through the soft ice, ourselves!" Black Wolf pointed out.

* * *

We gathered a huge quantity of wood, from kindling to large, downed tree limbs. There was no way of knowing how thick the ice would be or the depth of the water at this section of the lake. We picked a spot about 30 paces from shore where we arranged a layer of rocks which would keep the initial combustibles out of the melted ice until the fire was well underway. The fire-heated rocks would also help to accelerate the liquidization process. Then we created a cone-shaped formation of timber, with kindling sitting on the rocks at its center. The largest timbers were piled on the outside and they were quite substantial. Once those big timbers were caught up in the fire, it should continue to burn until either the wood was consumed or it fell into the lake's waters. The resulting structure was larger than our huts. After the kindling was ignited, we stayed only long enough to make sure the fire would not falter before retreating to the safety of the shore.

It was still morning, so the mammoths would not return to the lakes for some time. The sky was a clear blue but the relentless winds whipped the landscape.

"What now?" asked Dor.

"Perhaps we could find a place where we would be sheltered from the wind and we could build a small fire to warm us as we wait," Bror proposed.

"Yes, that would be a good idea," Puh agreed.

We moved some distance away to a small grove of trees that helped to break the fierce gusts of wind. I fervently hoped that the powerful gale did not blow down the wooden pyre that we had so carefully erected. So far, it seemed to be burning quite well. Although the flames looked tiny from our vantage point, the downwind-slanting plume of smoke was quite large.

"How do you hope to direct a mammoth to our trap?" I inquired.

"I do not know," Puh said, shaking his head. "I am still thinking on it. We could attempt to set upon it like a pack of wolves and hope to drive it forward to the thin spot in the ice, but I really do not expect the mammoth would feel badgered enough to want to escape from us. Their instincts tell them to stand their ground and face the threat."

Ria had been resignedly subdued ever since she had realized that Puh was determined to go through with this hunt, but suddenly she looked up at Puh.

"What if the mammoth cannot tell where the threat is?"

"What do you mean?" Puh responded.

"I mean, what if I was to conceal myself in the brush or behind a tree and shoot arrows into it? My little arrows will not do it any great injury but they will inflict pain. Would not the creature want to flee from an unseen antagonist that is raining down little stings on its body?"

"That might work!" Fish Hawk exclaimed excitedly.

"Yes!" Bror chimed in. "That would be just the thing!"

"How close would you have to be to hit the animal?" Puh asked cautiously.

"Well, the farther away I am, the more difficult it is to hit the target, but after all, we are talking about a mammoth, not a rabbit. I should think that twenty paces would be close enough. I could lie in wait near the head of this trail and when a bull appears, I could pepper it with a little encouragement to make it wish to escape me by bolting down the relatively sheltered trail to the lake. I could follow at a safe distance and let fly a few more arrows to make sure that it keeps moving."

All were silent as we watched Puh, deep in thought. I looked out toward our fire and noted that the flames were now moving up the wooden cone. The fire, fanned by the strong winds, was quickly growing in size and strength. Puh paced back and forth for a moment. I pictured the area at the head of this trail. It opened out onto the grasslands and it was the only trail to this lake partially bordered by trees and brush on each side. This would provide cover for both the hunters and possibly a confused mammoth who may wish to evade the vicious pricks of Ria's tiny spears. There were a few lonely clumps of trees between the open plains and the trail but they were not enough to shelter a full grown mammoth. However, they could give Ria a sufficient hiding place.

Puh seemed reluctant to come to a conclusion, but there was no doubt about it: her plan made sense.

"All right," Puh finally agreed. We will all position ourselves at the beginning of the trail. Tris, Ria, and I will select a stand of trees where Ria can shoot her arrows into the first young bull that comes along and tries to use the other route to the lake. If the rest of you conceal yourselves somewhere close by, we will be near enough to assist one another if something goes awry. But if the bull takes our path to the lake without any aid from Ria's arrows, we would let it go and follow at a distance. If good fortune is with us, he may simply stroll down the path and find our trap all by himself."

We all nodded. We were only too eager to give this novel strategy a try. I was also looking forward to seeing Ria set her tiny spears into motion again.

"Assuming that the mammoth falls into the trap, then we stand at its hind end and wreak as much havoc on its rump as we can?" Fish Hawk asked. "In hopes that we can open up enough grievous wounds that it will fatally bleed out?"

The Dreamer II: THE GATHERING

"Unless one of you has any better ideas," Puh started. "If so, I would be happy to hear them. We still have a lot of time during which we can devise a new plan. Or two."

Again, my attention was diverted to the fire on the lake. The wind-blown flames now erupted into the sky, as they had in my Dream. We continued to talk, pausing to eat and drink a little, until later in the day when a crash came to our ears as the burning wooden structure fell into the waters of the lake.

We stared out at the opening in the ice as the last remnants of smoke were still drifting away. It was almost beyond belief that only moments ago, such a big fire had been vigorously alight on that spot. Now, other than a few pieces of smoldering wood floating on the water's surface, the blaze was simply gone. We walked down to the lake for a closer look. I noted that bits of white were falling on us and at first I thought it was ash from the fire, but then I realized that it was snow. The blue skies rapidly disappeared behind clouds and the rate of snowfall steadily increased. Puh looked up at the sky, too.

"Just in time," he said, smiling. "Now, if this water will freeze over quickly so that the snow will disguise the trap, everything will be ready by evening."

We returned to our fire and kept watch to be sure that our handiwork was indeed being obscured. It seemed to take forever for the black hole in the ice to finally turn gray and then white. The dark skies gave the appearance of impending nightfall, so we made our way back up the trail in order to be in our assigned places when the mammoths decided to head for their evening haunts. Also, we were anxious to be off the trail as soon as possible so that the falling snow would cover our tracks and help to hide any lingering human scents that might be detected. We wanted to give them no reason to avoid the area where we had spent the day.

Although cloudy skies usually meant that temperatures were warmer than they were under clear conditions, the biting cold was unrelenting today. Thankfully, however, the howling wind had mellowed considerably. As the snow fell at a great rate I hugged myself for warmth. While we waited in our stand of trees I thought about our snowshoes, which were back in our huts. We might need them for our trek home if this blizzard did not ease up.

Ria unslung her bow from her shoulder and placed it inside her coat. Seeing our questioning looks, she explained.

"It is very cold. I do not know that my bow will not snap when I draw back. I hope my body heat will warm it enough so it will retain its flexibility."

"Part of the bow still hangs out in the cold," I observed. Ria was too small for the whole bow to fit under her coat. Feeling emboldened, I went on.

"Would you like me to keep it under my coat?   I promise to handle it with great care."

Ria looked into my face for only a moment before placing the bow in my hands.

"Many thanks, Tris," she said quietly.

Puh smiled at me and touched my shoulder as I tucked the bow beneath my coat.

* * *

The snow began to pile up around us. It was now ankle deep and I could feel its weight on my eyelashes when I blinked, but we made no attempt to brush the snow away. The more it covered us, the better we would be camouflaged.

At last, an old bull mammoth came into sight. This was not a tired, elderly bull such as we had joked about earlier. This was a magnificently huge old beast. His step was unhurried and confident. He nonchalantly ambled along as though he had nothing to fear.

Puh shook his head. Not this one. We let him pass us, actually hoping that he would not choose to go down the trail and fall into our trap. With a sigh of relief, we saw him take the open route to the lake. Only later did I realize that he was probably too big to use the trail. His great height and girth would have brushed the edges of the path on all sides.

A little while later, we were startled to see the same old bull emerge from the direction whence he came and he strode off, a little hastier this time, for some other locale.

"He knows that something is wrong," Puh whispered after he was gone. "I wonder what has happened at the lake…whether some other animal has already sprung our trap…whether he was able to pick up our scent…"

Then, another bull came into view. This one was young, probably not many years on his own. He was a strong handsome animal and he was our target. Moving slowly and smoothly, I passed Ria's bow to her. She nodded her thanks and slipped off one of her mittens, holding it in her teeth. Ria pushed her hood back and drew a number of tiny spears from their container, her focus never leaving the mammoth.

The bull seemed to be following the same path taken by his predecessor. I exchanged glances with Puh, willing the mammoth to change his mind and take the trail that ended at our trap. We would only have a few moments before the bull was out of range and the opportunity would be lost.

But Ria acted without any input from either Puh or me. Steadying her bow arm against a tree, she pulled back on the bowstring and sent the tiny spear airborne. When it struck the mammoth, he started and let out an odd sound, like a grunt. Ria pulled back once more and another arrow hit the animal, this time farther back on his body. Again, the creature gave a startled cry, slightly louder this time. A third strike finally spurred the bull into motion. He changed his path and began to stride in a purposeful manner for the trail.

We did not speak, as silence is an essential quality in a hunter, but Puh hugged Ria and kissed her, and we grinned at one another in triumph. We waited until the mammoth was out of sight before leaving the shelter of our stand of trees and met with our companions at the beginning of the trail.

We still did not speak, communicating only with nods and gestures. Keeping to the brush on each side of the trail, we ran through the falling snow, arriving at the lake behind the bull. It was standing near our trap, its tail swinging with agitation. Ria poised an arrow and shot it straight into the bull's rump, just to the side of his short little tail. This caused the mammoth's entire body to jerk and he took a step forward. His head swung from side to side, as though he was looking for the source of these continued assaults. Whilst I was thinking that we did not want him to turn around and come back at us, Ria let another arrow go, this one hitting the base of the tail, probably lodging in the bull's spine. The mammoth took a few quick steps forward and then the ice gave way under his forelegs. His head went down with a great resounding thunk as his tusks hit the solid ice in front of him.

This was a curious spectacle. We all gathered and looked down at the furiously struggling mammoth, his hind legs desperately trying to find traction on the slippery wet ice at the back end of his body, as his forelegs dangled uselessly in the water while his head was propped up awkwardly by his long tusks, which were hung up on the edges of firm ice at the opposite side of the trap.

We knew that we had to get down there and deliver our blows before the mammoth's throes further weakened the ice around it and made it impossible to get close to him without increasing our own chances of falling through. We quickly descended upon the beast, approaching from behind. As we neared, I saw the trickles of blood that discolored the long brown fur at each spot where an arrow had pierced the mammoth's skin. The mammoth's sides were heaving with effort and he was groaning and making panicked cries.

As Puh had said, the thinnest skin was up by the animal's anus, *up* being the operative word in this case. This was a chore for the tallest of us—Black Wolf, Fish Hawk, and me. While Puh and my cousins used their spears to make their deep wounds in the backs of the mammoth's still active legs, Black Wolf, Fish Hawk, and I drove our spears in as close to the poor brute's anus as we could. This seemed to me as though it might possibly be the most undignified way to meet your death I had ever heard of, but if Vosh and Vit demanded a mammoth for their sister, this unfortunate beast would have to suffer its fate.

As we worked our weapons to widen the wounds, vast amounts of steaming blood poured from the hind end of the bull, turning the snow at our feet and the lake waters within the hole a brilliant red. Suddenly, Great Gran's words came to mind: *Stand back next time.*

Just as I pulled back on my spear and stepped well back, the mammoth delivered his own blow. He trumpeted mightily and thus emptied his bowels, releasing a copious shower of clumpy manure. Sadly for Black Wolf, he had been standing between Fish Hawk and me, and he caught most of the excrement squarely in the face and chest.

We were too shocked to respond for a moment, but then we rushed to Black Wolf's aid, who had been knocked off his feet at the impact of the weighty blast. As the moaning behemoth breathed his last, we all regrouped at the left side of the beast, standing by a very unhappy Black Wolf.

Bror looked soberly at Black Wolf, who was busily employing handfuls of snow to scrub the still-warm dung from his face.

Bror shook his head.

"Oh, that is indeed unfortunate."

 **Chapter Eleven** 

"Unfortunate?!" Black Wolf sputtered. "Unfortunate does not even begin to describe this wretched mess!"

Fish Hawk was laughing so hard he could no longer stand. He sank to his knees on the snow-covered ice, eyes nearly shut and with tears of mirth streaming down his cheeks. Although we Old Ones do not laugh aloud as The People do, we too had to appreciate that the sight poor Black Wolf presented did look rather humorous. Puh and Ria were on each side of Black Wolf, helping to clean him off. Puh grinned with an amused twinkle in his eyes. Black Wolf noted this.

"It is not funny," Black Wolf insisted. *"Really not funny!"*

"I know it is not, old friend. I'm afraid that sometimes you are braver than you should be," Puh said. "I am very sorry that this has happened to you,"

"Then why are you smiling?" Black Wolf persisted.

Puh's grin widened.

"Because all I think of is Saree's current favorite expression for things that do not go her way and how appropriate it is for this situation."

"And what expression would that be?" Black Wolf inquired sourly.

"*Poop!*" Puh replied simply. "Come, let us get off the ice. The pool of blood around the mammoth is melting the snow and the snow is the only thing that is giving us any traction."

Not only did we not want to be slipping on the red-stained ice, but we also did not want to get any more of the beast's blood on us than we already wore. The snow was still falling fast and thick, but the place where we had sheltered earlier was still in the lee of the wind, so we returned there to continue the process of removing dung from Black Wolf.

I began to rebuild the fire, both for warmth and light, as the sun was now almost ready to set below the horizon and darkness would soon be upon us. We could not spend much time out here. Puh, Ria, and I hastily brushed off Black Wolf while Fish Hawk stood by, still tittering.

"Bror," Puh said, turning to Bror, "would you and your brothers go down to the mammoth and lop off its tail? I will need to bring proof of the kill to Vosh and Vit and the tail will definitely provide that."

Bror nodded.

"Yes, Uncle Tor." Bror motioned to his brothers to accompany him. "Let us go before we lose all light."

"Bror," Black Wolf called after him.

Bror stopped in place and turned back to face us.

"Yes?" he asked.

"Watch your step!" Black Wolf advised.

Black Wolf's words brought to mind the scene we had left behind at the rear of the mammoth which was liberally splattered with blood and manure.

"That, we will," Bror assured him.

Moments later, the tail was in our possession and we broke up the fire before we retraced our steps to Vosh and Vit's home. When night came, navigation was difficult in the falling snow, with no moon or stars to guide us. It was late when we arrived at our destination, but Puh did not care.

As we approached their domicile, Puh shouted.

"Vosh! Vit! We have killed your mammoth."

The two heads appeared at the hide doorway.

"You have?" Vosh said with evident surprise in his voice. "That is wondrous news! Come in and tell us about it!"

They might have regretted their offer of hospitality; when we crowded into their main room, their noses wrinkled with disgust at the strong odor that accompanied us.

Puh held up the severed tail and then gave it to Vosh.

"There is not much to tell. It is a young bull and you can see by the tail that he is an adult. He looked to be healthy. There should be plenty of good meat on him."

"The hide might have a few perforations in it," Ria added.

"That is no matter," Vosh waved her remark aside. "Where is the beast located?"

"He is at one of the smaller lakes next to the Great Lake. Follow a path through the brush and you will see the mammoth directly before you," Puh replied.

Vosh and Vit looked at one another, quite pleased.

"I will take you there tomorrow," Puh continued, "if you want further proof of the kill before you give Ria to me."

"I think they have ample proof to show that their conditions have been met," Ria stated. "Vosh, I want you to give me to Tor right now."

Vosh nodded.

"As you wish, Ria." Vosh casually passed the mammoth's tail to Vit and stepped closer to Puh and Ria. Grasping Ria's hands, he spoke. "Tor, son of …?"

"Orr." Puh supplied.

"Tor, son of Orr," Vosh restarted. "I give you my sister Ria." Vosh placed Ria's hands in Puh's as both smiled broadly at one another. "Um…it is quite late, I hope you understand that we are tired and wish to sleep in preparation for tomorrow's butchering."

"I understand perfectly," Puh nodded. "Sleep well."

We nodded our goodbyes as we took our leave.

"That is the shortest pairing ceremony I have ever heard," Black Wolf said as we walked back to our huts, "and I am so hungry that I could eat the frozen elk meat just as it is!"

Ria was clearly elated, regardless of the brief rites.

"Chew on some dried meat while the elk cooks. I will slice it very thinly so it will soon be ready," she said cheerfully, speaking to Black Wolf but looking adoringly at Puh. Puh was also peering at Ria, his facial expression mirroring hers.

"I will cut the meat," Puh told Ria. "You need to keep your fingers warm. You must have nearly frozen them while you were shooting your arrows today."

Puh and Ria's pairing feast was a humble one, but they were both so happy that I do not think it occurred to them to want anything more, except maybe to bring this long journey to an end and to be home again. That was what I desired, as well.

* * *

We left shortly after daybreak. Ria had no interest in saying farewell to her brothers, so we departed with no formalities. I realized only later that we had spent so little time with Vosh and Vit that we had never discussed the Gathering with them nor the fact that other people had been suffering from attacks, as well. I also wondered why no one had mentioned the existence of these brothers the first time we had arrived at the Gathering, so that their testimony could have been sought for Willow Woman. However, if anyone had come out to ask for their attendance at the Gathering, I was sure the price for their efforts would have been one mammoth.

* * *

It had snowed all night but even though the precipitation had stopped, the skies were still covered with clouds. The winds were mercifully light. The snow was now deep enough to require snowshoes. We took turns breaking the trail, so that no one bore that burden for too long.

Poor Black Wolf still looked thoroughly disheveled and begrimed, but he did not complain and neither did we, even though the reek of excrement followed him wherever he went. Earlier that morning, I noticed that Black Wolf's coat and winter leggings had spent the night outside of his shelter. I had exited my shared hut and saw the soiled garments frozen stiff just outside of his hut, as though they had been standing watch throughout the night. Black Wolf's hair still needed a good washing to get the rest of the filth off of his person, but sadly, his beautiful new suit of winter clothing would never again be quite the same.

* * *

We had traveled some distance when we came upon a deserted camp consisting of two moderate-sized shelters and a large fire pit. This was no hastily erected over-night camp; it was well used.

These shelters were different from ours. Ours were circular and about as wide as a man was tall. These were rectangular with a center ridge pole that supported a roof which extended all the way to the ground. Since the structure was covered with snow, it was difficult to see exactly how it was constructed, but it seemed to be mostly comprised of sections of tree trunks and branches. The roofs were covered with hide tarpaulins, and the front and backs were thatched with a combination of materials including smaller branches, reeds, grasses, and mud.

The site appeared only recently abandoned. The fire pit still contained the remains of a smoldering fire and the tracks were fresh. The shallow narrow tracks also told us that this camp belonged to men of The People.

"This is curious," Fish Hawk pointed out. "Why would men of The People be here?"

"Curious, indeed," Bror agreed. "And where are they going?"

"Their snowshoe tracks lead into the woods," I said, pointing toward the broken snow. "They would have been wiser to take the trail. It will be tough going through those tangled woodlands."

"Why is it that we leave the trail?" Puh asked me. He was not asking because he wanted to know; he was asking because he wanted me to think on it.

"Well, we leave the trail when we are hunting and want to sneak up on our prey," I responded.

"Exactly," Puh said. "But what is their prey?"

"Deer? Boars?" I suggested.

"Homes of Old Ones whose men are away," Ria proposed.

"We should follow them!" Black Wolf exclaimed. "I think Ria is right."

"Yes," Fish Hawk started. "I think Ria is right, too. Men of The People do not come up here to hunt. I believe we have blundered onto the band of pillagers."

This was not good news to me. I desperately wanted to go home. Morning Star might give birth to our baby any day now. But there was no denying that we were obligated to find out whether these men were in fact the same ones who had been attacking the homes of our fellow people.

It was easy to follow the trail they had left in the knee-deep snow. I noted heaps of various household items were visible in the lee of the thick brush, where drifting snows had not yet covered them. There was no attempt to sort the items by type, or preserve their condition. Everything—tools, eating and drinking vessels, clothing, hides—all appeared to be thrown down carelessly.

We did not stop to examine these caches, but we did point them out to one another as we passed. Our pace quickened. I, for one, was angry to see all those hard-won objects and stores sitting out in the elements, so far from their original owners.

I knew that as we neared the Great Lake region again, the forests would dwindle and we would be out in the open grasslands once more. What were these men after? If they intended to hunt, there were plenty of animals to pursue, but if they were looking for more dwellings to raid, there were only Ria's brothers, who were now one mammoth richer, and my Muh's estranged kin.

I wondered if they had somehow heard of the newly slain mammoth and were readying to descend upon Vosh and Vit. If Vosh or Vit had met with someone while we were preparing to kill the beast, it would not have surprised me to know that they might have bragged about their anticipated windfall. But given the scarcity of people in this area, that scenario seemed unlikely.

However, it was to an entirely different location that we were led. The narrow, broken trail continued through the forest, weaving around thickets and densely packed groves of fir trees, finally coming out at a large homestead, from which rose a column of thick black smoke. We surveyed the setting from the edge of the woodlands.

"That is not smoke from a chimney!" Puh said. "It looks as though their house is on fire!"

"You are right!" Fish Hawk agreed.

"Yes, let us go down…" Black Wolf started, but he suddenly stopped as a man came into view. Then, two more men joined him. They were men of The People and their arms were loaded with an un-identifiable array of goods.

A boy of the Old Ones came out and attempted to wrest some of the items from one of the men, but a woman, presumably the child's mother, followed the boy and quickly dragged him away. The men laughed at the retreating pair.

"This is too much!" Bror stated, and he began to move forward, but Puh held him back.

"You are right, it is too much. But let us go around to the other side of the dwelling and get a closer look before we confront these men."

We circled through the surrounding trees and brush, stopping when we reached a spot where we gained a clear view of the front of a partially earth-bermed house. It was not the house that was on fire, but a pile of the family's belongings. Four more men stood at the fire, tossing occasional items into the blaze.

"All right, let us go. Ria, you stay here," Puh spoke, pausing to kiss Ria. "Stay safe. We will not be long."

"No," Ria insisted. "I go with you!"

There was no time to argue. We stepped out from our hiding place and quickly closed the brief span of snow-covered earth between us and the raiders. The men looked up in surprise and hastily dropped anything in their hands so that they could arm themselves with their spears. I noted that Ria's bow was again under her coat, but she had a handful of her tiny spears grasped between her fingers.

The group of men, now joined by the other three we had seen earlier, stood close together, spears at the ready, until one noticed Ria and laughed, pointing at her.

"Ha! Another feisty boy is coming at us, but this time, he has brought his toy spears!" The other men chuckled at his words. The man, who seemed to be their leader, went on. "So tell me, Boy, what do you intend to do with those toys?" The man, still laughing, turned to his companions to see whether they were enjoying his levity.

"This!" Ria replied.

In an instant, she had drawn her bow and sent one of her arrows flying, hitting the man in his left buttock. This was an unexpected development for both sides. The man howled with pain, twisting and turning in an effort to see the injured part of his body. Suddenly, he no longer found the situation quite so funny.

"One of the men has a blanket that belonged to me," Ria whispered to us.

"Are you sure?" Puh whispered back.

"Yes. It was made up of a lot of small pelts. It shed terribly, but it was very soft and warm. The man on the right has it rolled up and he is carrying it on his left shoulder," Ria answered. "I do not recognize anything else that the other men hold."

"I know these men," Fish Hawk added in a hushed tone. "They were friends of my brothers Snow Leopard and Badger Boar."

I examined them more closely. They did look vaguely familiar. Were they some of those who had helped to abduct Morning Star from our pairing ceremony?

Black Wolf's eyes widened as he came to the same realization.

"I remember this lot! They stole my daughter!" Black Wolf did not bother to lower his voice as these last words came out. In fact, they were quite loud.

"Your daughter and my mate," I agreed. I wanted to shout at them: *What is the matter with you?! Why can you not leave us alone?!* But that would have been useless. They hated for hate's sake. They perceived that we Old Ones were different from The People. We were on the lands they desired. They wanted us dead and gone.

Two of the men were helping the leader to free the arrow from its lodging place, but the procedure did not appear to be going smoothly. The patient yelped with each pull. Although Puh, Black Wolf, and I were well covered by our winter clothing, the raiders were slowly realizing our identities. We were the three who had chased them down last spring and killed a good number of the comrades. They looked to one another for confirmation that they were of one mind and slowly lowered their spears, laying them on the ground. Black Wolf walked up to the tallest of the men, looking him up and down. He was nowhere near as tall as Black Wolf, but he was a big man. All the men involuntarily made faces and backed away from the pungent stench that Black Wolf brought with him.

"You!" Black Wolf barked at him. "Take off your coat and outer leggings! I will take yours and you will wear mine."

"Yes, Black Wolf," the man stammered. Black Wolf was conspicuous enough that he was known wherever he went. "But my clothing will be too small for you."

"They will be fine," Black Wolf muttered at him. "My mittens and boots will cover any gaps. You are lucky that I do not throw these stained garments on the fire and leave you to freeze to death after what you did to my daughter…and all these good people, too!" Black Wolf indicated two women and several children who now stood in the doorway of their home, watching the scene intently. *"Criminals!"* Black Wolf went on. "Steal my daughter from her pairing ceremony and then drag her all over the countryside…and made us run all over the countryside after them! And I *hate* running! We should have left you tied to trees and let the wolves eat you!"

Just as Black Wolf was putting on his newly acquired outer attire, three men of the Old Ones approached at a run.

"What has happened?" one of them called out to us.

As they drew nearer, I could see that two of the men were quite tall. One was my height and the other, slightly shorter. These men were obviously flummoxed. They looked from us to the group of raiders, whom we were keeping at bay with our weapons.

The women and children now emerged from their home and quickly explained.

"These men," one woman pointed at the miscreants, "burst into our house and started rummaging through our things…bringing everything outside where they lit fire to it!"

"They said they would kill us if we got in their way," the other woman said. "Then these men came and made them stop," she added, motioning toward us.

"Are you all right?" the tallest man asked, "was anyone hurt?"

"Yes, we are all right," one woman answered.

"Then go inside. You can tell us more later," he continued.

"Yes, go in now," the shorter of the three chimed in. "It is much too cold to be out here without your coats."

Then the three men turned their attentions to us.

"I do not know how you came to be here in time to come to our aid, but I am grateful," one of the men said. "I am Inlee, and this is my brother Trae and my mate's brother, Sere." The man peered closer to me. "You look familiar. Do you know me? Do you have kin in this area?"

I shook my head. I had never seen any of these men before. I could guess that they were somehow related to my Muh, since her clan had settled near here. They were older men, but the two brothers' whitening hair showed vestiges of the same dark red that Muh had owned and they were tall, the same as Muh had been.

"I am Tris." I replied. "I think you might have known my mother, Awna. This is my Puh, Tor…" I started to name the others in our party, but the brothers drew in their breath sharply.

"Awna? You are Awna's child?" Trae cried out.

"Yes," I answered. "And this is…" but I was interrupted once more.

"We have not heard Awna's name in many years! Our Muh and Puh would not allow us to speak it. She was our littlest sister. I always wondered what had happened to Awna."

The brothers now gazed at Puh, who was standing by quietly, appearing grief-stricken as he always did, at any mention of Muh.

"Tor, how you have changed," Inlee said, but he grasped Puh's forearm in welcome. "How is Awna?"

Puh hesitated.

"I am afraid I do not bear happy news. Not only about Awna, but also regarding your oldest brother, your half-brother, Bakkae. Awna has passed. Bakkae perished, too, some years ago. I am very sorry to have to tell you this."

The brothers seemed to be markedly disappointed.

"To be truthful, I had expected that Bakkae would have passed by now," Trae began. "He would be nearly fifty winters old if he was still alive. That is about as old as one can expect to live. But, Awna…poor Awna. I hoped to see her again."

* * *

Even though we would have liked to talk more with these people, we soon realized that we had to decide what to do with the band of robbers and it was therefore necessary to cut short our clan reunion. Fish Hawk knew every man in the group of thugs—his name, his kin, and his history.

"Black Wolf, do you know where Willow Woman was going? Now that we have caught them in the midst of committing their crimes and I can verify the identity of each man, we can bring these men before her for judgment," Fish Hawk suggested. "As Head Elder, she can do whatever she likes with them."

"Yes, I do know where she was going," Black Wolf grinned. "And it is not too far from here. But I like Ria's idea of shooting arrows into them until they resemble porcupines."

The men looked at Ria fearfully. I could appreciate their level of concern.

Fish Hawk brightened as a thought came to him.

"Or, we could take them out to the grasslands and stake them out on the ground and then drive a herd of wisents to stampede over them."

"Yes!" Black Wolf laughed. "And then *shoot* them full of arrows until they resemble porcupines!"

* * *

But in the end, neither of those things took place. We chose to take advantage of the available daylight and make a quick trek to Willow Woman's winter abode which, under normal circumstances, would be nearly a full day's hike.

However, we did not have a full day to deliver these villains Willow Woman. So, moving at a fast pace, we walked and sometimes jogged in snow-shoes the entire distance. The disarmed thieves were tied together in a string held by Black Wolf, and they were forced to go out in front and break the path ahead of us.

* * *

The Dreamer II: THE GATHERING

It was after dark when we arrived. Willow Woman seemed pleased to see us, despite the fact that Black Wolf had managed to ruin the exquisite winter clothing she had given him. She was just about to begin her evening meal, and we were invited to dine with her. Famished, we set upon the food like a pack of hungry wolves, our beards and mustaches gradually thawing as the frozen condensation from our breath melted and dripped while we ate.

The robber band stood there, looking defeated and miserable, as they waited to be recognized. Willow Woman had already been given a brief introduction to their circumstances and she gazed briefly upon them from time to time, appearing to be deep in thought. After a while, she addressed them.

"Please feel free to sit."

All but one did. The man still on his feet spoke.

"If it is all right, I would prefer to remain standing." This was the leader who had unwisely goaded Ria into firing one of her tiny spears at him. Although the arrow had been removed from his posterior and the wound was minor, he was still not inclined to rest his weight on that part of his body.

"By all means, stand if you wish," Willow Woman granted. "I have been thinking on the deeds that you men have been carrying out and also on the kind of mindset required to concoct and go through with such acts. I am a person with a lively imagination, but I must say, even my mind reels at these repellant thoughts." She paused as her piercing eyes settled on each man, causing them to squirm with unease. Then she went on, "I can think of only one thing to do with you. That is to brand you as Outsiders. You will live outside our society and outside of our lands. If you are spotted, you will be killed on sight. Tomorrow, you will be escorted to the northeastern border and let go. Remember my words well. You will be killed if you set foot back on these lands again."

"You are very generous to let us go, but will our spears and knives be returned to us?" the leader asked.

"No," Willow Woman said adamantly.

"But the Bone Crunchers live to the northeast!" the man persisted. "And how will we hunt? We might starve to death!"

Willow Woman responded with a non-committal noise, but it left no doubt that she really did not care about their future difficulties.

"Slow Bear!" Willow Woman called out.

A large man came through one of those swinging wall panels. He had admitted us to Willow Woman's chambers, so he was already familiar with the situation.

"Yes, Willow Woman," he responded.

"Slow Bear, bring some of the other men and escort these fellows to a place where you can keep an eye on them. They are now Outsiders. At first light, they will be taken from here to the northeastern border and let go, never to return, on pain of death," Willow Woman instructed.

"Yes, Willow Woman," Slow Bear said again and disappeared, but only for a moment. He came back with a sizable troop of friends and, together, they herded the band of dispirited criminals out the door.

They were barely gone when Willow Woman smiled at us charmingly.

"Now we have reason to celebrate! Let us enjoy our food, and then I will make sure that each one of you has very comfortable accommodations for the night. Especially you, Black Wolf. But first, I will need to give you a bath."

"*A bath?*" Black Wolf repeated, seeming hopeful that she was speaking in jest. "While it is true that I do need a good scrubbing, is it not rather cold for bathing? That is, if we can even find a stream that is not frozen solid."

"Oh, I do not mean to have you bathe outdoors! No, I mean to have some water warmed and poured into my bathing vessel. Then I will personally bathe you." Willow Woman leaned closer to Black Wolf, as if to emphasize the great honor she was bestowing on him.

Black Wolf blanched, presumably apprehensive at the thought of being submerged in a vessel of water like a handful of grains, left there to swell before cooking. And it was possible that he could also be troubled at the thought of what a personal bathing might entail, as well.

"I think I can manage to bathe myself," Black Wolf said meekly.

"But I will be so much more thorough!" Willow Woman promised, pressing up against Black Wolf and tickling his ear.

"I have no doubt about that," Black Wolf acknowledged resignedly.

* * *

After we had all been settled in for the night and I waited for sleep to come to me, I realized that Willow Woman had scarcely looked at me and did not once refer to me as The Big Red Buck. I somehow felt slighted at the snub.

* * *

When at long last we returned home, it felt as though I had been away forever. But, in actuality, we had only been gone for about one and a half moons. We were greeted by our many dogs: my family's Rooph, my Raena, Black Wolf's multitude of dogs, and Bror, Dor, and Lor's pups.

"I feel as though I am visiting my cousin Gray Elk, the dog breeder!" Black Wolf laughed.

We had to push aside the dense pack of furry bodies to gain access to the house where our families awaited us. Much to my relief, Morning Star was there. She rushed toward me, looking much slimmer and carrying our infant. Morning Star placed one arm around my neck, carefully holding the baby to one side so it would not be crushed between us as I hugged her.

"Oh, Tris," she said, "I am so glad you are home!" We kissed one another repeatedly.

"And I am so glad to be here," I told her. "The baby…when did you have it?"

"The baby is not an *it!*" Morning Star said with a grin. "He is our Fox."

Morning Star proudly showed me the fair-skinned, red-haired little thing. He was sound asleep, even though the room was quite noisy as dogs barked and everyone talked at once. "Here, you hold him, Tris."

"Let me remove my pack and coat first." I quickly slipped off the pack and coat, and eagerly held out my hands for my son.

Morning Star placed the tiny hide-wrapped bundle into my arms. He felt warm and surprisingly solid for such a small being. I was overwhelmed by an emotion I had never known before. This was my child. Morning Star and I had made this baby; he was ours. I felt as though my chest would burst with these feelings. Tears came to my eyes. In a flash, I saw all those times that Puh had cast aside all regard for his own safety to run to my aid. And the countless times he had simply been there for me and my siblings. This was what it meant to be a father. You would do anything, up to and including giving your own life, to ensure that your child is safe and well cared for.

The room had gone quiet as everyone looked on. Morning Star wiped the tears from my cheeks and kissed me.

"Oh, Tris, I hope you are happy! Is he not beautiful? He looks so like you."

"Yes, I am very happy," I assured Morning Star. "In fact, I could not be happier! You are well? The baby is well?"

"Yes, we are both fine," Morning Star answered.

"He is a big boy," Little Fawn said, caressing the baby's red curls. "He just turned one moon old and he has already grown so much!"

"*One moon old?*" I repeated. "I had counted nine moons from our pairing and I did not expect that he would to be born until sometime around now."

"He was big," Great Gran stated flatly. "Morning Star is little. He simply had to come out."

Black Wolf glowered at me darkly, hands on his hips. I well understood what he was thinking. I shrugged at Black Wolf helplessly, but his expression only became more severe.

At that moment, Morning Star happened to look up from affectionately stroking the baby's cheek and she noted the wordless exchange between her father and me with some alarm.

"Black Wolf, honestly! I never..." I stammered.

"Yes, Da!" Morning Star hastened to add. "You heard Gran. The baby just got so big that he had to come out."

Black Wolf seemed to consider this and suddenly laughed.

"Well," he said, "you can never be sure when a baby will arrive."

Little Fawn had been cooing to the baby but then left us and put her arms around Black Wolf.

"You have been away from us for so long," she told him. "And, oh! You are so thin!"

"Like a buck…" Puh began but was cut short by an elbow to the ribs from Black Wolf.

"It is just that I so missed your good cooking," Black Wolf quickly explained.

* * *

When we went home later that night, it felt as though Morning Star and I had begun an important new phase in our lives. We were now a family of three. Even though I should have been exhausted after all that time on the trail and at long last, making love to Morning Star, I could not make myself sleep. Morning Star dozed in utter contentment with her head on my shoulder and her arms holding me tightly, but I kept looking over at our slumbering son, marveling at the little person we had created. My eyes ached with weariness. I desperately needed to rest.

* * *

A vivid scene opens before me. Under a bright yellow sun, three boys are tussling in an early summer meadow as the surrounding grasses and flowers sway in the breeze. One boy is big and fair like me, one boy is big and dark, and the third boy is also fair, but he is smaller and wiry in build. The larger red-haired boy speaks to the others, "We three will always be together. And as long as we are together, we can do anything!"

finis

 **Author's Note** 

First, the obligatory disclaimer: resemblances to persons either living or dead to any character in this novel is purely coincidental. I can only say that there is a bit of myself, however minute, in each character.

Second, regarding the description of how Tris and his Puh retrieved honey from wild bees: I have based this on my experiences tending my bees, which was done in regular street clothing as opposed to typical beekeeper's garb. I knew my bees and their behavior. I would *never* advise anyone to approach or attempt to access a hive without using the proper gear unless they also have the experience and confidence to do so. Those who choose not to wear protective clothing during these processes do so at their own peril.

Third, as you may have guessed, the figurines described in Chapter Six are based on the *Venus Figurines* which were created during the Upper-Paleolithic period. A great deal of speculation has surrounded these works of art. Who made them and why? Did they represent a bountifully fertile or pregnant woman? Or were they simply intended to embody the female form in all her natural glory, strictly for viewing pleasure? You also may have guessed that Willow Woman's appearance was based on the Venus of Willendorf. The other figurine described was based on the Venus of Hohlefels.

Fourth, although considerable effort was put into making this work as historically accurate as possible, the constant influx of new discoveries and ever-changing theories make it impossible to ensure that the novel's details will hold up to the test of time.

The Neanderthal may not be with us as a distinct people, but I do not think that they went extinct. I believe they were assimilated into populations of Cro-Magnon peoples. Nature may have selected against certain Neanderthal traits in ways that would help modern man survive, such as, for example: a slighter build that would not require the great caloric and protein demands needed by the Neanderthal, but they, or at least portions of their DNA, are with us even yet.

Fifth, to elaborate on the Introduction, this book reflects my personal (admittedly unscientific) opinion, but I believe that these early peoples were probably much more advanced than is often thought. I think that peoples' life skills must have ebbed and flowed throughout history as climate and habitat changes contributed to the waxing and waning of their living conditions. As the world offered a warm, reasonably wet place for people to live, they thrived, and no doubt contrived to discover ways to improve their quality of life. Their numbers may have increased until the climate became less friendly, when both they—and the flora and fauna on which they depended for their survival were stressed, leading to the deaths, if not the extinctions of many species, both human and animal. Discoveries were lost until times were favorable for people once again, and then forgotten technologies were embraced by a whole new population.

At the time this story takes place, temperatures were generally ten to twenty degrees lower than they are today; indeed, the last Ice Age pushed many forms of life to their extremity of survival. Many species did not persist to the present day, including the Neanderthal, whose numbers were never very great at any time.

For those who are following this series *The Dreamer III – The People of the Wolves* will be released in the summer of 2018. There will be at least ten to twelve books before this series is complete.

Lastly, many thanks and much love to all the family and friends who have acted as my cheering section and sounding board throughout this project.

With warmest regards, E. A. Meigs

Index of European Ice Age Animals

Antelope (Saiga Antelope) These small antelope (24 to 36 inches tall at the shoulder weighing approximately 80 to 140 pounds) ranged over a good part of the northern hemisphere. They are exceptional in appearance due to their unusual muzzles, which feature a long, flexible snout that looks much like a truncated elephant's nose.

Aurochs (Extinct) Predecessor of domesticated cattle. Size varied between 61 to 71 inches at the shoulder, with weights of 1500 to 3300 pounds. Their horns could reach up to 31 inches in length. Sometimes aurochs is spelled "auroch", but from

my readings, I am lead to believe that but the "s" is often included even when the animal is referred to in singular form because it is an alternative form of spelling "ox" and isn't intended to indicate plurality.

Boar Wild boars are the plows of the animal world. They are built for digging. Their heads and massive

shoulders make up a good part of their bodies and their large, sharp tusks, which continue to grow throughout the life of the animal, are very effective at turning over soil. The largest adult male boars can reach weights of nearly 800 pounds and attain a shoulder height of 49 inches. Sows (females) are much smaller and they lack the mane and thick shoulder/back "shield" of the boars. Their tusks are also of a more modest size. The coloring of their coats varies from anything between white and black, but most tend to run towards darker shades.

Brown Bear
(Eurasian Brown Bear) Although this bear is called a "brown bear" its color can range from black to a tawny light brown. Males average 550 to 650 pounds but very large specimens can exceed

1000 pounds. Females weigh 330 to 550 pounds. During pre-history, the brown bear did consume some plant matter, but it was generally carnivorous.

Cave Bear (Extinct) This was a very large, stout bear. The average male weighed in at 880 to 1100 pounds.

Females averaged a little over half that (495 to 550 pounds). Despite their size, bone analysis and other indicators suggest that cave bears were primarily herbivores.

Cave Lion (Extinct) (European Cave Lion) These

efficient feline predators were some of the largest known cats in animal history. Based on skeletal remains, it is speculated that the males may have reached 11 ½ feet in length from nose to tip of the tail, and weighed over 880 pounds.

Chamois A medium-sized goat/antelope. They are 28-31 inches tall at the shoulder and range in weight from 55-132 pounds. Besides being a fine source of meat, their hides were used to make garments.

Crow (Carrion Crow) A large black bird, approximately 18 to 21 inches in length with a large, heavy beak that is well adapted to catching and eating small prey such as mice, frogs, insects, etc., and scavenging off the kills of other animals.

Elk (Eurasian Elk) ("moose" in North America) A medium-sized elk/moose, now extinct in many parts of Europe. They average from just over 600 to just over 1000 pounds, with shoulder heights at 5.6 - 6.9 feet.

Fallow Deer A medium-sized deer, about 30 to 37 inches at shoulder height and weighing 66 pounds (small doe) to 220 pounds (large buck), although unusually large bucks may tip the scales at 330 pounds. Their winter coats are brown, but they are  freckled with white dots on their backs and sides during the summer.

Giant Deer (extinct) (Irish Elk) The giant deer was one of the largest deer ever to walk the earth. Commonly, it has mistakenly been called an Irish elk, although it was neither exclusive to Ireland nor an elk. 

This huge deer averaged nearly 7 feet in height at the shoulder and carried antlers with a spread that could span 12 feet. They are estimated to have weighed nearly 1200 to just over 1300 pounds but larger individuals could have reached upwards of 1500 pounds.

Horse The Eurasian Ice Age horse came in many

different varieties. They were more than likely the size of modern ponies and appeared in all colors, spots and stripes. They may have resembled the Przewalski's horse that still exist today or the now-extinct Tarpan horse.

Ibex (Alpine Ibex) A moderate-sized, dun-colored mountain goat. The bucks' horns sometimes reach 39 inches in length. The does' horns may grow to a length of nearly 14 inches. Similarly, bucks achieve a much larger body size (35 to 40 inches at the withers and weighing from 150 to over 250 pounds) than the does (29 to 33 inches at the withers and 37 to just over 70 pounds).

Lynx (Eurasian Lynx) The biggest of all species of lynx. Approximately 24 to 30 inches at the shoulder, and including its short tail, it may be 31 to 51 inches in body length. The largest males weighed nearly 100 pounds, but the typical lynx will run between 18 (very small female)  and 66 pounds (good-sized male).

Marten (European Pine Marten) A small, weasel-like animal with dark brown fur, often with blond markings or a blond bib on its chest.  At a little less than 3 ½ pounds and about 21 inches in length, the marten was hunted for its beautiful, silky fur.

Mink (European Mink) A small mink,

even the largest is just under 20 inches in length and only about 1¾ pounds. They have been prized for their dense, luxurious winter coats.

Porcupine (Old World Porcupine) This rodent wears an impressive coat of quills, some of which may be up to 14 inches in length (Crested Porcupine). These species of porcupines come in a variety of sizes: the smallest adults run from 11inches to 34 inches long, and may weigh between 3.3 to 60 pounds.

Red Deer (European Red Deer) Another very large species of deer. The buck weighs in at 350 to 550 pounds (48 inches at the shoulder) and does run 260 to 370 pounds (45 inches at the shoulder). These deer, unsurprisingly, are known for their

reddish coats. During autumn, the males often have a short mane on the backs of their necks.

Red Fox The biggest of the fox species, the adult ranges from 14 to 20 inches tall at the shoulder and weigh from 5 to nearly 40 pounds. These animals were often harvested for their fine fur.

Reindeer (Also known as caribou) This important game animal consists of several different subspecies and varied in size from 120 to 550 pounds. Color varied as well, but all subspecies shared many of the same basic characteristics, such as a fairly

impressive set of antlers (in most reindeer, both the bucks and the does grow antlers) and a two-layered coat of fur, featuring a woolly undercoat that thickens dramatically each winter and an overcoat of longer, coarse, hollow hairs.

Roe Deer (Western Roe Deer) This small deer

averages just over two feet to two feet, 6 inches at the withers, and a mere 33 to 77 pounds. Nonetheless, they were an important source of meat for prehistoric humans.

Sheep The actual breed(s) of ancient sheep that roamed

Ice-Age Europe are unknown, but it is recognized that sheep were hunted and eaten by early man. It is possible that the Mouflon (shown in image) is the modern day link to prehistoric sheep. The Mouflon have a shoulder height of less than 3 feet and weigh from 75 to 110 pounds.

Snow Leopard This beautiful cat is well adapted to life in a cold, mountainous habitat. It has a stout build and long, dense fur that varies in color from white to pale gray, with dark gray to black spotted markings. It is about 24 inches at the shoulder with a weight of 60 to 120

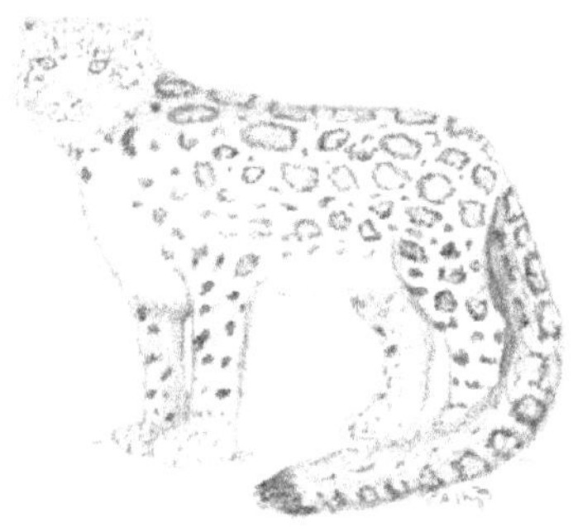

pounds, although larger males have been noted at 165 pounds. Their fur was considered to be very desirable and they have long been hunted for their pelts.

Vulture (Eurasian Griffin Vulture) This large scavenging bird may have a wingspan of over 9 feet and weigh as much as 33 pounds, although most individuals range from 14 to 25 pounds. It is known that early men consumed the meat of vultures.

Wisent (European Bison) An impressive animal, the wisent is the heaviest land animal that still resides in modern day Europe. Fully grown specimens range from 5 to 6 ½ feet at the shoulder and weigh 660 (small female) to more than 2000 pounds (large male). The wisent was an important source of food and hides for prehistoric humans.

Wolf (Eurasian Wolf) These are the largest of the European or Asian wolves. Their sizes vary greatly from 70 to 212 pounds. Although their coats could be black, white, or even reddish, by far the most common color was a grey/buff and white combination of medium length, dense fur.

Wood Grouse (Western Capercaillie) This Eurasian bird is the largest of the grouse species, weighing as much as 15 pounds. The cocks have an average weight of 9 pounds and a wingspan of 36 to 48 inches. The hen is considerably more modest in size, with a weight of approximately 4 pounds and a wingspan of 28 inches.

 Woolly Mammoth (Extinct) This large mammal lived in Eurasia and North America, and was similar in size to today's African Elephants, but with considerably longer tusks, a shorter tail, and much smaller ears. The males of this huge species could attain heights of up to 11 feet at the withers and weigh over 12,000 pounds. Females were somewhat smaller, although still impressive in size at up to 9½ feet at the shoulder and weights up to nearly 9000 pounds. Their hairy hides came in a wide range of colors that could be

anything from blond to quite dark. They were protected from the extreme Ice Age weather conditions by a double fur coat that consisted of a short, dense, woolly undercoat and strands of long outer guard hairs.

Woolly Rhinoceros (Extinct) Looking much like a  modern rhinoceros in a heavy fur coat, the woolly rhinoceros sported two horns on its long snout and carried its thick body on short, stout legs. This animal averaged about 4000 to 6000 pounds, with a shoulder height of about 6½ feet. The larger front horn that grew from the woolly rhinoceros' nose could reach lengths of 24 inches.

About the Author
E.A. Meigs

I was raised on Cape Cod (Brewster, Massachusetts, USA) at a time when the Cape was still a rural area made up of woodlands, marshes, beaches, streams, and ponds. There, my life was divided between the land and sea. My father was a commercial fisherman, backyard boat builder, and an outdoorsman; so I had an early introduction to boats, working in the commercial fishing industry and spending lots of time in the local fields and forests. When I wasn't on a boat or roaming around the great outdoors, chances are I was reading or writing. I have been a compulsive writer literally since I could first put words on paper, producing my first full length novel at ten years old. Even at that age, my goal in life was to someday find a way to combine my love of nature, the outdoors, and writing.

After raising a family and embarking on a long and varied career that included many years working on and around boats and in the commercial fishing industry; a stint with Florida Fish & Wildlife in a small field office; and other jobs that actually allowed me to use my writing skills, I awoke one day with *The Dreamer* in my head. I began writing the novel with the intention of producing just one book, but as the story progressed it became apparent that the plot would require much more than one volume to tell the tale.

I have two wonderful adult daughters and eight delightful grandchildren. I am an avid camper and I strive to get out hiking as often as possible, daily, when my schedule allows.

9 780998 125954